BLACK RAINBOW

J. J. MCAVOY

This ebook is licensed to you for your personal enjoyment only.
This ebook may not be sold, shared, or given away.

This is a work of fiction. Names, characters, places, and incidents are either products of the writer's imagination or are used fictitiously and are not to be construed as real. Any resemblance to actual events, locales, organizations, or persons, living or dead, is entirely coincidental.

Black Rainbow
Copyright © 2015 by JJ McAvoy
Ebook ISBN: 9781625178794
Print ISBN: 9781517705077

ALL RIGHTS RESERVED.

No part of this work may be used, reproduced, or transmitted in any form or by any means, electronic or mechanical, without prior permission in writing from the publisher, except in the case of brief quotations embodied in critical articles or reviews.

NYLA Publishing
350 7th Avenue, Suite 2003, NY 10001, New York.
http://www.nyliterary.com

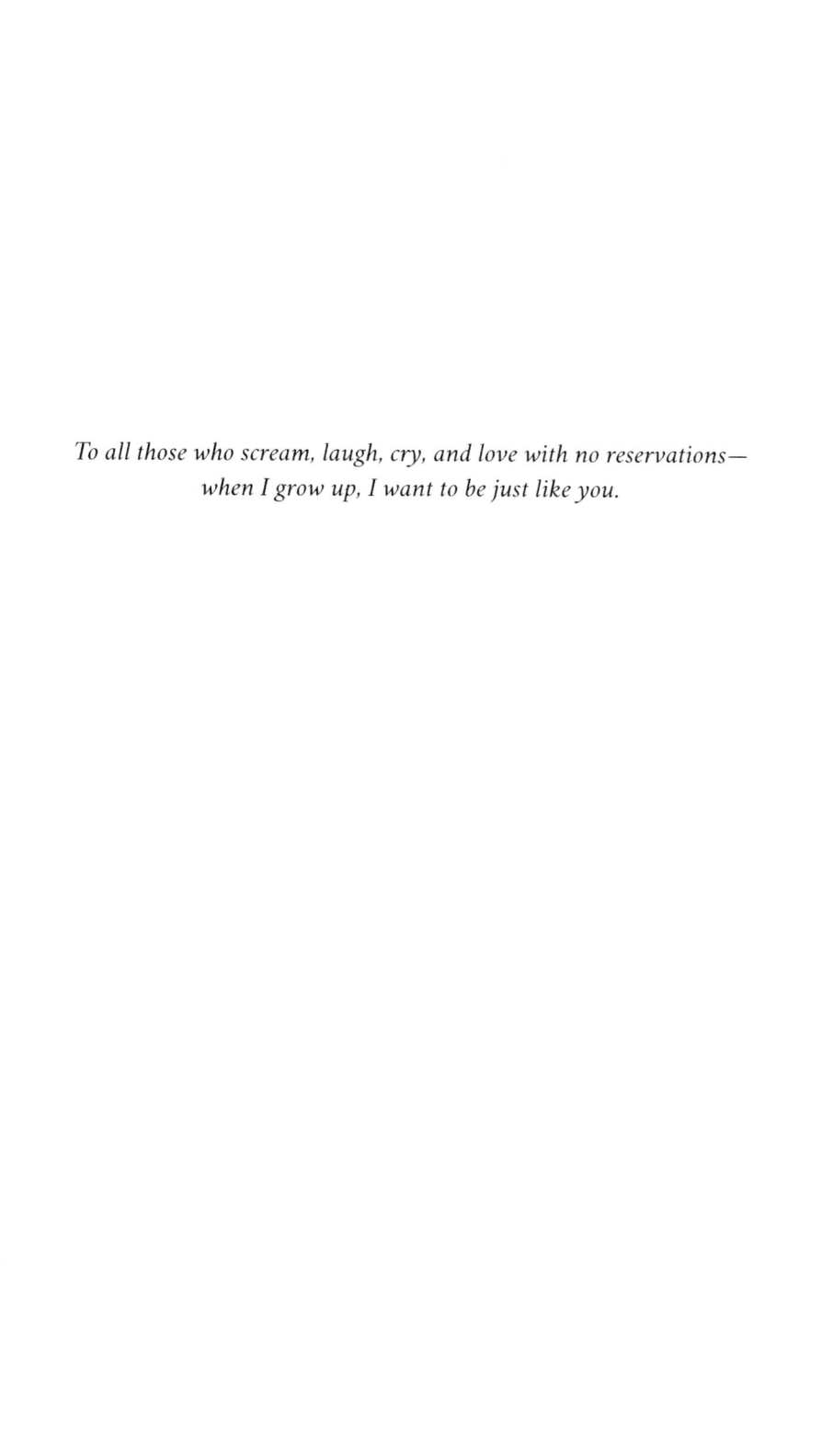

*To all those who scream, laugh, cry, and love with no reservations—
when I grow up, I want to be just like you.*

PART ONE

PAST & PRESENT

1

PRESENT

LEVI

This was going to be the worst week of my life. It had to be. After the week I'd just had, I knew there was not a thing in the world that could top it. I had met the woman of my dreams, and I'd fucked her all across the city. How could anything top that?

I was tempted to call her now, or swing by after work, but we'd made a deal; it was meant to be just a one-week fling. After our week was up, we agreed that we'd both go our separate ways.

Why had we made such a stupid fucking deal?

Sighing, I scrawled my name on the board for the fresh new lambs. I was always surprised that many of them had even graduated high school, and the fact that they had been accepted into Harvard Law made me wonder whose pockets had gotten fatter.

I was known as *El Diablo* by most – well – *all* the law students, even the ones that managed to pass my class. Regardless of what they thought of me, almost all of them applied for jobs within my firm after graduation. It led me to the belief that they were all masochists... I had taught them well.

"Come in, and sit anywhere," I told them as they filed in.

As I listed over two-dozen books on the board, I heard a chorus of whispers echo though the class, but this didn't stop me from moving on to my second column of titles.

"If you haven't read any of these books, get out. You will fail, and once that happens, there is no hope for you. I do not care if your mother was sick, your house caught fire or even if you were taken off the planet by aliens. If you want to pass this class, and if you want to be a lawyer, working for it isn't enough. You'll need to bleed for it," I said, placing the chalk down.

I waited for a moment, smiling to myself as I heard a few students rise from their seats and leave. It was the same story every time I chose to teach.

Thank God I only teach one class.

"My name is Professor Black. Now that we have weeded out the weak..." My words trailed off as I turned to face the class.

There she was, my girl, sitting in the front row, dressed in tight, dark jeans, with one of my shirts under her blazer. Her brown eyes went wide, and her mouth dropped open as she stared back at me.

Flashes of her lying naked in my bed, with myself embedded deep within her, as I kissed down her dark skin, of me gyrating against her hot, sweaty body in the club, of making love in my car, all of it, came rushing back to me.

Fuck. This can't be happening.

Looking up, I found what appeared to be a hundred eyes, focused on me. I cleared my throat and began again. "For those of you who have stayed, I expect that you've heard the rumors, and let me assure you, they are all true. By the time you are finished with this class, I'm sure you will have more to add to them, but for now, come up, sign your names, and grab a syllabus."

She didn't move. She remained in her seat, her gaze transfixed on me, looking as mortified as I felt. One by one, I watched them come forward, but not her.

Finally, she got up, grabbed her things, and then stopped. She looked as though she was trying to decide whether or not to run.

Run Thea! Please, for the love of God, run.

But of course she didn't. With her head down, she came forward, signing her name as *Thea Cunning*, before taking a syllabus from my desk. I took a step back from her. I couldn't touch her... not after everything we had done together.

I had screwed one of my students, repeatedly.

Shit.

THEA

"Who can pay attention with him up front?" a girl whispered to her friend beside her.

"I heard he's a total Nazi, but he's one of *the* best lawyers in the state. If you're in good with him, you might even get a place at his firm. Even a recommendation from him and you're set," the blonde whispered back.

The moment I saw him, I just knew that I was going to be in for one hell of a semester. I had screwed one of my professors. Hell, I had licked honey off his chest! This was not supposed to happen. It was supposed to be one week of amazing sex, and then we'd never ever see each other again!

This morning I had missed him, but I had known it was over. I needed to focus on school and on getting my life together. I had promised myself that I would do this; that I wouldn't let anything get in my way, yet here I was, staring at Levi... and to think that just two days ago I had... *Oh God.*

I had to transfer. I was going to transfer.

"Ms. Cunning," he called, and I jumped slightly.

"Yes, that's me," I muttered, raising my hand, knowing full well that he knew who I was. He didn't even look up, he just kept reading the other names.

God had the most twisted sense of humor.

2

PAST
DAY 1

THEA

All I really needed was a drink. No, not just a drink, but vodka. I was willing to drink it straight from the bottle. It was only by luck that I saw the lights of the upcoming nightclub called Twenty-Four through my foggy, rain-covered windshield.

Parking as close to the entrance as I could, I grabbed my purse before dashing out of my car and into the rain. This was a bad idea. It was pouring, I was annoyed, and I didn't have someone to take me home if I got drunk… which I most likely would. But right now, I didn't care, because what I really needed was a drink.

I sound like an alcoholic. Jeez.

The bouncer looked at my ID, and then at me as I stared passively back. He nodded and waved me in. I didn't pay attention to any of the couples grinding onto each other as I made my way across the dance floor, and to the bar.

"Vodka anything, fast," I said to the bartender who wore a top hat atop an unruly mop of brown hair.

"Tough day?" he asked, his eyeliner eyes narrowing, as he poured me the nectar of the Gods into a glass.

I downed the whole thing in one shot, before coughing and taking a deep breath.

"You could say that," I sighed, waving for him to pour more.

"Please tell me you're not a recovering alcoholic," he half joked, pouring more into my glass.

I smiled at that. "Maybe."

His brown eyes brimmed with worry, and I rolled my eyes. "My mother died two months ago. Today is her birthday, and right now, I really don't want to be at home, alone with all of her crap. So just keep them coming."

"I'm sorry."

I'm not sure if I made him feel better or worse, but this time he filled the glass, and I tried to be more civilized.

"What's your name? Because I believe you and I are going to be very close by the end of the night," I muttered sipping.

"Tristan," he said, then added, "I'm sorry about your mother, hon."

"Don't be, she was a horrible person," I muttered truthfully. "I'm Thea."

"Nice to meet you Thea. Drinks are on the house."

"No, it's okay, I don't want any pity."

"It's fine. I'm screwing the boss," he said, dropping me a wink, and I couldn't help but laugh.

"If you keep giving away drinks, you will be screwed all right."

"You're the first customer I have ever had that's fought me on free drinks."

"I'm sure but—"

"No buts," he replied, cleaning a glass. "Drinks are on the house."

"Fine. How about the house pays for the first three drinks, and

I pay for the rest?"

"How many do you plan on having?"

I shrugged. "As many as it takes until I'm numb?"

"Are you always this honest?"

"Only to the person who's controlling the booze."

He laughed, shaking his head at me. "Fine, the first three are on the house. Did you just move to Boston?"

"Yes and no." That was all I was giving him, and he nodded, accepting my answer as good enough.

I was just about to ask for a couple slices of lime, when the lights in the place dimmed. A blue light illuminated the stage as a *very* attractive man, took center stage with nothing but a guitar in his hands. His hair was dark, almost black, like a starless night. His eyes were a deep emerald color, so striking that even in the dimly lit bar I could see them. Every time the light hit them, I felt myself being drawn in more and more.

Sitting on a stool, he played softly, almost as though he was trying to put us all at ease.

"This song isn't dedicated to anyone… yet," he whispered into the microphone, which gained him a few whistles and claps.

Rolling my eyes, I turned back to my drink.

"I carry a smile when I'm broken in two, all because of someone like you," he sang.

"What the hell?" I whispered to myself.

"Fooling the world; none of them know you as I do. Why not me? Why never me? Standing right here you masterful puppeteer."

I don't know if it was the lyrics, or just the way that he sang them. Either way I found myself unable to look away from him, even to drink. It was as though I had come here just to hear him sing.

I sat watching as he ran his hands over the strings of the guitar. I was transfixed, bewitched, and overwhelmed. I could feel my throat closing up.

"I should go," I muttered to myself when his song was over.

But I simply sat there, staring down at my drink and unable to move.

Finally, I lifted my glass and swallowed its contents, and Tristan, my good old trusty bartender, poured me a new glass. I didn't feel like crying. In fact, I didn't have any more tears to spill. I was just tired. I had spent the last three and a half months with my mom. We fought, we cried, and then she died – in that order.

"Can I buy you a drink?" a voice behind me asked.

I turned to find the same devilishly handsome man from the stage, standing right beside me. He stood over six feet tall. He was fit, but not in the bulky, bodybuilder sort of way. His skin was fair and flawlessly smooth, his lips were full, his features were chiseled and well defined, yet still, it was his eyes that truly captured my attention. Without being aware of it, I leaned in towards him and smiled. He was totally at ease.

"Tristan, should I let him buy me a drink?" I turned to the man behind the bar. Tristan snorted, looking over at the man who waited for a yes.

"No, I don't think so."

"Thanks man," the man said, frowning at Tristan while I laughed.

Tristan replaced my drink, which I had not yet finished, with something new and pink.

"Still vodka?" I asked him.

"Still vodka," he nodded.

Smiling, I turned to the Casanova and shrugged. "Looks like I already have a drink, but, seeing that you're empty-handed at the moment, I'm happy to buy you one," I teased. I turned and dramatically rapped my knuckles against the bar. "Tristan! Give our friend here something *manly*."

They both laughed at that.

"I'll have what she's having," he said taking the seat beside me.

"You do see this drink is pink, right?" I asked him.

"I think I'm comfortable enough with my sexuality," he

winked.

This was usually the point where I left guys at the bar, but for some reason, I just shook my head. I didn't want to leave yet.

"You were good, by the way."

"What?" He smiled as he leaned towards me.

I pointed to the stage and grinned. "Your song, what did you think I meant?"

"Nothing," he laughed. "And thank you, I didn't think anyone noticed."

"Why wouldn't anyone notice?"

He raised an eyebrow and looked out over the dance floor. Following his gaze, I noticed that everyone was glued to each other, and no one seemed to care what kind of music was playing. It was Sunday, so I guessed everyone wanted to end their weekend on a high note.

"At this point, they might as well not have clothes on." I tilted my head to the side, watching as a man's hand worked its way up his partner's dress.

"That's what they're working towards," he laughed. "I'm Levi by the way."

"Nice to meet you, Levi," I said trying not to seem interested. He was attractive, but I was more the type who'd rather look than touch.

Yeah right.

"This is the part where you tell me your name."

"Really? Do you do this often?"

"Do what?" he asked with a frown.

"Sway women with your sultry music, then offer them a drink while staring deeply into their souls with your sexy green eyes, in order to get their names."

"Sultry music? Sexy green eyes? Are you sure you aren't the one that does this often?" He grinned so wide it was contagious.

Damn him.

"You're good."

"I'm sure you're better."

Oh damn him to hell.

"Dance with me," he said, extending his hand.

"I may be black, but I have no rhythm whatsoever," I informed him. "I'm a terrible dancer, and I mean awful. I'll step on your toes—"

He didn't seem to care, because he took my hand anyway, and I shivered at his touch... *I bloody shivered*, as he led me towards the middle of the dance floor and pulled me closer.

"You're going to regret this," I told him.

"Believe me, that's not possible," he whispered, spinning me around until my back was pressed against his chest.

I stopped breathing. I was afraid if I did, I would moan. I could feel him, all of him, behind me.

"Just relax, give in to the music," he whispered into my ear, and once again it was like I had no control over my body.

He's definitely done this before, I thought to myself. But I didn't say anything. I just lifted my arms up and wrapped them around him as the music blasted around us. His hands softly grazed over my thighs.

"I still don't know your name."

"That's because I still haven't told you," I whispered, turning back to him. His hands went to my waist and we both stared at each other.

I really couldn't take it anymore. Maybe it was the alcohol, or because he was insanely attractive, or because I just wanted to feel something, but I closed the gap between us. That was all the invitation he needed to take charge.

His arms wrapped around me, and his hands found a position on my neck as he drew me in for a kiss. He tasted amazing. I grabbed him by his hair and pulled him closer. I wanted... *needed* more of him. Before I knew it, I was pressing myself against him.

Releasing his hair, my hands slowly wandered up under his shirt, and I savored the feel of his smooth, rock-hard washboard abs, while his warm, almost feverish hand cupped my breast, relaying a promise of things to come.

Finally, we broke away from each other for a moment so that we could breathe. I wanted him so badly, I would have taken him right there on the dance floor.

"My name is Thea," I whispered.

"Your place or mine, Thea?"

"You think you're going to get lucky?" I asked him, and he kissed me again. The moment he did, I moaned into his mouth and gripped onto his hair. But he pulled away all too soon.

"I think I've already gotten lucky," he smiled.

"Your place it is then," I whispered, and he took my hand.

I barely remembered to grab my purse before he led me out of the club. By the time we got into his car, we both were trembling. As we drove through the city's streets, I took the time to admire his profile in the intermittent glow of the passing streetlights. His fingers gently traced patterns along the sensitive skin of my thigh. It was such a small, mindless action; still my breath caught in my throat and my mind went blank. Before long, my hand wandered into his lap and I groped him through his pants. He didn't say a word as we drove, but I could feel his mounting excitement.

He pulled up right in front of a beautiful townhouse in the better part of the city. Somehow I managed to regain a little bit of my composure as he opened the door for me. Anyone looking at us wouldn't have guessed anything indecent was happening, yet the moment I touched his hands, I felt myself flush, and a wave of heat spread over me.

He fumbled with his keys, trying to get the door open, and I reveled in the fact that he was either extremely nervous or so excited that he couldn't think straight. I took pride in either prospect.

The second we were inside, he spun around and pinned me against the door.

"Thank God," he said against my skin.

He brushed his thumb across my hot, swollen lips, and lightly trailed his fingers down to my waist. His touch lingered for only a moment before he dragged my shirt up over my body. Lifting me up, he carried me towards his couch, allowing us both to fall back onto it. With him on top of me, I could feel the length of him through his jeans, but that wasn't good enough. Pulling on his belt, I bit his lips impatiently, and he laughed as he understood the urgency of my actions. Moving away from me, he rid himself of his clothes and returned to help free me of mine.

The way his hard body felt against mine...I wanted to touch all of him, but when I tried to reach for him, he pinned both of my hands above my head, and proceeded to gently kiss and lick my nipples. He teased me slowly, enjoying how I shook under him. I felt like I was losing my mind.

"Damn you," I sighed.

But when one of his hands trailed down my stomach and between my legs, I couldn't help but melt in his hands. This wasn't foreplay; it was torture.

"Fuck. You look so sexy..." he hissed, as if I were doing anything to him.

His grip on me loosened as I kissed along his jawline. Finally free, I allowed my hands to wander back to him, and this time he didn't stop me as I gripped him. I tightened my hold on his member, moving my hand up and down agonizingly slow, torturing him, just as he had done to me. His breathing shortened, and his eyes seemed to darken as he watched me work him. I liked the fact that he seemed to be fighting an inner battle, trying to control himself. But I didn't want him to be controlled, I wanted our torturous version of foreplay to end.

"Condom?" I asked him.

"Back pocket." He nodded to his pants on the ground.

With my other hand, I grabbed it and tore the wrapper open with my teeth. Then, without wasting any more time, I put it on him.

We watched each other as I positioned myself over him. I could feel him, he could feel me. He grunted in frustration and grabbed my waist, flipping me onto my back and thrusting forward.

"Yes," I moaned as he pinned both my hands above my head with his right hand, and he used his left hand to grip my thigh.

He grunted, slamming into me.

"Yes!" I cried out, as he thrust into me, harder and harder, with so much force the couch moved with us, and I didn't even care. My breasts bounced freely, and he grinned, kissing them both before kissing my lips.

I opened my mouth, allowing our tongues to dance around each other.

"So tight," he hissed.

"Harder!" I demanded, not caring who heard me.

He made me feel so good.

He released my hands, and I immediately grabbed for his shoulders as my legs wrapped themselves around him. He kissed the sides of my face, then our lips once again met.

"Come for me," he whispered, and I nodded, unable to speak.

As my mouth parted, and my breasts pressed against his chest, I arched my back and pressed into him until I could no longer contain myself. "Levi!" I cried out.

"God, you're beautiful."

I tried to catch my breath, but for the love of God I couldn't. I moaned as he held me and trailed kisses down my neck. I pushed him onto his back and mounted him once more.

I looked down at him and grinned, riding him hard. I pinched my nipples, allowing him to watch as I bounced on him. His hands worked their way to meet mine. He cupped my breasts, and I covered his hands with my own, keeping them in place as he thrust upwards into me.

"Thea—" He bit his lip, fighting back his moan.

With my hands on his chest, I took in the sight of him; wild, sexy, hungry for me. I loved it.

"Come for me," I repeated his earlier sentiment.

He grunted his release. He rested below me for a moment, gasping as did I. I didn't want to get off him and he pulled me downwards to kiss his lips.

"You think we can make it into the bedroom next time?" he teased.

"There's going to be a next time?"

"God, I hope so."

I smiled, "Say when?"

"Twenty minutes?"

I raised an eyebrow at him, "What am I going to do for twenty minutes?"

"We are going to keep up our energy." He kissed me again, and I returned it. "Don't go anywhere."

"I wouldn't dream of it," I told him, admiring his physique as he walked away.

Smiling to myself, I settled back onto the couch for a moment.

That was fucking amazing. He was amazing. It was like he knew where I wanted to be touched and when. He wasn't even afraid to bite me. I never minded a little pain with my pleasure.

"What do you want to eat?" he called out from the kitchen.

I rose from the couch and stretched, not caring in the slightest that I was naked. As far as I was concerned, he had already licked, bit and seen it all.

"I have crackers, I can make sandwich—"

Walking up behind him, I placed my hand on his back and he jumped. Looking at me over his shoulder, he swallowed, unable to tear his gaze away from my naked form.

"Do you have strawberries?" I asked him.

"Hmm?"

Gazing past him, I spotted them in the door of the refrigerator and reached under his arm to get them. The cold air made my nipples harden, which I knew he noticed. Taking the can of whipped cream, I sprayed a little into my mouth and licked it off my lips.

"You don't mind?" I asked, waving the can at him.

He shook his head. "Not at all."

"I love whipped cream, don't you?" I whispered placing a squirt of it onto my finger.

I offered my finger to him, and he took it eagerly. He sensuously sucked the cream from my finger and ran his tongue along the length of it before allowing me to slide it out of his mouth.

"I'm loving it more and more each second," he whispered, and I handed him the can.

"It's your whipped cream, you should taste it from where you want."

"You're driving me crazy," he whispered, more to himself than to me, as he took the can and sprayed a squirt of cream onto my shoulder. I tilted my head to the side, giving him room to lick it off of me.

Next, he placed it on my breasts, but before he could lick it off, I took a strawberry out of the carton and allowed its tip to glide through the dollop of cream before I took a bite.

"These are some really good strawberries," I whispered.

He stared at me without saying a word, and I could see that he was awaiting my next move. Eager to please, I took another strawberry, and repeated the action before giving it to him to taste.

He accepted my offering with a smile, "Now I *know* I'm dreaming."

"Then enjoy it; I know I am," I said to him.

He couldn't stop himself as he licked along my skin, working his way downwards. I moaned, enjoying the feeling of his lips.

"Oh, I plan on enjoying this!" he whispered, cupping me between my legs. I gasped, but that didn't stop him from placing two fingers inside of me, "I think our twenty minutes are up."

"Time sure goes by fast here," I laughed. "What do you want

to do?"

"I want to fuck you until you can't walk straight," he said as he pressed me against the counter top.

I smiled, "Let's get started then."

"Ahh," I groaned, grabbing the side of my head as I sat up. Damn vodka always did this to me.

Looking around, the first thing I noticed was that this was not my room. The second thing I noticed was the sound of the shower running.

Shit, I thought, as the memories of last night flooded my mind.

Tiptoeing around, I searched for my clothes on the bedroom floor. Moving into the living room, I found my bra and skirt, and I hurriedly redressed myself.

"Making your escape?"

I snapped back to see… Levi? *That was his name, right…* To see *Levi,* dripping wet and clad only in a towel, which was loosely draped around his waist, accentuating the V shaped cut lines on his hips.

"Seriously, do you have to look like that in the morning?" I sighed, trying to draw attention away from myself, as I got ready.

"Like what?" he questioned.

I waved my hand up and down in front of him before giving up in frustration, "Never mind. Thanks for last night, it was umm… I should go—"

"Do you want breakfast?"

It was at that moment that I noticed the heavenly aroma of bacon and eggs. The smell was so alluring that my stomach growled. Truthfully, I longed to indulge in a good, hearty breakfast, but I couldn't stay.

"No thank you, I should really get going. We really don't need to do *the thing.*"

"The thing?"

"You know, where we both try to have a civil conversation after a one night stand."

"Actually," he corrected with a smile, "it was a four night stand; one in the kitchen and shower not to mention our first go on the couch and then in my bed—"

"Yep, got it…"

"Thea," he called, moving towards me, and I found that I had to force myself to not look at him.

Urgh! Damn him!

He cupped my face, "We could make this awkward, like you are trying so hard to do, or we can have some breakfast."

"I'm going to end up screwing you again."

"So?"

"That would mean that we spent two days together."

"One night and half of the morning is hardly two days," he chuckled, letting go of me. "If you want to go, then go, but you can't blame me for wanting to spend a little more time with the best lay I've ever had."

"You must say that to all the women you pick up at bars," I smiled.

He shook his head and grinned. "Have breakfast, and then I'll drop you off at your car."

"Fine, I'll stay for breakfast," I said, "but only if you put on a damn shirt or something."

"You're wearing mine." He nodded at the shirt I'd coveted.

"Well, you ripped mine," I retorted.

"Touché," he replied, and with that, he moved aside and gestured for me to enter the kitchen.

"Do you mind if I use your bathroom first?" I asked him.

"Yeah, go ahead."

"Thanks," I muttered, happy that I at least had my toothbrush and other necessities in my purse.

. . .

LEVI

Once she was gone, I rushed back into my room to get dressed as quickly as possible, seeing as how she appeared to be a potential flight risk. She was drop dead beautiful, sexy, funny, and just sinfully amazing in bed. At the very least, I needed to get her number. Hearing another door open and shut, I rushed out in a panic, and was dismayed to find that she hadn't returned to the kitchen.

"You keep records," she called from above, allowing me to breathe freely once again.

She stood on the upper level of my town house, along with the rest of my music and books. Climbing the stairs, I tried my best to be as relaxed as possible.

"Yes I do. It's old fashioned—"

"No, I like it. Everything sounds better on vinyl anyway," she said, running her hands over my collection.

"I always say that, but no one believes me with their smart phones," I snickered.

She stopped sifting through the pile and gasped. Then, she wordlessly lifted a record from the stack and held it up to her face. Her entire expression transformed into something I couldn't quite decipher.

"Curtis Mayfield — *a Curtis Mayfield album!*" she crooned.

"You know Curtis Mayfield?" I asked, kind of surprised.

Most people didn't listen to music like that anymore, unless of course, it was in a commercial.

She looked at me like I was crazy. "Talk about soundtrack to my childhood! My grandmother was big on records. You really have a cool collection here."

"Thank you, music's a hobby of mine."

"And your first love is books I'm guessing?" She laughed, looking at all the books I had scattered everywhere. "Law books too."

"You got me. I'm really a nerd."

She laughed, and it was beautiful. Her whole face seemed to beam. "Six pack abs, plays the guitar, listen to records, and is a book nerd... better watch out or I might just start to like you."

I hoped so.

Moving closer to her, I took the record from her hands and set it down on my old gramophone to play.

"Dance with me."

"That's how I ended up naked in your bed the first time."

"I know," I told her, flashing my best smile.

I took her hand, and once again it was like I was on fire. Just touching her had that effect on me. It was crazy. She broke out into laughter as we let the '70s take over. She no longer seemed shy about dancing as we both jumped around each other. Whenever she laughed, I felt the urge to laugh with her. She was...beautiful.

As the song slowed down, I pulled her in, spinning her around. She landed so close to my lips. What was this? Why did I want to kiss her again so badly? I didn't even know her last name, and yet it was like every part of me was crying out for her. She swallowed slowly as though she was fighting the same battle I was.

Finally, I took the risk and kissed her. It was supposed to be a soft, simple kiss. But I couldn't even control that. Her tongue slipped into my mouth, and I gripped her ass, lifting her up. Her legs circled around me as I pushed her up against the wall. I could feel her pulling at my pants as I shoved her skirt back up.

"Just a quickie," she said to me between kisses.

"Yeah, just a quickie, to get it out of our systems," I nodded, turning her around and remembering how good she felt last night.

"Mmmm," she moaned with her hands on the wall, as I slammed her hard from behind.

Her back arched, and my hands slipped the shirt she wore, *my shirt*, from her shoulders.

Groaning in frustration at not being able to take off her bra, I simply pulled it down to where her skirt was instead, and enjoyed the feel of her in my hands. Every part of her was real and mine. Leaning back against me, she moaned into my mouth as we passionately kissed.

"Ahh!" she moaned, as I pushed us both against the wall.

So fucking good, I thought to myself. I simply couldn't get enough of her.

"Levi," she called out for me, and I brushed her hair aside, bringing her head back to my face.

"Scream my name," I told her.

"Make me," she challenged.

She was perfection.

"This is crazy, right?" I finally whispered, putting my car in park beside her truck.

"What?" she asked quietly.

"The fact that we had sex, I can't even count the amount of times, and yet, I still want you," I confessed, leaning back against my seat.

"Yeah, it's crazy," she muttered, then she went silent. Finally, after what felt like an eternity, she spoke. "I don't know, maybe there was something in those drinks… because I'm not saying I don't want you either."

"You aren't looking for a relationship are you? Because I can't—"

"Believe me, I can't handle a relationship," she replied, cutting me off.

For a moment, I felt as though we were on the same page. What could be the worst thing that happened if I ask for sex? Sex seemed to be all she wanted as well.

"How about we just… I don't know, fuck for the next week? I don't have to work until next Monday, and maybe by then we'll—"

"Have it out of our systems?"

I looked at her and nodded with a laugh.

"Just one week?" she verified.

"One week. Sex, food, us, and then, we get back to reality."

She went quiet for a moment, and then grinned widely. "That's dangerous Levi. I'm going to ruin all other women for you."

"It's a risk I'm willing to take."

"How about we alternate days? We'll spend tomorrow night at my place and then the day after at yours?" she asked me.

"Sure," I said as smoothly as possible. On the inside, I was dancing like a mad man.

She reached into my pants and grabbed my cell phone, after she made a point of grabbing another part of me first. I smirked but didn't say anything.

"Do you like cats?"

"Like pussy?" I asked innocently.

She looked at me with a blank expression before we both broke out into a fit of laughter.

"No, like normal cats, with four legs, fur and whiskers."

"I don't *hate* cats," I said.

"Okay, I only ask because I have one. I just wanted to make sure that you weren't allergic or something or that it isn't going to be a problem," she said, placing my phone back into my pocket. "I put my number in your contact list. Come over around eight tomorrow night."

"You just moved to Boston?" I asked.

"Yes and no," she replied, dismissing the question. "I'll see you at eight, Levi, and don't be late," she said, kissing my cheek before getting out.

For some reason, I knew this was going to be the best week of my life.

3

PRESENT

THEA

For the entire duration of the lecture, my thoughts were filled only by him... and not in the way they should have been. How could I have missed the fact that he was a professor? I thought he was just a lawyer. When I saw the law books in his house, I wanted to ask him more about it but held myself back. I wonder why he never said he was also a university professor. Should I have pressed him more?

"This class is still too big," he said as he paused.

Crossing his arms, he leaned against his desk and looked over the rows of seats, his eyes scanning all of our faces. When his eyes met mine, they narrowed in what appeared to be disgust, and an anger so intense, I wanted to turn away. It was as though he was screaming at me to get out. But I wasn't going to move, I wasn't going to just let him bully me out of his class, sex or no sex.

"How many of you have heard of the Zukerman Case?" he

asked, and a little over half of the class raised their hands. I, unfortunately, was not included in that half.

"All of you who didn't raise your hands, you can go now," he stated.

One by one they grabbed their bags and laptops. Once more, I was not included in the group despite my qualification. With my phone in my lap, I began Googling as quickly as I could.

"Ms. Cunning, did you not hear me?" he called, causing me to jump.

"This a law class right? Don't I get to plead my case?" I contested.

His eyebrow raised. "You wish to plead your case as to why you deserve to be here when you aren't prepared?"

"Yes."

"Well then, plead away. You have one minute."

Standing up, every head in the room turned to face me. "You asked us to raise our hands about *the* Zukerman Case and yet you did not clarify or specify which one you were referring to."

I heard a few snickers, but I knew he wasn't amused. "Wouldn't it be obvious? It was one of the most high profile cases of this year."

"Yes it was, but so was the Zukerman Case of 1956," I replied. "The syllabus we picked up said this is criminal law of not just recent history, but the past as well. I *could* have raised my hand because I knew of *a* Zukerman Case, however, that would have made me seem like a fool or a liar if your follow up question was in relation to the details of the case." I licked my lips before continuing. "Between *the* Zukerman Case and *a* Zukerman Case, it's impossible to know which specific case you were referring to since no further details or clarifications were provided. Hence the reason why I did not raise my hand, Professor Black." I stood tall, trying not to look as nervous as I felt.

"It seems you have saved your seat, Ms. Cunning, by a matter of technicality." The corner of his lips twitched. It was fast, but I saw it, and though it was wrong that I took a little pleasure in it, I was happy that I made him smile instead of being happy that I saved myself.

He turned to face the rest of the class. "Let this be a lesson to the rest of you. You are in the running to become lawyers. If someone tells you no, then you find a loophole and jump right through it. Even the smallest technicality can change the outcome of a case. Though, I do hope you don't Google your arguments ten seconds before you are called upon."

How did he know?

"You meant to refer to the Zukerman Case *1957*. The Internet isn't always a reliable source," he added.

Shit.

He didn't bother going into any further details before moving on to the Zukerman Case that he was initially referring to. I hadn't known, but he had been Zukerman's lawyer. The man was charged with arson and robbery, but Levi had been able to totally shred each one of the prosecution's witnesses, and had gotten a police officer kicked off the stand for perjury.

It was... awe-inspiring.

As he played us the video, he highlighted everything that the prosecution had done wrong, and I found myself baffled by him. The man on the screen, and the man I had been in bed with, were two different people. He was a monster in the court room, not caring in the slightest about how the witnesses felt, as he hammered every part of their credibility to the point where one woman looked as though she was about to suffer a mental breakdown. The man who had kissed down my spine and made me breakfast in bed was nowhere to be seen at all. It seemed that there were two of faces to Levi Black, and I, despite it all, wanted to know them both.

All too soon, class was over, and as people left, I found myself unable to move. There was so much that I wanted to say to him.

I stood up, taking a deep breath and hoping to stir up the

courage to speak to him, when all of sudden, he walked right past me as if I wasn't there.

"Levi—"

"It's Professor Black, and class is over. If you wish to speak to me any time after class you'll have to call the office and make an appointment. Good day, Ms. Cunning," he replied, already out the door.

"Asshole," I murmured under my breath.

But what did I expect? Were we just supposed to laugh it off and pretend like nothing had happened and that everything was okay?

Grabbing my stuff, I headed out as well, and before I could stop myself, I was already searching though the crowded hallway for him.

"Who are you looking for?"

Jumping, I turned to find my little sister staring intently at me.

Selene and I, in my opinion, looked nothing alike. Yes, we both had dark skin, brown eyes, and hair that went past our shoulders, but our facial features bore no likeness or similarities. Plus, she was in this phase where all she would wear was black makeup and dark clothing.

"No one," I said, looking at her. "I thought you were going to call me when your flight came in?" I added in an effort to change the subject.

"Jeez, hello to you too! It's not as if you haven't seen me in months or anything," she pouted.

She was a baby, and even at sixteen, she would stay that way. Not that I wanted her to grow up or anything.

"Selene, we talked almost every day—"

"Except for last week. So, who is he?"

"What? No one. There's no one," I repeated, searching for my keys as we walked outside.

It was only September, but there was still a chill in the air. At this time of year, back home in Maryland, most people were still wearing shorts. I tried not to think about my life back there too much, because the truth of the matter was that I missed it, badly. It was my home, more so than Boston had ever been.

"If you're going to be a lawyer, you need to learn how to lie much better than that, and to hide the evidence." She grinned and pulled out a pair of boxers from her purse.

"Selene!" I hissed, trying to shove them back in there. "What in the hell is the matter with you? When did you go to the house?"

"Since *someone* didn't answer her phone, I had to take a taxi to the house and then another one here," she said, rolling her eyes at me.

We headed to my old, beat up Honda, and she stood on the passenger side, patiently waiting for me to unlock the doors.

"I was in class."

"I figured, but I was wondering why there were so many boxes left. The proof was on the bathroom floor. So, are you going to tell me who he is? Does he go here? Is he hot? If he used our shower, he'd better be hot."

"Selene, don't worry about it, it was nothing, and it's over."

"So, does that mean I can keep this?" she asked, dangling Levi's watch from her index finger.

"No," I said, as I snatched it back from her.

"How will you get it back to him?"

"I'll mail it."

"You know his address!"

"Selene, I swear if you don't stop, I'll make you walk home," I told her.

"Ooh, I'm so scared!"

Little sisters, no matter what anyone tells you, they are a pain in the ass.

"Whatever, I'm happy for you," she muttered, leaning back into her seat and staring out the window. "I hate this place, and I know you hate it too. But you're forcing yourself to be here, so if something good comes out of it, at least it wouldn't have been a complete waste."

"Selene, you didn't have to come back here. You could have stayed with Grams and finished high school—"

"We're a team, remember?" She smiled, but her smile didn't reach her eyes. "Where you go, I go. Sorry it took me so long to come, but I was waiting for—"

She was waiting for our mother to die.

"It's fine," I told her. "She was bedridden for most of it, and I didn't want you to have to see her like that anyways."

That was a lie. The truth of the matter was that I did want her here, but it wasn't only for our mother's sake, but for her own… so she could finally let go of everything and move on. So she could have some closure. But no matter how many times I told her that the cancer had spread, or that mother's condition was worsening, she didn't seem to care.

"Yeah, well, I'm still sorry."

"Every time I start to think you're a pain in the ass, you always act so sweet, even if you do look like Marilyn Manson."

"Shut up!" she squealed, and punched me playfully.

We both laughed. It was our thing.

LEVI

"Can you repeat that again?" Tristan asked over the phone, as I headed into my office.

"You know the woman I picked up from the bar? Turns out she's a law student… one of my law students."

I fell back into my chair.

Why God, why?

"Are you laughing, you prick?" I snapped.

"Come on man, give me a break!" he chuckled, "The great, strait-laced, Levi Black has finally slipped up, and has ventured over to the dark side. And you've always been so careful. How did that not come up once during the whole week you were together? Didn't you guys talk at all?"

"We were preoccupied—"

"For 168 hours? And you're still alive? How?"

"Why am I talking to you?" I grumbled.

"Because I'm the person that will judge you the least. Just wait until I tell Bethan how her big brother isn't so righteous anymore," he teased.

"I hate you. I truly hate you," I muttered, pitching the bridge of my noise.

I am Levi Black and my record was spotless; I didn't mess around with students, I didn't lose cases, and I sure as hell didn't air my dirty laundry in public. It was because of that reason that I was everyone's go-to. Senators, governors, celebrities, I was the guy that powerful people called in to clean up their mess, no matter where they were in the world. The only way I could do that was to not have any messes of my own. Thea Cunning was… well, I don't even know where to begin!

"It was just supposed to be sex."

"For a week."

"It kept getting better and better. She's like a Venus flytrap, once you're in, you're in, and there's no getting out."

"Ahh, man," he groaned.

"That's not what I meant!"

"Look, if it's bothering you that much, just kick her out of your class. Isn't there some clause in your contract that allows you to take on as many students as you want?"

He was right. I had taken on teaching when I had just opened my own firm, in the hopes of stealing the best graduates for myself. Six years later, I was still here, even though my firm had as many capable associates as we needed.

"I know. But I only get rid of the weak, and weak she is not. She stood up to me today. It usually takes my students a few weeks, but she did it on the first day."

"Are you sure this was just sex?"

As I was about to formulate my answer, a loud knock interrupted my thoughts.

"Come in," I called to the door, and to Tristan, I said, "Tristan, I gotta go."

"Is someone really there, or are you trying to avoid the question?"

"It was just sex, and it's over," I muttered into the phone as quickly as I could. "I don't do relationships, you know that. And someone really is here. Enjoy your day off, we might have a big client by the end of the day." I hung up just as my secretary came in, her lips were drawn into a hard line. Her eyebrow rose as she handed me a file.

"Good afternoon, Betty, how are you?"

"Umm hum." She shook her head at me. "Mr. and Mrs. Archibald will be coming in at two, then a phone conference with the governor at five, followed by six messages to return… all from your ex-wife," she added.

"Tell Mr. and Mrs. Archibald I will be meeting with them at their home shortly. The press must be going crazy by now, and it would be best if they stayed inside. See if you can push the call with the governor to six, and if my ex-wife calls again, hang up."

"Then she'll come here."

"Call security?"

"Really? And if the media finds out that Boston's top defense attorney had his ex-wife thrown out of his office, what do you think will happen?"

"I will get a round of applause." *And rightly so*, I thought, because my ex-wife was, for want of a better word, borderline insane.

"Mr. Black, I am sixty-five years old, do you think I *want* to deal with your ex-wife?"

"Good point. Forward all her calls to one of the associates to handle. It's not like they do much of anything anyway."

She shook her head and turned around.

"Thank you Betty!" I called out cheerfully.

Betty had been with me since the very beginning. I had left my firm six years ago with nothing but a box of awards, which meant nothing to anyone anymore, and an album full of pictures that I later burned.

They all said I was a fool for walking out, that I should have just stuck it out. Betty was the only person that came with me. Six years later, I still took immense pleasure in stealing their clients and beating their asses in court. *It was the little things in life.*

Reaching into my bag, I searched for my proposal, but I stopped when I felt the lace at the bottom. Opening it wider, I saw the pair of teal lace panties that she had worn the first night we spent at her place, with a note from her:

For the long trip home, it was fun.

Thea.

Just the mere sight of them caused something deep within me to awaken, and as I felt the texture of the material against my fingertips, I could feel myself growing hard.

What sort of a mess had I gone and gotten myself into?

PAST
DAY 2

THEA

Brushing my teeth for what had to be the eighth time, I spun around, observing myself in the mirror, and dusting off the yellow button down shirt, and black skirt that I'd decided to wear.

I was so excited that I was shaking.

I was twenty-three, damn it. I should be past shaking like a schoolgirl at the thought of a guy coming over.

It seemed that no matter what I tried on, nothing looked good enough. My hair didn't look right, and I felt like if I ate or drank anything, I would need to brush teeth again. Plus, I was sure that I'd gained weight.

Get it together Thea. It's not like you both haven't done this already. Your clothes are fine. Your hair looks nice. And you've only gained a pound but that could just be stress...Right?

"I should change," I said to my reflection, as I turned and moved over to the closet. Before I could give my appearance another thought, the doorbell rang.

Shit.

Taking a deep breath, I forced myself to not give in to my absurd urge to bolt down the stairs. Pausing, I looked myself over in the mirror that stood in the entryway, and I rubbed my finger over my teeth relishing the clean squeak they gave off. Eighth time's the charm, I supposed. Then, taking a deep breath, I opened the door to what would prove to be the most pleasurable week of my life.

"Wow," he whispered.

"Now that's how you say hello." I beamed, taking in the sight of him. He wore a pair of casual, dark jeans and a blazer. His hands were behind his back and he rocked back and forth on his toes, grinning mischievously. I suspected that he was hiding something behind his back, but before I could question him about it, his grin widened as he brought forward a chilled bottle of wine for my inspection.

"You didn't have to bring anything," I told him, as I took the bottle from his hands.

"What type of house guest would I be if I showed up with empty hands? Besides, you just moved in, right?" he asked, as I made room for him to enter.

"Yeah. I moved most of boxes into the other rooms. It was just too much for me to sort through alone."

"If you need help, I'm great with a box cutter—shit, that sounded awful…"

I laughed, I couldn't help it. One moment he was overtly sexual, and the next, he was so cute and sweet, that it was hard to believe.

"It's fine," I told him. "Have you eaten? I ordered pizza because I felt that making dinner would be a little too—" I paused and made a face.

"Too relationship-y?" he finished with a grin. "Pizza's good."

Nodding, I headed for the kitchen, and he followed. I handed him a wine opener from one of the drawers and turned around to reach up for the plates I had unpacked just this afternoon.

"Glasses?" he asked. "Or do you want to drink out of the bottle?"

"I'd say bottle, but I wouldn't want you to judge me, or get any ideas about the kind of girl I am," I teased.

"Honesty. I like that in a woman," he said, taking a swig before handing the bottle to me.

"Then let's get real honest," I said with a grin as I swallowed a mouthful of wine. "Do you really want to eat pizza right now?"

"Not even a little bit," he muttered.

Taking my hand and pulling me to him, he molded his lips onto mine, and as I tried to place the bottle on the counter, it slipped from my hand and shattered against the floor. Neither of us paid the bottle any heed, and as my hands moved up his neck, his hands slid down the length of my torso to the bottom of my thighs. Then, he lifted me up onto the kitchen table and ripped open my blouse.

"I liked that shirt," I complained, as he kissed down my neck.

"I liked that wine."

"Touché—Ah!" I hissed, as he gently bit the top of my breast whilst reaching inside my bra to tease my nipples. As I wrapped my legs around him, drawing him closer to me, I reached for his belt and began to unfasten it, but he stopped me.

"Not yet," he whispered, trailing kisses from my mouth all the way down to my bellybutton. With ease he took my skirt off, and his fingers played around with the lace of my underwear.

I gasped as he rubbed his fingers over me. Pushing the lace to the side, he continued trailing his kisses downward until his head lingered between my thighs. Grabbing onto his hair, I shivered as he licked me.

"Levi."

He didn't stop. He began, slowly, softly, but then, just as if someone had flipped a switch inside his mind, he grew wild... just the way I liked him. My back lifted as his tongue, followed by two of his fingers, entered me. Gripping onto his hair, I held him tight, rocking my hips towards him.

"Urgh..." I couldn't even form words.

"You should see how you look right now," he said. Kissing his way back up my body, his fingers remained, vigorously stroking my sweet spot. Pleasure rocked through me, and I bit my lower lip, trying in vain to smother the loud moan that had been building deep within the core of me.

His teeth grazed my earlobe, and I could feel his hot breath against my neck as he whispered, "I know you can be much louder than this, Thea. Moan for me. Come for me."

"God! Yes!" I screamed, as I allowed myself to let go.

As my climax reached its peak, I threw my head back and dug my nails into his shoulders as though he were the only thing in the world that was holding me to the earth.

My lips parted as I watched him lick his fingers clean... as he licked *me* off his fingers. I was sweating, and my breathing was ragged. My heart felt like it was going to explode out of my chest. I had climaxed, but I wanted more of him. I needed *all* of him.

I kissed him passionately as I wrapped my legs around his waist to pull him in closer. As our tongues tasted and teased each other, I pressed myself against the length of him desperately trying to convey my need. Thankfully, he understood.

"Take me to your room," he demanded, breaking our kiss.

Nodding, I slid off the counter, making sure to avoid the broken glass, and stepped out of my panties. Then, I took his hand and led him into my bedroom.

The distance, no matter how small, between us was enough to drive me mad. He brushed my hair aside and kissed my neck, each step towards my bedroom felt too long... too damn far away. And

I couldn't help but want to stay in his arms longer. I loved how he touched all of me with no reservations.

"This is a clothes-free zone," I whispered, as we finally entered my room. To illustrate my point, I rid myself of my bra as I stepped though the threshold. "House rule."

"Who am I to go against the house rules?" he muttered, unbuttoning his shirt. I lay back on my bed watching him. "Aren't you going to help?" he asked.

"Not even a little bit," I replied, biting my bottom lip in anticipation.

To my disappointment, he stripped quickly, and his boxers had barely touched the floor before he pounced on me.

I laughed as he hovered above me. "Before the week is out, we definitely need to work on your stripping routine."

"Will you give me a few pointers?"

I gently sucked his bottom lip. "I don't strip, but I'm sure we can work something out."

I ran my hand down his chest, enjoying the feel of his heated flesh as I traced each line of his muscles. As I trailed my way downwards, I took hold of him. His member stood hard and proud in my hands, throbbing with need, and his mouth parted slightly, as he let loose a low hiss.

His thumb grazed my lips, then he slid his palm up to caress my cheek, his strong touch was firm against my jaw line. "If you take hold of that, you better know what to do with it."

I let go in order to push him back. He fell onto the bed and I sat up on top of him. "You better be able to handle it," I teased.

LEVI

There are some things guys know they can only dream about. We never say them out loud, and we try not to think about them until we're alone… where we can fantasize all we want. But having her, a beautiful, fun, confident woman, kiss down my chest, all while her hands worked me to the point where I needed to grip onto the sheets in order to maintain some semblance of control... it was too much. Each and every second I spent with her, my control was slipping. I'd wanted to take this a little bit slower, to enjoy it—

"Fuck! Thea," I gasped, sitting up as she took me in her mouth. I stared down at her, captivated by her ability to leave me shivering me in her hands. "I can't think, fuck, Thea. Ah—"

My hands were in her hair before I even realized it. She swirled her tongue around the tip of my head, and I could feel the urge building inside of me.

No. Not like this.

Holding her head steady for a moment, I took charge, and I flipped us both around, pinning her hands above her head.

"So, I take it that you couldn't handle it?" she grinned, licking her lips once again. Fuck me. She was doing it on purpose.

I parted her thighs with my one free hand. Feeling her velvety lips part, and her body go rigid in anticipation, I paused and pulled back slightly. She wasn't the only one who could be a tease. Then, as she frowned in frustration at her delayed gratification, I slammed into her, allowing her to have all of me at once.

"Ah goddamn!" she screamed, her head twisting back pleasure.

"You were saying?"

"I—"

Slam

"Levi—"

Slam

Slam

She gave up trying to speak, and instead struggled to free her hands from my iron grip. But I refused to let her go. She begged to touch me as her body shook and trembled, but watching her under me, seeing the pleasure rippling through her with my every thrust, I soon found that even I was struggling to hold back.

"Baby, please," she begged, and at that, I let go of her hands, and took ahold of her hips. I changed my pace and sped up my thrusting, grunting with each thrust.

"Yes. Ahh," she moaned, as she wrapped her arms around my neck, and pulled me to her lips. Our tongues circled each other, matching the rhythm and intensity of our writhing bodies. When she opened her brown eyes to look at me, there weren't enough words in that moment to express the depth of our affection and our longing for each other. I never wanted this moment to end.

"Levi."

"Thea."

We both called out for one another as we finally came. When it was over and our afterglow had begun, we collapsed into each other's arms. Neither of us spoke; we just leaned back against the bed and relished the scent of our sex.

Her head rested against my chest, and as she settled down against me, my hand slid down the length of her body and came to rest on her ass. Without thinking, I squeezed it, but she didn't say anything, she simply let me be.

It was things like this that made me feel as though she was just a dream. Things like this didn't happen to me. I worked, I had a few hook ups here and there, and then I went back to work. But never in my life had I ever been so infatuated with someone.

"What's your last name?" I asked her.

"What?" She turned her head and looked at me.

"Your last name, what is it?"

"Don't tell me you're already getting attached," she teased.

I frowned at that. "It feels dirty to me— dirtier to be doing this and not at least have an idea as to who you are. Don't you think so?"

"It's Cunning," she said simply. "Thea Cunning."

"I'm Levi Black."

"Sexy name," she giggled. "I'm guessing that's your alias, it can't possibly be your real name."

Reaching over the edge of the bed, I searched for my pants.

Finding them, I fished my wallet out of the back pocket and flipped it open to show her my ID.

"Now I know your age, height, date of birth—?" she taunted, "What if I'm some kind of crazy stalker?"

"I'm a lawyer," I told her. "I can get a restraining order if needed."

"Ooh, a lawyer," she said, not sounding the least bit impressed as she sat up and wrapped a sheet around herself, much to my disappointment.

"Most women find that highly impressive."

"I guess it's okay, but I prefer brain surgeons," she said with a wink as she rose out of bed.

"Where are you going?"

"I'm going to heat up some pizza; I'm starving!"

"I'll go with you," I said as I stood up. I grabbed my boxers as she took one of my shirts to wear. "Must you look sexy in everything?"

"That's the hunger talking, come on." she laughed, taking my hand.

I like the way she laughed. She did it so easily, as if she didn't have a care in the world.

"Shadow! No!" she screamed, as she rushed forward to chase away her cat who was busy getting itself drunk off of the wine we'd spilled on the ground.

The brown and white cat tried to run away from her, but she caught it, and moved it over to the water bowl.

"Sorry about that," she said, looking up at me.

"It's fine," I said, as I bent and began picking up the broken shards of glass. She knelt beside me and wiped up the rest of the wine.

"Sorry about the wine as well. You said it was your favorite?"

"It's not really. I lied because I ripped your shirt," I said, nodding to the yellow top that lay on the ground, along with the rest of her clothes that were scattered all around.

"Well, I'm just going to have to keep your shirt as compensation then," she sniffed.

"You look better in it anyway."

Shaking her head at me, we dumped the glass shards into the bin. Trying my best not to stare at her, I looked around her kitchen. It was a little outdated, but still nice. Wait—

"Thea? How are you going to heat up the pizza without a microwave?"

Her eyes went wide as she looked around. "Damn it, I left it in one of the boxes."

"Then what have you been eating all this time?"

"Cereal and take out?"

I tried not to laugh at the look on her face.

"Hey, give me a break, I just moved."

"No judgment," I lied.

"Liar."

"Come on, let's search for your microwave."

"It's okay, we can use the oven."

"True. But then you still won't have a microwave to use next time. Now, where are the boxes?"

Sighing, she opened the door that led out of the kitchen and into what I could have only assumed was a garage. It was filled with nothing but boxes.

"What is this? Hoarders?"

"First of all, hoarding is a serious medical condition, one that I do not have, and secondly, what happened to 'no judgment'?" She crossed her arms over her chest and I couldn't help but notice her breasts as they rose.

"Excuse me," she said, interrupting my ogling, "are you staring at my boobs?"

"Yes," I replied, "but again, we aren't judging each other."

Shaking her head at me, she turned back into the garage, and pulled out a pair of boots for herself and a pair of sandals for me.

"Good thing my sister's feet are huge," she chuckled

"So is my sister's. She used to buy big shoes, and ask for a small box to take them out of the store with her."

"Ha! I thought my sister was the only one."

Smirking, we didn't really go deeper than that, nor did we need to. We hunted around for the microwave, and interestingly enough, it was a lot more fun than I thought it would be.

PRESENT

THEA

That bastard was gunning for me, I could feel it. This was only the sixth class, and he had already given us a pop quiz. The moment he said the words, his eyes flickered over me. It was as though he meant to challenge me right then and there. Plus, with his Darwinian style of teaching, if we all failed, he'd kick us out without a second thought. I had heard a rumor that all Professor Black needed was a total of twelve students to be in his class, and at the moment, there were twenty of us. And on the first day, there had been over fifty.

Everyone he kicked out would go to the other law professors, in the hopes of sitting in on their classes. It was said that only the top twelve students got offered a position within his firm after graduation. This group of students were known as the twelve disciples, and come hell or high water, I was determined to be a part of the twelve.

I had spent the last week reading everything I could find on

Levi Black. To students, he was *El Diablo,* but in Law circles, he was called *The Cleaner.* The reason for this was that he hadn't lost a single case since he had opened up his own firm, and he was known for being the one who cleaned up everyone's messes, legally speaking.

Levi Black and Associates was one of the leading law firms in the country. The name partner, Levi Black, graduated Harvard Law School at twenty-three, the same damn age that I was just starting out on. After graduating, he received a job offer at Spencer and Hill, where he worked for five years, before leaving to start his own practice with a college friend. However, two years later, and after a nasty divorce, he left the company and started his own firm at the age of thirty.

Now here he was, six years later and on top of the world, and all I could do was wonder: who in the hell was this person? *Time* magazine quoted him as saying he wanted to "shape the next generation of young minds." He was a natural born genius with a hunger for winning at all costs. He could have studied anything but chose law. They all made him seem like he was the Goliath of lawyers.

No matter how hard I tried, I couldn't make this version of him match up with the Levi I knew. He wasn't a savage workaholic lawyer; he played the guitar at a club, he sang with me in the shower, he ate cold pizza in his underwear, and laughed at all of my bad jokes. I knew that people sometimes put up façade when they first meet people, but even at two o'clock in the morning, he was still just as kind as the first moment I met him.

"Ms. Cunning, shouldn't you be more focused on your quiz than on the light fixture?"

I jumped as he startled me out of my daydream.

Be one of the twelve.

"Yes, of course, but I've already finished, and wasn't sure if I was allowed to leave early," I said as I handed him my write up.

He looked at the clock. "It took you twenty-one minutes?"

"Sorry it took *so long*," I replied dramatically.

He read it over it, and placed it back down in front of me. I couldn't stop myself from shivering when his hand accidentally grazed against mine. And to make matters worse, he noticed.

"Everyone," he called out to the class, "thanks to Ms. Cunning, you now have five minutes left to complete the assignment."

A few people turned to glare at me, but I was too focused on trying to stop my hand from shaking to pay them any heed.

Was that too cocky? Fuck no, this is Levi Black. And I was going to be one of the disciples.

For some odd reason, I had a sneaking suspicion that he was the one who had started calling his selected students the *twelve disciples*, just so that he could praise himself, the asshole.

"Time's up," he snapped.

As we passed our papers down to him, a few people opted to save themselves the embarrassment and simply stood up and left. I counted.

Sixteen. At the rate he was going would there even be twelve of us left?

"The four students who just left, never speak to them again," he stated as he took the quizzes and dropped them into the trash. "This quiz wasn't meant to test your analytical abilities, it was meant to test your mental strength. Can you work under pressure? If you can't, then you don't deserve to be a lawyer. However," he boomed, "that is just my opinion. There is a loophole for ninety-nine percent of everything, and after a week here, the four students who left—I no longer care to remember their names—did not grasp the lesson that Ms. Cunning understood on the first day; you have the right and the ability to present your case and therefore defend your right to remain in the class."

Was he praising me? No. He couldn't be.

"Even if you don't have the strength now, you fake it. You fake it as if your life depended on it. You research the hell out of it, and even if you're dumb enough to get the date wrong, or finish a quiz early without properly quoting the text, or me, then you still fake it. Because if you can believe your lie, you can sell doubt to others. To win a case, all you have to do is instill doubt in the thing opposing you."

Asshole! Praising me, my ass. The son of the bitch was still making a fool out of me. Damn I hated him. I hated him so much, I wanted to claw at his face.

Or his back. The thought slyly slipped into my mind and I flushed.

Damn it. Why can't I think straight? Why?

"Who here has heard of the Richard Archibald Case?" he asked, and we all raised our hands.

He pointed to a guy who sat behind me. I turned to look at him, and I noted that he wore a plaid shirt and cowboy boots, and that his eyes were blue, and his hair was a dirty, sandy blonde.

"Atticus Logan, rise and use this moment to impress me."

"Alrighty then—"

"Sit back down, Mr. Logan," he said, causing a few snickers. "Your southern charm might be nice for some people, but here you're wasting words, which means you're wasting my time. Next, you, girl in the glasses, Ms. Vega is it?"

She stood up quickly, knocking over her all of her things, but she wasn't even bothered. "Richard Archibald, age sixteen, son of the multimillionaire, Andrew Archibald. On Friday September 12th, he was arrested and charged with second-degree murder and manslaughter in the death of two high school students, who attended one of his parties, where he gave them the new heroin pills that are now on the streets. It's basically heroin in a capsule."

"Thoughts?" he asked.

"Second-degree murder is ridiculous," someone up front said.

"Wasn't one of the kids his ex-girlfriend? And they said that he knew the batch was bad. The prosecution could call it a crime of passion," Vega added.

"Hearsay." Levi replied.

"He deserves manslaughter, but I doubt he will get it," I stated out loud, and they all turned to focus on me.

"Go on," Levi prompted, leaning against his desk.

"Come on, whether or not he knew the batch was bad doesn't matter. The substance is still illegal, and therefore, any death attributed to it is a crime. If this kid wasn't rich and white, this wouldn't be news. He would be made to serve his time, and we would move on."

"Why is it always race with you people?" Atticus snapped behind me.

"Excuse me?" I exclaimed. "With 'you people'? Did I just become the poster child for black people everywhere?"

"There you go, twisting my words. I'm just saying that whenever anything happens, 'African-Americans' are always the first ones to pull out the race card. I bet if the kid was rich and black, it would still be news."

"Oh, that's such bullshit. If he were black, the media's reaction wouldn't be one of surprise at all. After all, a black kid with drugs is a thug. A white kid with drugs has made a few bad life choices. There is a systematic issue in our legal system—"

"Oh please, go preach to someone else. This kid didn't force anyone to take the drugs. They may be *underage*, but they're all smart enough to know what could happen to them. Blaming this kid is wrong, and saying he deserves manslaughter, is lazy."

"I moved to the north to get away from 'you people.' " I muttered.

"And I came here to piss people like you off, sweetheart."

Sweetheart?

Sweetheart!

"You—"

"Both of you will be working with me on this case," a familiar voice up front said, with the finest trace of amusement in his voice.

"What?" We both turned around to gape at Professor Black.

"I've been asked to represent Richard Archibald, and I have decided to choose the two of you to work alongside me and my associates. Ms. Cunning, since you adamantly believe he should already be in jail, I'm sure you and the prosecution will be on the same page, which should keep me one step ahead. Atticus, you've given an angle for this case. Free will, the two that died should have known better. So for that reason, you are both now working with me. The rest of you better step your game up. That's it for the day," he concluded, leaving us all stupefied.

Once again, I waited for everyone to leave, and I glared at Atticus as he winked at me before walking out the door. I wanted to throw something at him, or at the very least stick my tongue out like a petulant child.

Yeah, that's mature.

"Do you need something, Ms. Cunning?" Levi asked, drawing my attention back to him.

"What, you aren't just going to walk out?"

Shit, it just came out of my mouth.

He said nothing as he gathered his things, and prepared to leave.

"You should take me off this case."

He paused, "Why? Because of our prejudices towards it? I told you it can be useful in formulating a—"

"No," I interrupted him and I wanted to say *because we shouldn't spend anymore time together.* But I just couldn't.

He looked at me, but it felt as though he was looking through me. His eyes narrowed and his stare grew cold, "Do you want to be here, Ms. Cunning, or are you just wasting my time?"

"I do!" I interjected.

"But you're willing to walk away from the chance of a lifetime because of *that*?"

"I never said that."

"But you were thinking it, I can tell by your hesitation. So either you're not strong enough to keep your personal and your professional life separate, or you don't have the confidence to be here. Either way you still look weak."

"But I'm not. What happened—"

"Thea, nothing is bigger than what you want to do with your life. If you want to be a lawyer, you can be a damn good lawyer, and you don't let anything get your way. In fact, you use whatever you can to your advantage."

He couldn't be serious.

"You're saying I should use *that*... use *you* to my advantage?"

He shrugged. "What's done is done, and can never be undone. Maybe you don't get it, but if you want to be a lawyer, you have to be the best there is, otherwise you're not worth anything to anyone. So do whatever you have to do to get to the top. Considering who your mother was, I thought you would be the last person I would have to explain that to. You fought for your seat, so don't just give it away. Not now, not ever."

Clenching my jaw and my fists, I stepped right in front of him. He was so close that one wrong move would inevitably lead to us kissing, and yet in this moment, I didn't have that urge.

"First of all, *never*, under any circumstances, bring my mother up *ever* again. Secondly, I *want* to be here, I *want* be a great lawyer, and I will not let anything you do rattle me, because like you said, that was in the past. But don't make it seem like I tricked you or lied to you. You never told me you were a professor. Lastly, I will never use *that* as a stepping-stone for my career. I will never give anyone the ability to say that I got to where I am because I fucked my professor. I will be great, and that's because I earned it, just like you did."

I dug into my purse and left his watch and boxers on the table. Then without another word, I turned and started for the door.

"Wait," he called out to me.

Damn it, why can't I just leave?

"What?" I snapped.

He threw my underwear back at me. "Since we're returning things now."

Glaring at him, I stuffed them into my purse and stormed out.

Damn him.

LEVI

Damn her.

I had spent all week researching everything I could about her through the Harvard database, only to be hit with surprise after surprise. Thea Cunning, age twenty-three, was the daughter to Margaret "The Shark" Cunning.

I had written my very first thesis on *The Shark*, how she, in her whole career, had only lost three cases in twenty-five years. She was the original gangster of criminal law. Having her working on your case was basically like having a get-out-of-jail-free-card in court. We still studied and referenced her cases today. After learning that, it suddenly made sense why her daughter wasn't the slightest bit rattled by me. Having *The Shark* as a mother must have been like having the ultimate crash course in law.

Thea graduated valedictorian at Towson High School Law and Public Policy and went on to graduate from Princeton University, summa cum laude, in three years with a degree in English studies. Apparently, she had been on track to follow in her mother's footsteps, but instead opted to take a two years hiatus when she moved back to Maryland. And now, she was currently attending Harvard Law on a full scholarship. Her hobbies were listed as volleyball, tennis, photography and creative writing. Her biggest achievement, according to her file, "has yet to be realized, and thus, nothing else matters." She came back to Boston after her mother's diagnosis of stage four-lung cancer and was currently living in her old childhood house.

"Why?" I questioned, sighing to myself when I got home.

Kicking off my shoes, I fell back onto the couch.

"Why, what?"

"Damn it, Bethan!" I jumped up.

My sister, and her giant pregnant self, came out of my kitchen, with the carton of rocky-road ice cream she had pillaged from my freezer. She was dressed in sweats, a Guns N' Roses shirt, and on her head, she wore a beanie.

"Don't yell at me!" she yelled back.

"I wouldn't yell if you didn't scare the hell out of me. What are you doing in my house?" I demanded, trying to sound as though I were really angry.

"We were out of ice cream?" she replied, wobbling over to take a seat on the chair.

"So instead of going to the grocery store, like a normal person, you came over to steal mine?"

"You always sucked at sharing," she replied, taking another spoonful.

I was tempted to snatch it back from her.

What kind of man takes away food from a pregnant woman?

"Bethan, please tell me you have a more logical reason to come here, or I swear I'll call Tristan."

"Is that supposed to be a threat? You'll call my husband? Who do you think dropped me off here?"

I hated them both.

"Bethan—"

"Okay, okay. Tristan told me you've been sinning all over the city with a girl, and then she turned out to be one of your students."

"I don't want to talk about this with you—"

"Levi, for thirty years you have been the good one, the smart one, the shining star, and I've never once faulted you for it, or even been jealous of you, because honestly, your life seemed to be a pain in the ass. But now, I'm a human incubator for a tiny person, which means my husband no longer lets me go to the bar I founded because I scare away the customers. Mom keeps taking me out to buy me dresses with ruffles…*ruffles,* Levi. People are in my face every ten seconds, screaming about the joys of motherhood, and honestly, it feels like I'm dying. My feet hurt, I have to pee every twenty minutes, and I can't drink. I've never been so bored in my whole life! So, I'm coming to you big brother, to cheer me up, or so help me, I will end up being the next person you will be defending in court, when I snap like a toothpick."

When she snapped?

"Whatever you're drinking, or whatever you smoked, you need to stop," I said slowly, and she threw the couch pillow at me.

"Tell me about your one-week lover."

"Of all the people you had to marry, why did it have to be my best friend?"

"Objection! Avoiding the question."

Rolling my eyes at her, I laid back down— "We went out for a week. It was just pure fun, and then, the morning after the week was over, I saw her in my class, the end."

"Why didn't you kick her out? Isn't that your "scary Professor" thing?"

"I tried, but she's smart! If she were any other student, I'd seriously be interested in her career path."

"Well, if it was just a one week thing, then you should both just move on like adults, right? And not let it mess things up."

That's right. So why couldn't we—I— do that?

"So, then," Bethan continued, "why'd you come in all gloomy?"

"Because I'm a masochist."

"Too much information," she cringed.

"I put her on a case I'm working on," I told her. "I did it without even thinking about our situation. I was thinking about how I could use her to win the case. What's worse is when she brought it up after class, she was so close to me, I wanted to—" I broke off my sentence, unable to say the truth of it out loud.

"So, maybe it wasn't just a one week thing."

"It was," I said quickly. "It has to be. We made that very clear from the start. One week of sex, and that was it."

"So, that's all you guys did for a week? Screw each other's brains out?"

I paused, not wanting to relive our week in my mind while my sister sat on the chair staring intently at me. I chose my next words very carefully, trying my best to mask my emotions and not give too much away. "We didn't have sex *all* the time."

"Okay, let's think of this in another way. If she wasn't your student, would you have broken the one week thing and asked her out again?"

Fuck me. I would have. I had planned to.

I stared at my sister and made no effort to reply.

"I'll take that as a yes."

"It doesn't matter," I said. "None of it matters. She's my student, I'm her professor. That's as far as our relationship goes. She has promise, and I will see to it that she gets what she needs out of my class."

Bethan remained quiet, then with careful deliberation she asked, "No, but seriously, what did she do to you in that week? I've never seen you act like this over anyone."

That was the million-dollar question that even I didn't have the answer to.

What had she done to me?

PAST
DAY 3

THEA

"You've got to be kidding me with this," I laughed, opening his freezer. "And you were judging me for eating cereal."

"I have a sweet tooth, what can I say?" he replied, as he came up behind me, wrapped his arms around my waist, and kissed my shoulder. "Pick your ice cream already."

"There are so many choices," I mused.

And the truth of the matter was that my reaction wasn't unwarranted. Half of his freezer was stacked with every carton of ice cream that I could think of. They were all lined up perfectly as if we were at an ice cream parlor.

"Well, you can't go wrong with chocolate," he whispered, as he cupped one of my breasts through his shirt. I was always wearing his clothes now. Luckily, he didn't seem to mind.

"What?" he asked, as I stifled a laugh.

I reached in, grabbing a carton of vanilla instead, before wiggling out of his arms. "Nothing."

"You're a horrible liar," he said as he followed me into the living room. I jumped onto his grey couch... we had already broken it in at least four times.

"That comment you made about chocolate... it sounded like something out of an '80s porno."

"Well excuse me! As a child of the '80s, I'm not sure what to say to that—"

"It's all right," I chided as I dipped my spoon into the carton, "but the '90s were so much better."

He snorted, eating the ice cream off my spoon before I could. "Oh please! All that sex is messing with your head."

"Are you kidding me? The cell phone—"

"There were cell phones in the '80s too, you know."

"That giant rock that people carried around like cavemen does not count as a cell phone," I informed him.

"My generation suffered so yours could have that nice flip phone," he shot back. "In the '80s, *Madonna* was amazing, and so were *New Kids on the Block*. Plus, Will Smith became the fresh prince, and on top of that The Simpsons—"

"The Simpsons came out in 1989, that belongs to the '90s."

"What comes after the 19?" he tilted his ear to me.

"It's called rounding up."

He rolled his eyes at me. "The '80s had The Breakfast Club."

Damn it.

"The '90s had The Breakfast Club 2."

He paused for a moment, looking shocked— "Did you just compare the original Breakfast Club to its sequel?"

"Well you can't just throw the Breakfast Club card on the table like that, at least wait until I list a few more '90s classics, you jerk." I sulked, knowing I was beat.

"And I still had my Michael Jackson card to play, because *Thriller* was the shit."

For some reason, I felt as though I'd let my whole generation down. Scowling, I stuffed my mouth full of ice cream. He looked at me, awaiting my comeback, but my brain was as frozen as the ice cream I was consuming.

"It doesn't matter what you say, I'm not saying the '80s win—"

He kissed me before I could finish.

Falling back against the arm of the couch, I wrapped my hand around his neck as he hovered on top of me.

"The '90s had you," he said, his voice softer now.

"You're buttering me up," I pouted, as he undid the buttons of my shirt. "Smart move, Mr. Black."

He grinned, already kissing down my chest— "I thought so too."

Closing my eyes, I dropped the ice cream… he made me shiver more anyway.

LEVI

She snored. It wasn't loud, or obnoxious; it was kind of cute actually. She was wrapped up in the sheets, her legs peeking out slightly, and she held on to my arm as she slept, but I didn't mind. It was odd that I didn't mind. I really didn't know much about her, but I found myself *wanting* to know her.

"I can feel you staring at me,' she whispered, as she shifted beneath the sheets.

"You snore."

"I do not!" she shot back immediately, sounding both embarrassed and hurt at my remark.

I laughed. "You do."

"I know," she gave in with a laugh, as she covered her face with her hands.

I laughed along with her. Her laughter was infectious.

"It's all right, it's actually cute."

She looked at me for a moment like she was trying to read me, but with a little sigh, she gave up and rose from her position and stepped out of bed, taking the sheets with her.

"I'm going to take a shower."

"Okay, then I'll make us something to eat," I said, already on my feet.

She paused turning back to me, "You cook too?"

"Yes?"

"Please tell me it's like, only eggs or something."

"What? No, I can cook."

"Damn it, Levi, I like my men just under perfect, thank you!"

"Would you like me to burn one side of the toast?"

"You'd better." She glared, and I kissed her lips quickly.

"Don't worry Thea, I'm nowhere near perfect."

"So you say."

She kissed me back once more before she headed into the bathroom.

"You're amazingly weird, has anyone ever told you that?"

"It's all part of my charm, Mr. Black."

Snickering, I shook my head at her and headed into the kitchen, wondering whether or not she really wanted me to burn her toast.

"I'll just make one burnt and the other one fine."

What was happening to me?

THEA

With Levi in the kitchen making us breakfast, I knew that I had at least twenty minutes to myself. Taking my bag from under his sink, I grabbed my curling iron, shaving gel and my stick of deodorant, along with everything else I needed to make it seem like I was still a damned lady.

This morning I'd felt the roughness of my legs, and I wanted to die. I had planned on shaving yesterday, but he had joined me in the shower, and once again, I forgot everything that I was supposed to be doing with my life.

What was wrong with me?

I sighed, as I turned on the shower.

I didn't know much about him, but I wanted to. When we first thought of this one-week fling, I honestly thought it would just be sex, a short sweet conversation, maybe some food, and then we would be on our way until the next day. But instead, we were only separated for a few hours, which felt like forever.

"I'm getting addicted," I confessed to myself. "I'm getting too addicted to Levi Black."

This should bother me more—

"Aww, fuck!" I screamed at the self-inflicted cut on the back of my heel.

"Thea? Are you alright?"

I didn't say anything for a moment trying not to scream. It hurt like a mother—

"Thea?" he asked, as he opened the door.

Why hadn't I locked the door? Damn it! Can't I just be a little bit sexy sometimes?

"I'm fine," I called out, "it's just a little cut…"

He opened the shower curtain and I instinctively I crossed my hands over my chest in an attempt to conceal my nakedness, while trying to balance on my one good leg. I must have looked like an idiot.

"Come out of there, I have some topical."

"Seriously Levi, I'm okay."

"Look down," he instructed.

When I did, I just wanted to crawl under a rock for the rest of my life. Watching my blood go down the drain, staining his bath… it was gross.

"Fine," I sighed.

I tried to step out of the shower, but he stepped in front of me and picked me up. With me in his arms, he grabbed two towels off of the rack, and we headed into the bedroom. Placing me on the bed, I wrapped one of the towels around myself, while he pressed the second one against my bleeding foot.

Looking at him over, I noticed he was wearing a simple pajama bottom and light cotton shirt... but he also had glasses on.

Even when he wasn't trying to be sexy, he was sexy, while I, on the other hand, had been busy *trying* to be sexy, but had instead pulled an Edward Scissorhands on my leg.

Fuck my life.

"Sorry," he muttered, as I winced when the cream touched my heel.

"Oh please, don't say sorry, this is embarrassing enough as it is. So much for me trying to be sexy," I sighed.

He paused for a moment looking up at me like I was crazy— "I came into the bathroom to find you standing under my shower, wet, naked, and beautiful. Then, I got to carry you out of the shower like a man, and now, you're sitting on my bed, dripping wet, with nothing around you but a towel. The only thing that could make this sexier is this," he said as he reached up and pulled off my shower cap.

Goddamn it! I forgot I had it on. *Why, God? Why?!*

"You're sexy without even trying," he said, as he planted a light kiss on my kneecap, "now stop ruining this for me."

I remained silent, allowing him to finish bandaging me up. At least I had finished ninety percent of shaving my legs before I got hurt.

"I'll finish breakfast while you get ready," he said, as he stood back from me.

Reaching up, I grabbed the edge of his shirt, and as I sat up on to the bed, I allowed the towel to fall. He swallowed, his eyes fixated on every inch of me.

"I like you in glasses," was all I could think to say before he kissed me.

Moaning into his mouth, he lifted me up, moving us further onto the bed.

"You're killing me Thea," he murmured against my lips.

"God, I hope not. The week is just getting started!" I grinned, as I took his glasses off and placed them on his bedside table. Reaching for the box of condoms I noted, "You're running low."

"A box well spent," he replied taking it from my hand as I kissed him. It took him only a moment before he grabbed ahold of my waist and started thrusting.

"Hgh…" I moaned, gripping on to him.

When he squeezed my ass, I knew that this round wasn't meant to be a drawn out affair, he meant to go at it hard and fast. He was on his knees, squeezing my thighs, as he slammed into me over and over again.

"Levi," I gasped, as I let go of him, and leaned back to grab onto his headboard.

I called his name over and over again, but the only answer he gave to my calls were in the form of short grunts… until he slowed down, much to my frustration.

"What are you…?" I asked.

Opening my eyes, I found him watching me intently, a slight smile lingered on his lips. I knew that he took pleasure in seeing me beg for it. Each slow thrust forward drove me crazy. I wanted him, and he knew it.

"Faster," I demanded.

But he just smirked, going slower than ever. "I'm sorry, what?"

Damn him.

Letting go of his headboard, I pushed him onto his back.

"I said faster, and if you won't give it to me, I'll give it to myself," I said, as I planted a quick kiss in the center of his chest before sitting back up.

"Thea…" he gasped, as I rode him.

His hands went to my waist but I smacked them away.

"Thea," he grunted, his eyes closing.

"You should see the look on your face," I teased him, just as he had teased me.

He flipped me on to my back, his face only inches away. "Don't push me," he growled.

"Then don't hold back."

That did it. Whatever reservations he had left, disappeared as he once again buried himself deeper in me.

Slam.

Slam.

Slam.

"Yes!"

That was all that I could say, but it was all that needed to be said. His grip on me was so strong, it was almost painful, and even that made it feel better.

Pulling him to me, I kissed him again. I was rough and sloppy, but I didn't care.

"Levi."

"Thea," he whispered, right before falling on top of me. "I think I'm becoming addicted to you."

I laughed, "That's good, because I feel the same way. Let's indulge."

Because this was sinful in all the right ways.

PRESENT

THEA

"Well look what we've got here, someone is five minutes early."

There was only one person with that annoying accent, and he was the very last person I wanted to deal with in the morning.

"What do you want Atticus?" I pressed the elevator button two more times, willing it to come faster.

"I do recall Professor Black choosing the both of us for this case," he replied, stepping inside with me. "Anyway, I think we should introduce ourselves and be professional while we're here. Who knows, we might be working here in a few years' time. I'm Atticus Logan."

He held out his hand for me to shake.

"Thea Cunning."

"I hear every year Professor Black takes a student under his wing. You should know right now: I ain't losing to you, or anyone else. So don't get in my way," he stated, stepping out when the doors opened.

Do no harm. Do no bodily harm to the ass in the cowboy boots.

"So, you guys are the fresh meat," a voice chimed.

I turned, searching for its owner. That voice, it was so familiar...

As I turned, I found myself face to face with none other than Tristan. Tristan, the man who'd served me drinks at the bar, the man who had worn the top hat and guy liner. In the clear light of day, he looked completely different. His hair was styled perfectly, his shoes shined to the point where I could see my reflection in it, and he wore a suit that likely would have cost me my entire life savings. A point which said a lot about my current financial state of affairs.

"Mr. Knox, it's a pleasure sir. I was fascinated by your work in the Dreyer Case," Atticus said, already kissing ass.

"Where are you from?" Tristan asked him.

"Greenville, South Carolina," Atticus replied with pride.

"I was born and raised in Mauldin."

"You're kidding me."

"I never kid about my hometown."

Atticus looked back to me and winked— "A small world. You're my new found hero."

So this is the old boy's club people talked about.

"I heard you worked for *The Shark* at one point in your career," Atticus grinned.

The Shark? My mother, The Shark?

"Mr. Knox," I said interrupting Atticus, "it's a pleasure to meet you, *again*." I stepped forward extending my hand.

I was not going down with a fight.

"Again?" Atticus questioned, looking at me with a frown.

"Yes, Mr. Knox worked for my mother, Margaret Cunning," I lied.

Well, it wasn't a complete lie. I *had* met him before, and he had worked with my mother at one point, right?

"Yes, of course. I'm quite sorry to hear about her passing." Tristan smirked at me.

Atticus' mouth dropped open, and this time, I was the one who turned to wink.

"You're all late," Levi scolded, coming towards the elevator.

"We're five minutes early."

"You *were* five minutes early, but you spent those minutes, *my minutes*, may I add, chatting about your personal lives, right Tristan?"

"I couldn't get them to shut up."

They'd fucking set us up.

"Anyway, in this office, if you aren't a half hour early, you might as well not show up. So far, I'm rethinking the both of you," he responded, as the elevator doors closed.

"You were supposed to be on that elevator with him," Tristan said from behind us. "If you don't make it to the car before he does, believe me, he will drop the both of you on the spot."

Atticus and I glanced at each for a second, before I took off my heels and bolted towards the stairs.

"Are you insane? There are at least 60 flights of stairs!" Atticus yelled after me, but I ignored him, running as quickly as I could.

As I reached the 49th level, I pushed open the door and dashed towards the elevator, pressing the button over and over again, as if my life depended on it.

"Ma'am?" a security guard asked, coming towards me. Fortunately, the doors opened, and sure enough there was Levi reading his paper.

"I work for him!" I shouted, pointing to Levi, as I jumped inside.

He looked up at me, confused as I entered gasping.

"I would have been more impressed if you'd ran down all of

the stairs," he said, no longer interested in me. As I stood there trying to catch my breath, he continued reading.

"Fuck you."

"Excuse me?" he turned back to look at me, his eyes narrowing.

"Achoo," I sneezed. "Excuse me," I lied and he knew it, but I put my heels back on anyway.

"Where's Atticus?" he asked as the doors opened.

"I don't know maybe he just isn't hungry for—" I stopped, seeing Atticus already standing at the car door. '

Levi looked back to me. "He wins."

He allowed Levi to enter before cutting between us both and climbing into the spot next to Levi, which forced me to take to the front seat.

"We are going to see the Archibalds," he said. "Keep your heads down, don't talk to anyone, especially not the reporters, don't even breathe into their mics, and don't under any circumstance, make eye contact. The same goes for the Archibalds themselves. You are nothing more than flies on a wall, you take notes, and you keep out of my associates' way, because they sure as hell won't be paying attention to you. If you have questions, keep them to yourself. If you have thoughts and opinions, keep them to yourself, unless I ask from them. Understood?" We both nodded. "Good."

This was the first time I had ever seen him dressed to the nines. When he had been with me, it was always a variation of jeans, and a button down shirt, or just his boxers, or sometimes, nothing at all. At school, he was semi-casual. But no matter what he wore, he looked good in everything.

No, Thea no! This is work. Think about the case, not him!

When we made it to the Archibald's Multimillion-dollar Boston Brownstone, it was worse than I realized. The press was being kept at bay by a wall of guards on the stairs.

"If either of you screw up my case in any way, I will make sure that you won't be able to study law, let alone practice it," he warned.

Opening the door, the media crowd swarmed, and began shouting questions at us. As we began our trek to the front door, dozens of flashbulbs went off in our faces.

"Remember, keep your head down," Atticus whispered to me as we walked forward.

"Mr. Black, do you truly believe in light of the new evidence that Richard did not intend to kill his ex-girlfriend?"

"Mr. Black, do you think this be your first loss since opening your firm?"

"How do you think this case will affect race relations?"

The wall of guards parted, and we crossed over the threshold, finally safe from the prying eyes of the press. Moving into the house, it was madness. Files, papers and coffee cups were everywhere. His associates had been arguing with each other; however, they stopped their bickering the moment he entered.

"Where are we?" he said, taking off his jacket and throwing it onto the chair as if he owned the place.

"Mrs. Archibald is in the kitchen looking through photos, Richard is upstairs in his room, we check in every ten minutes, and..." the girl who was speaking froze.

"And?" Levi snapped at her.

"And Mr. Archibald took a flight into New York this morning," another one of his associates replied. "We've tried calling, but all his phones are off."

Levi's nostrils flared, and he clenched his jaw, as he stomped into the kitchen.

Atticus and I followed, while the rest of his associates went back to their case files.

"He's in New York?!" Levi really yelled for the first time since I had met him.

The older woman was dressed in a navy tailored suit dress with a strand of pure white pearls around her neck. Her red hair was neatly combed back, and pinned up, and as Levi stormed into the kitchen, she jumped slightly— "He said he had a meeting—"

"His son has been charged with murder. *Two counts*, I may add, and he goes off to a meeting in New York?" he snarled, his voice only one octave lower.

"You have to understand—"

"No. *You* need to understand. I told you both that the only way I was taking this case was if you gave me your complete and utter trust, your loyalty, and your commitment. Which means you do what I say and I said *not to leave the bloody house*! The moment the press gets word of this, it will be spun one of two ways; one, that your husband is not taking this seriously, or two, that he is so distressed at his son's actions, that he could not bear to be near him. Which way do you think helps us?"

"Neither," she said, staring at the floor.

"Exactly!" he yelled again, turning from her and back to the living room. "Smoke signals, carrier pigeons, I don't care what or how, someone get in touch with Mr. Archibald before the five o'clock news. And you two," he said, pointing to two of his associates, "come with me."

The two associates all but jumped out of their seats as they went back into the kitchen.

"Thing one, Thing two, stop standing around like mannequins, and start dialing," another associate called, throwing us a stack of phone numbers.

Nodding, we dropped our stuff and started making calls.

"Everything you ever dreamed of, right?" Atticus whispered with the phone at his ear.

I snickered, before remembering who I was talking to.

"How did you get down to the car so fast?" I asked.

"Window washers."

My mouth popped open. "You're lying."

"Nope. I jumped on, and they took me all the way down." He grinned. "Hello, this is Atticus Logan with Levi Black and

Associates, can you tell me if Mr. Archibald is in?" He paused as he listened to their response. "Thank you for your time, please call us if anything changes." He hung up and looked at me. "I told you I was in this to win, and I meant it. You'd better pick up the pace, because I'm not waiting for you," he said, as he dialed the next number.

My mother used to say law school was just the battle, and that being a lawyer was leading a war. I never really understood that until now.

"Game on," I replied.

LEVI

"Where is Ms. Cunning?" I asked, coming out of the meeting with Mrs. Archibald.

Things were getting worse by the moment, and the plea deal was starting to look more and more appealing, but she'd refused.

"She went to the bathroom and disappeared," one of my employees replied, without looking up from the case files.

"She probably realized that she was in over her head," he added, more to himself than to me.

Thea, admit defeat? That will be the day I sprout wings and fly.

Sighing, I noticed the Archibald's youngest daughter staring at us through the stairway rails whilst she chewed on the end of one of her perfect red curls. She lifted her hand and motioned me over. I crossed the floor and went to her. She cocked her finger at me, a sign that she wanted to tell me a secret.

I leaned down and she whispered, "The pretty lady is upstairs with Richie."

"Thank you." I petted her head before rushing up the stairs.

Damn you Thea. At least I have reason to fire you now.

"You spoiled, little, rich, brat," I heard her snap at who could only be Richard.

"Excuse me? Do you know who you're talking to?"

"Yes I do, a spoiled, little, rich, brat," she repeated, enunciating each word.

"I can have you fired!" he screamed at her.

"Go ahead, but before you do, use your brain for just a moment. The only reason you're sitting up here playing video games is because you said you have nothing to worry about, right? I mean, you have the great and all-powerful Levi Black on your case."

"Yeah, so what? He's never lost case, so why should I be bothered? This will all be over in a week, two weeks, tops."

"Levi Black is an *amazing* defense attorney, but he's not God. Even he can't stop the people from loathing your guts. That's why he brought me here, because I personally believe you should spend a few years behind bars. It would do people like you some good. My job is to see every reason why the state wants to throw you away, and find a counter for it. And so far, your lack of remorse, your inability to comprehend your own situation, and your superiority complex will be the death of you. I truly hoped that I was wrong about you. I'd hoped that it was all just a stereotype I'd formed in my head, but sadly, you are worse than I imagined. So please, go ahead and have me fired, you'll only be adding another nail to your coffin kid. And me? I'll get to go home."

"So you're just going to give up? What type of crack lawyer are you?"

"What kind of human being are you? Two of your friends died, in your house—"

"Don't you think I know that?" he snapped. "Just because I'm not sobbing all over the place, or cutting my wrists, doesn't mean I don't know. I didn't even want the stupid pills, but everyone stopped coming to my parties because I wasn't *fun enough*. Hector was the one who told me where to get the pills from in the first place!"

"Richard, why didn't you say that?" She dashed out of the

room, only to run right into me, sending us both sprawling unto the ground.

Once again, I could feel every curve of her, and I fought the urge to hug her to me. But all too soon, she was gone.

"Oh my God, I'm so sorry, Mr. Black."

"Never mind that," I sighed, standing back up.

Turning to Richard, who looked more like his father than his mother, with his pale skin and dark eyes, I addressed him, "You said Hector, the boy that died, was the one who told you where to get the pills?"

"Don't use that," Richard said quickly.

He was insane.

"Are you insane?" Thea asked him.

If it was any other day, and we didn't have the history we had, I would have laughed.

"You guys hear what they're saying in the news, right?" he whispered, taking a seat on his bed. "Hector was my best friend. We played little league together, and he always let me win because he knew my dad hated it when I lost. He was an honor roll student, he was the star basketball player, what do you think would happen, if we say that my black, best friend, told me where to get the drugs from?"

"That's why you never said anything?" Thea whispered.

"I'm not an idiot, Hector was a good person, and I don't want people to remember him as some drug pimp... and I don't want his family to hate me anymore than they already do. So please, don't use that angle."

"Is everything alright?" Mrs. Archibald came up behind us, and Richard's eyes went wide.

"We were just going over some details. But we're done now, thank you," I said turning, making sure that Thea followed as well.

"Am I fired?" she asked, when got to the end of the hall.

"You don't work for me, you're my student."

"Then, am I being kicked out of your class?"

She was too close to me.

"No."

"We were able to get in touch with Mr. Archibald, he'll be here in a few hours," Atticus informed me, bursting with pride.

"Raymond, take our eager young friend to go pick up Mr. Archibald, and babysit him at all times. If he so much as goes near an airport, tackle him."

I saw the small grin Atticus shot Thea, and the glare in her eyes as he left. They were already in full out war, which only made things better for me.

"The rest of you, pack up and go home. I expect to see you all in the morning, looking less zombified, if possible," I told them.

They all sighed in relief, packing up their discarded coats and jackets, shoes, books, and papers. The press had gone home for the evening, so our exit was significantly easier than our entry had been.

I watched as Thea waited at the curb for a taxi, even though my car was already here.

"Get in," I called to her, holding the door open.

"That's not a good idea."

"It's about the case, now get in," I said firmly.

She looked me over like she didn't believe me, and rightly so. I only partially believed it myself.

"Is your car at the office?"

"I took a cab," she replied.

Nodding, I turned to my driver and gave him her address. She reluctantly walked over and climbed into the back seat, sitting as far away as she could from me, as though I had some sort of contagious disease.

"You shouldn't have spoken to him."

She sighed. "I know, I'm sorry, I just saw him sitting there playing video games, and I lost my cool."

"It's fine," I said, "but only because you got something I can use out of it. If you hadn't, no apology would have been able to help you."

Her head whipped back to me so quickly I was surprised that she didn't hurt herself.

"You're going to use Hector?"

"Yes. What other choice do I have? Richard's screwed if I don't."

"He doesn't want to drag his friend through the mud. If you do this, he will hate you."

"Believe me, I will survive just fine. I'm his lawyer, not his friend. His parents are paying me to keep him out of jail, so that's what I'm going to do. His personal feelings mean nothing to me."

"Levi, you know what will happen if you do this—"

"Yes, he will return to high school, and never touch drugs again."

"Not that!" she yelled. "Every black activist in America will use him as the poster boy for injustice in the legal system. Hector's parents will get on every station claiming that their son, *their dead son*, was put on trial for one mistake. This will not be the end of it, and I'm sure Richard won't run *from* drugs, but run *to* it, or at the very least, alcohol, to help him block out the fact that he not only betrayed his best friend, twice, but that the world now hates him because of it. He will self-destruct, and when it happens, everyone will point and say that's what he gets."

I fought back a smile. "I thought you wanted him in jail," I said, "yet here you are; defending him."

She sat back, crossing her arms. "Your plan is stupid."

"Harvard education right here," I said. "My plan will give us a win."

"What's the point of winning if you don't help anyone? What's the point of it if you only make things worse?" she muttered, opening the door as we pulled up to her house.

She didn't even look at me as we exited the car and I walked her to her door.

"Fine," I said.

She stopped, turning back, "Fine?"

"We won't throw Hector under the bus."

"So what will you do?"

"I'm going to hold a press conference—well, no, *you're* going to hold a press conference, with Richard."

Her mouth dropped open, "I'm going to do what now?"

"Tomorrow afternoon, you will sit by Richard as he apologizes to everyone he has *offended*, and as he states that he never meant for anyone to get hurt. Then, you will say how Richard was just one of many students who threw parties where pills, and other illegal substances, are used and abused, and on top of that, you will state that the fact that the police haven't even bothered to focus their efforts on finding the dealer is in itself a crime. Most of all, you will do it convincingly. "

"If you know what I'm going to say, then why don't you just say it?"

I shrugged taking a few steps towards her and closing in the almost unbearable distance between us. At that precise moment, the wind shifted, causing her hair to flutter around her face. Taking advantage of the opening nature had granted me, I brushed her hair back into place.

"Three reasons," I whispered. "One: I'm your professor and I'm telling you to. Two: You and Richard have built up a rapport. You can't fake something like that on television, and that way, people will see that you really do believe he shouldn't be charged."

"And the third reason?" she asked as she took a step towards me, closing the distance between us even more.

"What do you think?" I asked her.

I waited for a second before her brown eyes narrowed at me— "It can't be about race if I'm sitting there. You—urgh!— You were planning this from the moment we left the house weren't you?"

I dropped her a wink and turned back towards my town car.

"This is not all right!"

"Use what you have Thea, I've told you that before. Don't let anything stop you from winning. The race card has been thrown on the table, so take it off and you'll have your name associated with one headline case by tomorrow. Don't let your *feelings* blow it for you. You're better than that, and I will not hesitate to kick you out of class if you fail, right after using you as an example to the others. Goodnight."

Getting into the car, I slammed the door shut, and as my driver pulled away from her house, I rested my head against the back of the front passenger seat, trying, in vain, to will my hard-on away.

Damn it. I had gotten too close to her.

PAST
DAY 4

THEA

"Do you play?" he asked, as he noticed the guitar hidden behind some of the boxes in my living room.

"I wish! My sister is pretty decent, though she just started learning," I replied, as he stood up from our small picnic of wine, popcorn, and sandwiches.

"Do you think she would mind?"

"Not at all," I said.

I had bought the thing for her anyway, so I figured that I was at least entitled to hear it being played every once in a while.

Taking a seat on the opposite end of the couch, he picked at the strings. With his head cocked to the side, and his eyes closed, he listened intently to the tone and the pitch of each string, pausing every so often to adjust the tuning. He strummed through all six strings, measuring them against his internal tuning scale.

Satisfied, he opened his eyes and smiled at me, then, as he drew in a deep breath, he began to play.

I closed my eyes for a moment and listened to the sound of his music. As I followed the melody, the tune took form and I opened my eyes to stare at him.

"I know this!" I said as I sat up excitedly, trying my best to not spill any wine.

He laughed, "What is it then?"

Shit.

"I know it, don't tell me!" I repeated, trying to remember.

Urgh.

He kept smiling, as his fingers slid up and down the neck of the guitar with ease. He looked so relaxed, as if he could spend the rest of his life shirtless with a guitar in his hands.

"Damn it," I cried out in frustration, *I knew this song!*

He glanced up at me, "Give up?"

"No. Don't I get to call a friend or something?"

"It's "More Than Words" by *Extreme*," he said with a grin.

"I would have gotten it," I muttered. "It was on the tip of my tongue."

"Okay," he said with a tone of teasing.

"Anyway, where did you learn to play?" I asked him, desperate for a diversion.

"My father taught me," he replied. "I was horrible at hitting on girls when I was in high school, so he taught me to play so that I could woo the ladies," he said with a chuckle.

"You had issues with girls?" I asked incredulously.

"It's so hard to believe because I'm so devilishly handsome, right?"

Rolling my eyes, I threw some popcorn at him, and he managed to catch a few in his mouth.

"Do you want to hear the story or not?" he asked with mock annoyance.

"Alright, so Mr. Sexy-green-eyes had girl trouble in high school, go on."

"First of all, try to imagine me twenty pounds lighter with no muscular definition, a crew cut, acne, and thick glasses."

I laughed. I didn't mean to, but I laughed.

"You're lying."

"God, I wish. There was even a rhyme."

"No!" I covered my mouth with my hand, trying to stifle the bout of laughter that was threatening to explode out of my lungs.

"Did you realize that Levi was left seaside and his face got stuck in beehives?" he repeated the taunt that had no doubt haunted him throughout his high school career.

"Kids are awful," I told him, feeling sympathetic.

Note to self: make sure Selene isn't being bullied.

"Yeah," he laughed it off, "my dad told me that girls were a sucker for a guy with a guitar. And me, being a horny fifteen-year-old boy, I saved up everything I had to buy myself one. And it worked to a degree; I was bullied less, and some girls thought it was sweet. When I grew out of my awkward years, everything changed though. My high school reunion was a blast for my sister and I," he said with a laugh.

"Was she awkward too?"

"Bethan? Ha! No, she's always been the rebel of our family. She was one of those rare few that never cared what anyone thought. She'd wanted to come along with me to see how the prom queen and the quarterback looked ten years later. She laughed for days. Everyone thinks of her as a wild child, but she's a lot more sensible than most people give her credit for. You know the club we met at?"

"Twenty-Four?"

He nodded. "She had stashed away every penny that anyone had ever given her, be it birthday money, or Christmas money or even her weekly allowance. She kept it all hidden under the floor-boards of her room. By the time she graduated college, she had almost twenty grand to her name. She took that money and put all towards opening that club," he said beaming with pride.

"Your parents must have—"

"Lost their shit," he finished. "They did. But it worked for her. *She made it work for her,*" he smiled.

He seemed to be really proud and fond of his little sister. In a way, she reminded me of Selene.

"I'm glad it worked out for you," I said, as I leaned even more into the couch.

"What about you, what were you like in high school?"

"Urgh. No." I groaned, not wanting to go there.

"Come on," he urged, "it can't possibly be worse than *the rhyme.*"

He had a point.

"Let's see," I mused, wondering just how much I should reveal. "Well, I was overweight and a teacher's pet, that about covers it," I nodded, wishing that I could have avoided this conversation.

"Overweight? You?"

Now it was his turn to be incredulous.

"Thank you, I'll take that as a compliment," I said. "But yeah, my grandmother was a chef, and even though she was retired, she still fed us every waking moment. Jesus, when I think back on it, it was pretty bad. That, plus my baby weight…" I shuddered at the memory, "If it wasn't for the few sports I played, I would have needed to be rolled down the halls."

He thought about for a moment— "Yeah, I can't imagine that."

"Oh, but you don't have to," I said, already regretting the decision I was about to make.

I stood up, moving towards a stack of boxes. After a moment, I found the one I was looking for. A box filled with my photo albums. Selecting the right year, I scanned through it briefly before handing it to him.

Putting the guitar away, he wordlessly flipped through the album. I sat forward, trying to gauge his reaction.

"It's not that bad," he finally said.

"I'm sorry, did you not *see* the photos??"

"I saw them. It wasn't that bad," he repeated. "By the way, your boobs were *huge!*"

Of course that's what he was looking at.

"I don't miss them," I told him, "they killed my back."

"You're slightly taller than most girls, so everything evened out alright." He paused, flipping to another page, then he laughed— "Okay this one is kind of bad."

"Thank you, I know." I tried to take the photos back from him, but he wouldn't have it.

"You were a teacher's pet," he echoed the sentiment I had expressed moments ago.

He smiled to himself as he looked over all my awards and photos with my teachers.

"I actually liked school."

"No judgment," he snickered.

And he was right. One of the things I liked about him, was the fact that no matter what either of us did, there was no judgment. But then again, after agreeing to this week, how could we really judge each other?

"You were the captain of the varsity volleyball team your sophomore year?" he asked, tapping one of the photos.

"Okay that's enough," I said, reaching over to sit on his lap and obscure his view of the book.

"You're playing dirty," he told me.

"Hey, a woman's gotta do what a woman's gotta do," I replied, before kissing him.

He moaned, and allowed himself to relax as he leaned back into the couch. As I had hoped, the book slipped out of his hands, and softly thudded to the ground.

I shifted my position and slipped my body between his legs as I caressed the side of his face and deepened the kiss. I slid the album under the couch, where it would remain unnoticed for another month.

The second my lips touched his, thoughts of the album immediately left my mind, and with a soft grunt, he stood up and lifted me off my feet, just as he had done in the shower earlier that morning. As I wrapped my arms around his neck, I could feel the almost erratic beat of his heart as he carried me into the hallowed darkness of my bedroom. He set me on my feet right in front of my bed.

"I want you," he whispered, his eyes roaming over me.

"So?" I crossed my arms...I had no idea why I was playing hard to get now...that was a lie. I knew why; it was the look in his eyes...the way he looked at me made my toes curl.

He took a step forward and grasped my hips, pulling me against him, so I could feel how hard he was.

His lips hovered over mine as he spoke; "When I say I want you, I mean I need you. I need to run my fingers over your skin, kiss down your back, and make you moan my name. I. Need. You. And from the look on your face, you need me too. *So* strip."

How could I not?

LEVI

"Ma, I'm fine. Can't we reschedule for some other day next week? I'm just busy right now."

"Levi you're supposed to be on vacation; you shouldn't be busy doing anything."

My mother was driving me crazy.

I balanced the phone between my shoulder and my cheek and allowed my mother to rant at me while I partially listened. Reaching into the fridge for the milk, I noticed that Thea was running out of almost everything. I felt guilty in that moment because I knew I was the one with the voracious appetite.

"I'm not working Ma," I replied as she asked me once more what I could possibly be busy with.

"Levi? Have you seen my— Oh I'm sorry, I didn't know you were on the phone," Thea said as she came into the kitchen dressed in a pair of shorts and an oversized sweater.

I missed seeing her in my clothes.

"Who are you with?" my mother barked from the other end of the phone.

I covered the speaker with my hand as I looked at her and sighed, "Give me a second?"

She nodded and turned around.

"Mom, I really gotta go," I said. "Tell dad I'm sorry about the game, and that I'll make it up to him. Bye."

I hung up before she could say anything else, but deep down, I knew that that wasn't the end of this conversation.

"Is everything okay? I'm not keeping you away from anything important am I?" Thea asked, as she grabbed an apple out of the ceramic bowl on her counter and polished it with the sleeve of her sweater.

More important than her? My father and his golfing buddies could wait.

"No, it's fine, my father's just been bored out of his mind since he retired."

"What did he do?" she asked, taking a bite out of her apple.

"He was lawyer."

"A lawyer? And he retired? That usually only happens for two reasons; he was either kicked out of the firm, or his health got the best of him."

The moment she said it her eyes went wide and she looked at me— "Shit. I'm so sorry. I have no filter."

"It's okay, honestly. Besides, you're right. He had a heart attack last year, and my mother put her foot down."

She stood there, staring at the ground, unable to meet my gaze. She was clearly embarrassed by her outburst, and self-conscious about what she should do next. Pulling her into my arms, I kissed her forehead. "It's fine." I told her once more. "Besides, I'm more interested in knowing how you could have guessed that."

"My mother used to be a lawyer. She left her firm because of health reasons too, but believe me, she put up a hell of a fight," she said as she shook her head.

"What was her name?" I asked, curious now. "Maybe I've heard of her."

"Maybe," she shrugged, wiggling out of my hands and going over to the fridge.

I noticed there was an invisible line with her. She was willing to talk about herself and her sister, but that was where it ended. She didn't give me too many details about anything. She was trying to keep me outside of her bubble… after all, we only had three days left. Yet still, I couldn't help but want to know more about her.

Where had the time gone?

"I was thinking that I'd head down to the farmers' market really quick, before I headed over to your place. You can hang out—"

"I'll come with you." I said

She balked, "That's okay—"

"Thea," I stated cupping the side of her face, "give me a minute to throw on a shirt, and then we can both go out together. We have three days left, so no running away from me. I want to make the most of our time."

"I wasn't running; I just thought you might want some space or something."

"If I wanted space, I wouldn't be coming to your place every other day," I said softly, pressing against her. "And I sure as hell wouldn't be this close to you. When we get back change into my shirt."

"Someone is getting demanding," she noted, looking at my lips.

"Someone is liking it," I replied, biting her bottom lip before moving away from her.

∼

Three

Two

One...

"You aren't paying for anything!" she yelled back at me.

She always had to get the last word in; her pride wouldn't let it go otherwise.

"Okay," I called back.

There was just no point in having this fight just yet, but there was no way in hell I was going to let her pay. On the other hand, our fights always left me turned on...

9

PRESENT

THEA

"I'm really sorry about what happened to Esther and Hector. Yes, Esther and I broke up, but we never hated each other. And Hector... Hector was my best friend. No one in the world knew me like he did.

"To his parents, who were always like second parents to me, I...I'm so sorry. I never thought that anything like this could have happened, and if I could go back, I would have never had the party. I'm sorry," Richard whispered in to my mic before stepping back.

He brushed the back of his hand across his face, wiping away his tears. Then, he crossed his hands over his chest and looked down.

Placing my hand on his shoulder, I smiled, trying my best to comfort him. I didn't want to mess things up for him. For the first time—well, the second time since last night—I realized that this was someone's life that we were fighting for. As I sat straight and squared my shoulders, I prepared to give my speech to the media.

"Richard Archibald threw a party, one of eighteen, thrown by students at his high school this year. In fact, Richard had thrown a party one week prior, to the incident in question, but no one attended because there wasn't enough alcohol or drugs for their liking. And so, he made a mistake, all for the sake of fitting in.

"There's no denying that this was a tragic loss of two young lives, but to lay the blame solely on a sixteen year old boy's shoulders is not only injustice but incompetence.

"Since this investigation started, not once has any member of the Boston PD asked for information on the drug dealer, who is, in my opinion, the real killer. He sold a bad batch of drugs to minors, God alone knows how many others fell ill and possibly died because of his distribution. There are still parties being thrown, even now, with kids just like Esther and Hector, who are only one pill away from overdosing. This isn't a racial issue, this is not about another privileged teen getting away with something. This is about the DA, and the Boston police, trying to make it seem as though they are tough on crime, when in all honesty they are chasing their tails, searching for a scapegoat. That scapegoat will not be Richard Archibald."

Standing up, I allowed Richard to get ahead of me so that I could whisper to him to ignore all the people and cameras and questions that were being hurled our way. When we entered the house, I took a deep breath as Mrs. Archibald hugged her son, and Levi spoke to his father. Then, I moved into the living room, where Logan and the rest of Levi's associates were watching the news.

"A little emotional, but not bad," one of them said.

As I looked around, I noticed Atticus sitting in the corner with his jaw clenched shut.

That was a first.

Looking at me, he shrugged as if to say 'not bad.' I smiled, knowing he was planning to do everything in his power to regain his lead on me.

"So what happens now?" Mrs. Archibald asked.

Before Levi could answer, one of his associates' cell phone rang.

"It's the DA."

Smirking, he took the phone— "Pete, how are you?" A pause, then, "A three-month stint in rehab? Have you lost your mind? He didn't even take a pill."

Everyone was on the edge of their seats and so was I.

"What do I want? I want all charges dropped and no further action to be taken against my client. That's the only deal I'm making, and if not, I will take this matter to court, and you will be forever remembered as the guy who tried to shaft a kid." He paused once more, and everyone in the room held their breaths.

I was sure that he was deliberately being dramatic, trying to freak us all out and give us heart attacks.

"Yeah Pete, I hear the words coming out of your mouth, I just don't like them."

Again with the damn pausing. Part of me knew it was because the district attorney was speaking, but another part of me knew that Levi was doing it on purpose.

"I'll speak with my clients, and let you know," he stated before hanging up.

Turning back to Richard he said, "The DA will drop all charges if you give them everything they need to know about the drugs. That means giving up Hector as well."

"Will anyone else know about Hector?"

"I doubt it, it would only make them look worse, and since the drugs are still being distributed, it would be like putting a Band-Aid on a cracking dam."

"Okay?" He looked up at his parents, who just nodded.

"Yes!" I squealed.

Suddenly a room full of eyes were focused on me. Realizing my outburst, I shrank back into my seat. "Sorry," I apologized.

Levi stared at me, shaking his head before taking the rest of the Archibalds into the adjoining room.

"Lame," Richard grinned at me.

"You wound me with your words, and just when I was beginning to like you."

Rolling his eyes at me, he turned to walk away and stopped, "I'm not saying thank you or anything, because it's kind of your job to help me—"

"Just go."

Little brat… but when I looked at the situation retrospectively, he wasn't half-bad.

When he was gone, Atticus came up beside me, and his baby blue eyes looked me over.

"How did you do it?" he asked

"Do what?"

"Don't play dumb! How'd you get to do the conference?"

I smiled. "While you were searching for Mr. Archibald, I was upstairs winning over the kid. I did say 'game on,' remember?"

He popped his jaw and nodded. "It ain't over yet, Cunning."

"I'm not going anywhere," I told him.

"Why don't you both just whip it out already, so we can measure?" Raymond interjected.

Raymond had light brown skin and dark brown eyes. He was one of the first associates Levi hired when he started, making him at least in his late twenties or early thirties.

Atticus and I ceased our spat, and moved to help the other associates pack up the case files that were scattered all over the ground. By the time we were done, a row of taxis were all parked in waiting outside of the house and Levi was already at the door with his jacket on.

"Good work, head home, you all look horrible," was all he said.

As he looked over to where I was standing, I immediately

looked away and raised my hand to signal the driver of our complementary taxi.

The moment the cab stopped at my feet, I threw myself inside of it. I didn't want to be left alone with him again…I didn't think I could handle it.

"Hello?" I answered my phone without thinking, as I gave my address to the driver.

Shit.

"You ran."

"You said to go home."

He snickered, and for some reason it sounded sexier over the phone. "You did well today."

"Are you going to call Atticus and tell him the same thing?"

I didn't want to be treated differently… and yet some small part of me did. I was just confused.

"I didn't need to call him, because unlike you, he didn't run away, he actually approached me while you were busy flinging yourself into the cab. After all, we just won a big case without even going to court."

Of course he did! Kiss-ass.

"I'll keep that in mind for next time—"

"Who said there was going to be a next time?"

"You just said I did a good job."

"I said you did well *today*. Tomorrow is a brand new day. Plus, there are still sixteen students left. Prepare yourself for Monday."

"Prepare myself?"

"Goodnight Thea."

"Wait…" I almost pleaded into the receiver, but he was already gone, "Urgh!"

"Tough day?" the cabby asked.

"No. Tough professor."

"Stick it out. I'm sure it'll be worth it in the end."

"God, I hope so."

If it wasn't, I was torturing myself for nothing.

All I wanted to do was get home as quickly as I could and crawl into bed. As I walked up to the front door, I slipped my heels off and relished the feel of the cool floor. I opened the door and was welcomed by Selene's loud greeting.

"You were badass!" she squealed, as she jumped up from behind the couch.

"Thanks—" I replied.

Before I could utter another word, a shiny glint caught my eye.

"What the hell is that in your nose?" I asked sternly.

"You like it?" she cooed, touching the ring.

I could feel my eyebrow twitch.

"Selene, that better be fake, or so help me God, I will rip it out of your nose."

"What's the big deal—?"

"Take it out. *Now.*"

"Thea!"

"*Now.*"

"Ah! Why do you always have to do this? You're my sister, not my mother," she snapped, as she took it out of her nose and handed it to me.

Opening the living room window, I threw it out into the yard. I heard it hit the walkway with a tiny *dink*, and then, it was lost from sight.

"Whether or not you like it Selene, I'm your legal guardian, and that sort of makes me your mom *and* your sister. When you turn eighteen, you can pierce whatever body part you like, but until that day, I don't want to see another piercing or hear about it."

"You sound more and more like *her* every day."

That hurt.

"That was low… even for you," I muttered.

She made no reply as she threw herself back unto the couch.

"Turn of the lights when you're done," I told her as I walked away.

Picking up my things, I dragged myself into my room. Falling onto my bed, I reached into my purse looking at the napkin that Levi had given me during our week together.

One free rant.

LEVI

"Congrats on the win. You didn't even need me for this one," Tristan said as he strolled into my office and placed his feet on my desk. He was the only person who could get away with doing that shit.

"For some reason, it almost feels like I didn't even do anything to earn my win." I said.

"Well, that makes it even sweeter," Tristan said. "Work smarter, not harder," he reminded me.

"I guess."

"Dude, seriously? You have to get her out of your system man, it's been two weeks already and you've spent more time thinking about the time that you were together, than when you were actually together."

"I've tried! Don't you think I've tried? It's her damn fault, and she knows it too. She told me she was going to ruin all other women for me, and she fucking meant it! I picked three women up and I couldn't even bring myself to leave with them."

"What was wrong with them?"

"They weren't her!" I shouted at him as though it should have been obvious. "They laughed at all the wrong times, and they couldn't even hold a conversation."

"Please remember you're comparing them to an Ivy League educated female, whose mother was a year away from being nominated to Supreme Court judge."

"You know?" I asked.

I hadn't said a word about that to anyone. I wondered who else might have known about Ms. Cunning's family history.

"Yeah, thanks for keeping that a secret, you prick. I nearly lost my cool when she said that I used to work for her mother."

She was telling people now? Well at least that was one less thing holding her back. She had a royal flush in her hands, and she wasn't playing any of her cards. If she wanted to make it, she had to stop treating her advantages as though they were handicaps.

"Is she anything like her mother?" I had never met *The Shark*, but that wasn't for lack of trying.

"The world cannot handle another Margaret Cunning. She was a genius… and such a cutthroat bitch, that people's heads rolled right off their shoulders as she walked by. I don't even know how to describe that year of my life. If you can make it six months with *The Shark—*"

"You can make it anywhere," I finished for him.

He nodded, as he grabbed a Snickers bar out of my desk. "I don't think she was on good terms with her mother though," Tristan said, as he tore open the wrapper and took a bite.

"Who?"

"Thea. At the bar I gave her my condolences for her loss, and she told me not to, because her mother was a horrible person. I don't know what that was all about, but most people tend to not speak ill of the dead, especially if that person is their own mother."

"Yeah?"

It was all I could think to say.

So what was her story? The more I thought about it, the less it made sense. She was living in her mother's old house, but she didn't have any photos of her anywhere. She never brought her up, and the one time I did, she was ready to bite my head off.

Why did Thea hate her mother? And if she hated her so much, why was she following in her footsteps?

No matter how many times I turned the story over in my mind, I couldn't make sense of it. Thea Cunning was a true woman, and like a true woman, she was an enigma wrapped up in a mystery.

PAST
DAY 5

THEA

"What's the matter?" I asked, taking a seat on his lap.

He shook his head, and wrapped his arms around my waist.

"Nothing."

"You're a horrible liar."

"Ah, my pride," he joked, but he didn't really seem to be in the mood for anything.

Sighing, I sat up, reached over the couch, grabbed a napkin from the side table, and quickly scribbled a note on it before I handed it to him.

"One free rant?" he read.

"Yep, you get one free rant, about anything, for as long as you need, and when you're done, I won't say anything. We'll just move on like it never even happened."

He looked at me for a moment before reaching over to get

another napkin off the table. He wrote on it and handed it right back.

"I'm not going to have anything to rant about within the next two days Levi."

"That's why there isn't an expiration date on it. Even when we're not together, you can call me up, and cash that in. If you don't promise to use yours, I'm not going to use mine."

"Fine."

Did he always have to be so difficult?

He lifted his pinky.

"You've got to be kidding me."

"You have to do it, or I won't believe you," he said with a grin so wide, I just wanted to kiss and slap him at the same time.

Sighing, I locked my pinky with his. "Yeah, this definitely makes it legal and binding."

"Can I cash this in yet?"

Closing my mouth, I waited.

"My ex-wife," he stated, pausing as if to test my reaction to those two words.

I ignored the alarms going off my head for a moment, and tried my best to stay composed and to keep my poker face in place.

"My ex-wife has been driving me insane for the last few weeks," he continued, and I noticed his grip on me tightened, just slightly. "We were only married for three years before I found out she had been having an affair with my business partner. I left them both to start my own practice.

"In the beginning it was fine. Neither of them bothered much with me, because apparently, they expected me to fail. Starting a new firm in this economy is almost impossible, but I was dedicated. I was going to come back and tear them both down.

"It's taken me a few years, but I've finally managed to get back on top. The only thing is that I no longer give a shit about either of them. I want to be the best lawyer I can be, for myself, not them. Fuck them. The only problem is, the higher I get, the bigger a target my firm becomes.

"My ex-wife's been trying to steal clients new and old. My former partner has friends in Capital Hill, you know, the financial fraud agency, and they keep trying to railroad me at every turn. I've been audited every other year since my first big case. There are days when I want to walk into his office with a bat, and do what I should have done the moment I found about their affair..."

I sat up more, wrapping my arms around his neck, but not saying anything.

"It's like high school never ended with them, grown adults acting like fucking children! And the only way I can fight back is to avoid them both and keep winning cases. But that isn't enough, I want to close off that chapter of my life completely.

"I want to forget about her. I met her once since the divorce, and you know what she told me? That I wasn't man enough, that I was too good, too nice. And for months I racked my brains, trying to figure out what the fuck it meant to be 'too good'.

"I'm sorry I don't drive a Harley, or feel the need to start brawls to prove I have fucking balls. She hurt me, I got over it, and now, I just want to work in peace. I sound... pathetic, don't I?" he groaned, dropping his head back.

"I know I said that I wouldn't say anything, but can I amend the conditions of your voucher for just one statement?"

"Sure, why not?" he muttered half-heartedly, keeping his gaze fixed on the ceiling.

Sitting up on my knees, right between his thighs, I kissed his cheek. "Your ex-wife has to be the biggest damn fool in the state, and she's probably kicking herself right now, which is why she's trying so hard to reinsert herself into your life. But it's her loss, my gain... at least for the next two days at any rate," I said, as I gently sucked and kissed my way down his neck.

He pulled me back, forcing me to look him in the eyes. "Is that's all you're going to say?"

"What more needs to be said? You used your rant card and now we move on. So can I finish now?" I asked, as I resumed kissing his lips.

He breathed out deeply and allowed himself to relax, as I reached into his pants and grabbed on to his member. I could feel him hardening in my hands with each stroke.

"Sometimes I think to myself that you, that this, is all a dream," he moaned, shifting under me.

"I'm one-hundred-percent real," I assured him as I gently squeezed, a simple reminder that we were both real, that we were both here, and that this was really happening.

Reaching up, he pulled the shirt off of me, grasping both of my breasts with his hands and I shivered at his touch. He kept his eyes on me, as he kissed the both of them, licking around my nipples before gently taking them between his teeth. I winced, both in pleasure and pain.

"Levi… ah," I moaned, as one of his hands slipped downwards from my breasts, and came to rest in-between my legs.

Letting go of him completely, I leaned back and rocked against his fingers.

"Damn… you. I… I… fuck I—"

"You what?" he grinned, as he slipped another finger into me.

He leaned back against the pillows and watched me as I ground myself against his hand.

"You… ah…" I moaned, as he increased the pressure on my nipples.

"I, what? Come on baby, complete sentences please."

"Fuck you."

"You already are," he grinned. "Or would you like me to stop…?"

And just like that, his hands froze, and I grunted in frustration, and crushed his lips against my own. My tongue slipped into his mouth, brushing against his, as tried to get him moving again. But instead, he pulled out, completely breaking away from my lips to lick his fingers.

He smirked as he regarded me. "How badly do you want it?"

"Mmmmmm," I whined.

"Use your words," he instructed.

That stupid smirk of his, and those damn green eyes— "I fucking hate you."

"Wrong words," he said, his tone cold and menacing.

He moved towards me then, faster than I ever saw him move. He was rough with me as he flipped me back onto couch, driving me downwards. I grabbed on to the armrest, bracing myself for his sexual fury.

He kissed my back, moving upwards until his lips barely brushed against the curve of my neck. "Since you can't say what you want, I'm just going to have to take what I want. Don't you *dare* move," he warned.

He disappeared from behind me, and I remained on the couch, my knees locked, my knuckles white against the armrest, and my heart racing in anticipation of the pleasure that was to come, as adrenaline surged through my body. I was frozen in place. Unable to move, even if I wanted to.

He returned seconds later, and kissed his way down my spine. I shivered, but I still didn't move. I could feel him right behind me, his chest hovering over my back and I could feel the heat coming off his body in waves. I shivered once more, and my skin broke out into goose bumps. He pressed himself against my ass, and I felt myself tremble at the heat of it. I wanted to clamp my legs together; he had made me so wet, it was almost embarrassing.

"How badly do you want it?" he asked again, as he pressed the tip against my opening.

"If you have to ask—"

Slam.

"Fuck!" he hissed, tightening his hold on me, as he slid his shaft in all the way to the base. My mouth dropped open. There simply wasn't enough words to describe the intensity of the pleasure I felt, and as he thrust into me, deeper and harder, I found that my hunger for him was insatiable. I wanted more, I *needed* more.

"More—please," I begged.

I knew the voice was mine, but it didn't sound like me at all. Since when did I sound like such a porn star?

"Yes!" I shouted, wanting more, more, more…

I moaned, my cries echoing throughout the house as I felt my climax nearing. I dug my nails into the chair and threw my head back, screaming his name at the ceiling. My head was spinning, my vision was blurred, my toes curled, I was reaching heaven in the most beautiful way.

"Fuck, Thea," he grunted, one hand on my hip the other on my shoulder as he fucked me harder.

"Yes. God yes!" He was amazing, he was fucking amazing.

"I can't—"

"Not yet," he demanded, but, I was seeing stars. Never in my life had I ever felt like this.

I couldn't hold back any longer.

"Levi!"

He gripped on tightly, burying himself in me over and over, until he stilled for a moment.

"Thea," he grunted before rested on top of me.

My hair stuck to my face, and my breathing was short as I tried to regain my senses.

"Mmmm…. we're definitely doing that again," I slurred, still drunk from the sheer force of my orgasm.

"Definitely."

LEVI

When she meant we were going to do it again, I didn't think we would end up doing it three more times: in the shower, in her kitchen, and on her bed. Jesus, I was spent. Her sexual appetite was becoming voracious, and I was surprised that she could still move, and that I could see straight.

She rested against my chest, reading her what she called her 'least favorite, favorite book,' *The Great Gatsby*. She was a little weird, but I liked it. Even without really knowing me, she still seemed to understand what I needed, and when I needed it.

I had been nervous to talk to her about my ex-wife, and I didn't want to make her uncomfortable, or do anything to kill our mood. But I had gotten yet another email from Odile, and I was just about ready to snap. I could only hope that she needed to use her rant slip soon so we could be on equal footing. I felt like I was depending on her way too much, and it had only been five days.

I blinked and brought my focus back to her. She had put her book down and was now staring at me.

"A penny for your thoughts?" I asked her.

She smiled; she had the most beautiful smile. "Only a penny, Mr. Black? What type of girl do you think I am?"

"You're right, my apologies," I said. "So, what's the price for a slice of Thea Cunning's thoughts?"

"One of your own," she answered, her eyes studying my face intently.

"I have far too many of them," I told her.

"So do I."

"And here I figured you just said whatever came to your mind," I teased.

I brushed her hair behind her ear.

"I do… sometimes."

"What were you thinking about then?"

"Why the hell is he staring at me like that? Doesn't he know what his eyes do to me… or, well, something of that nature," she replied once again, far more honestly than I imagined. "And you?"

"That I depend way too much on you, and I wish it were the other way around." I couldn't lie to her for some reason.

"What do you mean? You haven't depended on me for

anything."

She looked like she truly believed that. She had no idea how much of an impact she had on me.

Shaking my head, I looked to her book. "Why is *The Great Gatsby* your least favorite, favorite book? Is it because you hate Jay?"

"No! I hate Daisy," she said, as she sat up angrily.

This was going to be amusing.

"You hate Daisy?"

"She's an evil witch!"

"That's a little harsh," I laughed.

I enjoyed seeing her get so worked up.

"Oh please! First of all, she marries a man she doesn't love because he's rich. But I can forgive that, because, you know, it's the 1900s, women's suffrage is just starting to kick in. In fact, I felt bad for her because it was as though her parents were pushing her into it. But then she drank the Kool-Aid."

"The Kool-Aid?" I asked.

"Yes, the golden Kool-Aid of the rich and fabulous. The next time we meet her, Jay's back, and she's all like, 'let me forget about my husband and child, and go party at my former lover's house all the damn day.' "

"But she truly loved him," I said, realizing in that moment that I was now defending fictional characters.

She snorted and rolled her eyes. "Even if he's your true love, you're still married to another man. You either run away with him, or you stay away from him. You don't *keep* having an affair under your husband's nose. And what type of person meets her long awaited, true love and doesn't ask a few questions first? She just jumps onto his private boat, and parties around in his house."

"Gatsby is the one that called her there, why didn't he sweep her away?"

"Any man willing to take the rap for murder would have gladly run away with her. But nope, Daisy didn't want to just have her cake and eat it too, she wanted the bloody pastry chef as well!" she said, with a huff.

She was all worked up now, and she hopped onto her knees, waving the book in front of me.

"And the absolute worst part of it all is the fact that she didn't even have the decency to go to his funeral. She just ran away to live her perfect little life with her husband. She is a horrible, terrible human being, and I wish she would have gotten run over by a yellow buggy!"

I laughed. The look on her face, the passion and rage pouring out her, it was too funny.

"Damn it! Why'd you bring up this book? Now I look crazy," she groaned, hiding her face under the sheets.

Instead of remedying the situation, it only made me laugh more.

"Stop laughing at me! It's not my fault. Us English Lit majors tend to be a little weird about books, okay?"

"Thea," I said, trying my best to stop laughing as I reached for her.

But she turned away. Wrapping my arm around her, I held her through the sheets.

"I'm not laughing because I think you're weird... though you are for the record, but just a little bit." She smacked me before I could continue. "I'm laughing because you're amazing, and I couldn't help but wonder if you can get this passionate over a fictional story how you must you be with real people. You have a big heart, I can tell by the way you love your books."

She uncovered herself trying not to smile. "Nice save."

"I try," I said. "Now, read to me."

I handed the book back to her.

Once again, she wrapped herself around me, placing her head on my chest, and started from her least favorite, favorite part.

There were only two days left...

I don't think I can let her go.

11

PRESENT

THEA

Thea May Cunning
Age: 23
Height: 5'9 ½
Race: African American
Undergraduates: Princeton
Family:
Mother: Margaret "The Shark" Cunning.
Sister: High School student

"What the hell?" I exclaimed, as I walked into class and saw my information written on the board. I could tell by the handwriting that this was Levi's doing.

I'm going to kill him the moment he walks through the doors. I promised myself.

"He can't do this, that's my personal information," I protested.

"Actually he can," Atticus said as he leaned in behind me. "Or did you not read the paper he had us all sign our names on, on the first day of class?"

"What?"

"Wow," he shook his head at me, showing me a photo of the document on his phone. "I always have a copy of everything I sign my name on. The last line says…"

"I hereby allow Professor Black to use any and all information given to him by myself, for teaching purposes," I finished reading.

I hadn't been paying attention that day because I was just getting over the shock of finding out I had slept with my professor for an entire week, and now, it seemed that it had come back to bite me in the ass.

"And you want to be a lawyer," Atticus said disapprovingly. "My guess is that he got that information from your initial application. Good thing you didn't put your weight down, aye?"

I *had* written my weight down on the application… fortunately for me, he opted to not include that modicum of information.

Ignoring him, I turned back to the board, wondering how the hell he could possibly use this information, and what lesson he planned to teach us with this.

"Good, you're all here," Levi said, making an entrance.

He looked stunning, dressed in a pair of blue jeans, a white button down shirt, and a vest in place of his usual jacket… and to make matters worse, he had those glasses on again.

He's trying to kill me.

"Thea May Cunning," he said aloud.

I sat up in my seat, staring at him with all the fury I could muster, but he wasn't looking at me, he was looking at the rest of the students. "As most of you may have already heard, every year I choose one person to personally mold. And right now, Thea May Cunning is at the top of the list.

"So, what does that mean for the rest of you? It means that she is now the new public enemy number one. Everything on that board is what you'll need to know about her, to kick her off the top of the list. Her name will remain on the board until someone displaces her. And consider yourselves lucky, because the first person who gets their name on my board, never stays up there for long."

I now understood what it felt like to be a gazelle surrounded by a coalition of cheetahs. I could almost sense their salivary glands awakening.

Levi Black, you are such a fucking sadist.

"Do you hear that? It's the sounds of people sharpening their knives," Atticus whispered from behind me and I fought the urge to turn around and slap him with my notebook.

He was so damn annoying.

"Are you alright with this, Ms. Cunning?" *El Diablo* asked.

"No. But I accept that it must be done," I said with confidence, even though I felt like a mouse in a snake pit.

What else could I do?

"Professor? When you say Margaret 'The Shark' Cunning. Do you mean *The Shark*?" A guy in the front row asked.

"Off with his head!" Atticus whispered behind me.

"Get out," Levi said to the guy up in the front row. "And let him be a lesson to you all; I *do* believe there are such things as stupid questions."

"I want to defend my seat!" he objected.

I sunk into my chair, bracing myself for the horror show that was about to begin. Levi was going to eat him alive.

"You want to defend the fact that you didn't understand what quotation marks meant?"

Atticus snorted behind me, trying his best to contain his laughter. The guy, paused, thought about his defense, drew in a deep breath and suddenly deflated. He lingered for a second before grabbing the rest of his things and leaving.

As the door slammed shut, Levi turned to face us. "Fifteen left. Three of you aren't going to make it. I wonder who you are," he said with no emotion whatsoever. "Now, let's get started."

The moment the words were out his mouth, it was as though someone had rung the bell at a heavy weight fight. Everyone tensed, sitting on the edge of their seats. But for some reason, seeing my mother's name on the board gave me a sense of security.

"What do you know about Margaret Cunning?" he asked.

This? Her? She was the topic of today's class?

"She was a total bad ass!" someone yelled, and Levi shot him a look that cut him down a few inches and reduced him to something bite size.

"That she was, but can anyone use big boy words, and explain why?" Levi asked as he looked around the class.

"While at the DA's office, her first major case was Ayala Petroleum vs. the citizens of Blake. She was able to criminally charge Ayala Petroleum with over a dozen counts of manslaughter charges, resulting from their dumping of toxic waste into the Blake local river, *and* she won a class action suit, rendering the company bankrupt. She's my hero." Ms. Vega, the girl that Professor Black had called in regards to the Archibald case, said.

"After leaving the DA's office, she started her own firm, where she successfully defended the likes of Nol van der Stoep, the Danish Ambassador, and the novelist Zinachidi Okoli," Atticus added.

I had been jumping through hoops and bending myself over backwards for him, and all I asked him to do was to never bring up my mother again… And he couldn't even respect me enough to do that. He couldn't just let it go. According to our syllabus, we shouldn't have covered any material that pertained to her until the end of the term. So he was doing this just to get under my fucking skin… and it was working.

Watching him talk, I wanted to storm to the front of the class, and scream all manners of obscenities into his face. Didn't he get it? There were some lines you just didn't cross.

"Anything to add, Ms. Cunning?"

I bit the inside of my cheek. "I'm biased beyond measure."

"You cannot be biased with facts," he stated.

He was deliberately pushing me, and I was about to snap.

"When she was—" I paused, taking a deep breath I continued. I wouldn't let him win. "She was offered the position of a Supreme Court Justice, but due to her deteriorating health, she was forced to decline."

I sat up on the edge of my chair, waiting, praying that class would end. My leg bounced with anxiety, but it was nothing compared to the feeling of having you heart crawl up your throat. I could feel my eyes burning, but I refused to cry here. Finally he looked up at the time.

"Alright for next class—"

I was gone before he finished. I ran out of there as fast as I could, trying my best to breathe, but everything hurt.

Breathe, Thea. Breathe.

I leaned against the bathroom wall with my hands on my knees.

"Thea?"

No, please, no.

"This is the girls' bathroom, get out," I yelled at him.

"This is the guys' bathroom," he replied, and I looked around to find myself standing between two urinals...

"Of course it is," I remarked bitterly.

"Thea."

"Stop saying my name!"

His green eyes widened as he took a step back.

"Stop saying my name like you know me. You don't, Levi. It was over a month ago, and *that girl* is not me. So stop saying my name."

"I don't believe that." he said, as he leaned against the door.

"I don't care what you believe!" I shouted at him.

"Talk to me Thea, what's wrong with you?"

The world was shaking, or maybe it was just me. I didn't know anymore, and I didn't care.

"What's wrong with me? What's wrong with me?!" I shouted hysterically, "What the fuck is wrong with you? I told you that you were *never* to bring her up again, and what do you go and do? You make her the class' main discussion *and* to top it all off, you deliberately antagonized me to provoke a reaction! You're so busy talking a million words per second, you don't listen!"

Digging into my bag, I pulled out the napkin and threw it at him. The crumpled paper lay at his feet with the words *free rant* peeking out.

"Margaret "The Shark" Cunning," I spat, "the woman everybody always praises, as if she were some sort of saint, was a conniving, manipulative, vengeful and bitter woman. She let my father go to jail for a crime he didn't commit, while she ran off with her lover, my darling stepfather, who by the way, took great pleasure in molesting me when I was twelve. And when I told *The Shark* about it, she sent me off to live with my grandmother. I wet the bed for a year before I worked up the courage to tell my grandmother what had happened. By the time we went back for my sister, it was too late, he had already gotten to her and from what my mother told us, he was long gone. I suppose she must have seen it with her own eyes that time.

"My grandmother took us in, and I didn't have to see her face again, until I got a call from her doctor. All the poison and bitterness she had been bottling up had finally started to kill her. She'd pushed everyone away, and in the end, she had no one left. So against my better judgment, I came back.

"I think I was expecting some sort of an apology, but all she wanted to talk about was the fact that her life's work had all been in vain, because she had been forced to turn down that seat within the Supreme Court.

"So excuse me Professor Black, for not wanting praise her in front of your goddamn class. She is *The Shark* to me, because she eats her own young."

I ended my *free rant* and grabbed my things. I moved towards the door, and he stepped aside without saying a word. I didn't think about where I was going, I just ran. I ran from him, I ran from her, and I ran from the law.

I ran all the way home and threw myself into bed, sobbing heavily. I heard a movement next to my bed and I felt Selene crawl into bed to comfort me… she didn't bother asking. She didn't need to.

LEVI

I entered the house and made it to the bathroom sink just in time. My stomach was upturned, and as the reality of the situation hit me, all I could think about were her words. They haunted me.

I spat into the sink as a wave of vertigo swarmed over me. In all honesty, I wasn't sure how I had made it all the way to my house. Everything from the moment she ran out of the bathroom to now was a blur. I saw her fighting back her tears. Her whole body language changed, like she was being run over by a car each time someone spoke of her mother. The panic, the fear, her pain, I couldn't just turn away from her. Reason told me not to follow her, it was too risky. I could just swing by her place later. But she was in agony, and the risk meant nothing compared to that.

Now I felt like my soul was being stoned, and the realization that I had victimized her by forcing her to endure that lecture… I retched once more. This time, nothing more than a thin thread of saliva passed my lips.

I stepped away from the sink and wiped my mouth with the back of my hand. As my back pressed against the cool tile of the bathroom wall, I allowed myself to slide to the floor.

I lifted up her napkin. Of all the things I thought she would have ranted about, this was nowhere near my list.

As I sat there, lost in the painful memory of our conversation, my phone rang. Without looking at the caller ID, I answered, "This isn't a good time."

"Oh? Who's over—?"

"Bethan. I'm serious."

"What happened?" her tone changed.

I thought for a moment. "Have you ever seen a nuclear bomb go off?"

"Levi..."

"The people in the center, they don't feel anything. One minute they're alive, the next, they're just ash. It's the people who are far away that really suffer."

"Levi, I don't understand."

"A bomb went off today, and it was my fault. I saw the *Do Not Touch* sign, and I knew that if I did, that something bad would happen, but I just wanted to know what that something was, and then the bomb went off. I never expected it to be as bad as it was..."

"I'm coming over," she said.

"No, I'm fine."

"No you're not! Listen to yourself Levi, you're talking crazy."

"I just want to go back to that week, everything was better that week," I said, talking more to myself than to her. "I'll call you later. I gotta go."

I hung up, and threw my phone away into the corner.

When you find out that someone you care about was hurt, how do you help them? How do you help them after pouring salt on their wounds?

I could admit it now; I cared about Thea. It had taken me an entire month to come this far, and I had pushed her away... maybe for good.

PAST
DAY 6

THEA

"The sun, it burns," I joked, hiding behind his back when we got outside.

"I know, just push through it, *persevere*," he chuckled.

Holding hands, we walked down my street and into the town. I enjoyed the sight of all the leaves falling from the trees above us. The reds, golds, and oranges, they all made the world so much more beautiful in my eyes.

"What are you smiling about?" he asked.

I pinched my cheeks, not realizing the face I was making. "I love fall. It's my favorite season. You have to give it to Mother Nature, even when she's technically dying, she's doing it like a true lady and going out with style."

"I would have pegged you as more of a spring girl."

"You've pegged me? Have you been thinking about me, Mr. Black?" I teased him with a laugh.

He rolled his eyes, and placed his arm around my shoulder, pulling me closer to him— "Don't ask questions you already know the answer to. How can I *not* be thinking of you?"

I wanted to kiss him.

"Why spring?" I asked, curious as to his assumption.

The truth of the matter was that I needed to stay focused, or else we'd end up right back at my house, or worse yet, doing it somewhere in public. That thought alone caused a momentary throbbing sensation in all the right places.

Why did that excite me? What is he doing to me?

"Because it's the season that's full of life. It's bright and preppy."

"Preppy? And you were doing so well!"

Preppy?

"What's your favorite season?" I asked, as I decided to let the *preppy* comment slide.

"Winter," he said, "I love the snow, and the way it just blankets everything. It's beautiful, especially at the crack of dawn, when the world is still asleep, and the sun starts to come up."

It did sound beautiful.

"Sadly, it's only a temporary state. Before you know it, we silly humans go and muck it all up."

"Yes, all that blasted shoveling. Or would you rather everyone just stay inside all winter?"

"That would be glorious," he said with a smile. "Spend the fall stocking up on food, and just hibernate for the winter," he half-joked. "Imagine how much fun we could have!"

"As genius as your plan is, imagine how many people would snap if they were locked away with their families for four mouths."

"Even better! I would make a killin' in the spring."

I laughed. "You're a horrible person."

"Yeah, yeah. But I can still dream. Can't I?"

There was something about Levi I just liked. It was so easy to be around him. We didn't say much after that, until we got into town and I saw the long line coming out of the Young Thailand restaurant. It snaked around the freaking corner of the block! Apparently, their dinner was worth waiting for.

"Yeah why don't we just—" I began, but he ignored me and led me to the front of the line.

"Reservation for Black," he said as we got inside.

"Good evening," the hostess bowed at us.

She picked up two menus from the stack nearby, and beckoned us to follow her. She led us to a table at the storefront window.

"Reservation?" I asked, as she seated us and left. "Did you just trick me into going on a date with you?"

"How else am I ever going to ever get you to stop eating Frosted Flakes?"

"What's wrong with Frosty?" I pouted.

"It's sugar and fake corn, need I say more?"

"You're no better, with your granola bars!" I accused him.

"Not the same," he retorted, as he slid the basket of unleavened bread towards me.

"I'd eat more, but *someone* never gives me a break long enough to sit down and eat a full meal," I shot back, as I broke off a piece of the bread and nibbled on the end.

"Oh, that's a two way street baby, and you know it."

I knew that he was right, I just couldn't bring myself to admit it. Instead, I picked up my menu and pretended to be completely captivated by a list of food that I had never seen, had, or heard of, in my life.

He remained silent, letting the issue go, and the next time I glanced up, I saw that he was staring out the window, watching as the autumn leaves fluttered in the wind. As I looked at him, I realize just how attracted to him I was, and not just in a sexual way either. Sex had started our time together, but lately, it felt more personal than that.

Lost in my thoughts, I almost didn't notice that he had turned his attention back to me. I looked away, blushing because I knew that I hadn't been quick enough, and he had caught me ogling him. Knowing him, he probably assumed that I was having erotic fantasies about him.

Luckily, before he could say anything, a server came to take our order.

"What would you like to have?" Levi asked.

Crap. I hadn't really read the menu.

"Ah… the Larb Leuat Neua?" I said, picking the first thing that caught my eye.

His eye went wide, and he chuckled before he placed his own order.

"Are you sure?" he asked me.

I wasn't, but I nodded anyway. I had already committed, it was too late to back down without looking like a complete idiot. With a smile, he nodded at the server who collected the menus and left.

"Seriously?" he asked again, this time with a slight frown.

"What?"

"You hate raw food, right?" he asked, knowing full well that I did, after he'd unsuccessfully tried to get me to eat sushi.

"Yeah…"

"Larb Leuat Neua is basically a raw meat salad with mint leaves."

I opened my mouth, but no words came out.

People could sell that?

"If that's not what you really wanted, I can call the—"

"Nope, I'm good," I interrupted.

Note to self: when on dates, read the damn menu.

"Can we just pretend that that didn't just happen?" I begged, shifting in my seat.

I was always embarrassed when it came to him. It was as though my brain just went on hibernate, and I was left to fend for myself.

"What's your favorite color?" he asked.

"What?"

"I'm pretending that didn't just happen. What's your favorite color?"

"Teal."

"Teal?"

"I've always had trouble picking between blue and green; then one day I saw teal, and all was right with the world," I laughed.

Teal was my happy color.

He nodded, then looked at me as though he was waiting for something. Finally he gave up.

"This is the part where you ask me what my favorite color is, Thea," he said, rolling his eyes.

"Is it? This is a slippery slope we're on, you know. First it's colors, and the next I'm telling you my deepest, darkest secrets."

"Are you scared, Ms. Cunning?"

"I'm not, but you're just not ready for it yet, Mr. Black."

"Anything you bring to the table, I can take. But hey, if you're scared of—"

"What's your favorite color Levi?" I asked finally giving in.

He smirked, "I don't have one."

"Then what was…" I stopped, he did this all the time. "You really just like rattling me, don't you?"

"In every sense of the word," he said, behind the glass of water, and I shifted under his gaze.

He reached across the table, took my hand and rubbed the inside of my palm with his thumb. Though it was a small action, I felt myself melting into him. After six days, just doing this was enough.

We leaned back into our seats and relaxed, enjoying each other's company. When the server brought our food to the table, he didn't let go of my left hand. I tried to ignore him, but it bothered me how at ease he was. My pulse was racing, and he didn't seem to be bothered by it in the least.

Slipping out of my flats, I pressed my right foot between his legs, smiling innocently when he jumped.

"Thea," he said, as his back straightened, and his jaw tightened in an effort to control himself.

"Yes?" I asked, taking a bite of the rice he had ordered for me.

Meanwhile, under the table, my foot rubbed against him slowly.

"You're pushing me," he said.

"You're enjoying it," I leaned forward. "As a matter of fact, I can *feel* how much you're enjoying it, Mr. Black."

Covering his mouth with his hand, he sat there, trying not to give into what I knew he was feeling. Pressing harder into him, he tightened his grip on my hand.

"This isn't fair," he glared at me. "You're too far away."

"Sounds like your problem."

"Eat," was all he said as he picked up his fork.

Taking it as a personal challenge, and curious about how far I could take things, I increased the pressure a little as I continued sliding my foot against his hard-on. And just like that, his fork fell out of his hand.

"God damn it, Thea." He was smoldering now.

"You should really try this, it's good," I told him, as I pointed down to my food.

Finally, he reached down and restrained my renegade leg.

"You're gonna have to hold it for as long as we're sitting here," I told him, "and people might start to wonder what your hand is doing down there."

"You're evil."

"And yet still, you like me."

He let go of my foot, and sat there, not saying single word as I started again. The look on his face was priceless. It was a pleasure to watch him battle with himself to maintain control, and to remain cool and collected. And from the feel of things, I knew he wanted to get up and leave right now. But the moment he did, he knew that it would have meant that he was admitting his defeat, and he'd have to acknowledge the fact that he really had no self-control.

I knew him better than that. He'd always let me win the smaller battles. But this, this was something that I knew he would pay me back tenfold for, and each second I drew this out, would be a second more that he would seek out in revenge later on. And truthfully, I looked forward to every moment of it.

Even watching him eat slowly bothered me. I didn't want him to be able to eat. I wanted him to get us out of here. I want him to concede his defeat… he just needed a little push.

Lifting my other foot, I brought it up against him. That was it. He bowed his head, and clenched his fist, until finally, he got up, dropped a hundred on the table, and pulled me up.

"I wasn't done," I said to him, smiling to myself as I slipped my flats back on.

"I'll make us dinner," he said, dragging me out of the restaurant.

He looked down the length of the street, back to my house, and instead of going in that direction, he took my hand and led me to the nearby park.

"Levi…"

"You reap what you sow," he stated.

We bypassed everyone, all but running headlong into the woods. It was only when we couldn't hear anything but birds chirping, that he pushed me up against a tree, lifted my skirt up and grabbed on to one of my thighs.

"This right here, is to get me off, until I can thoroughly pay you back for your little stunt back there," he whispered.

"Levi, someone can come through here at any second."

"Then I'll just have to keep you quiet," he said kissing me as he thrust forward.

"Ah—"

I gripped on to his shoulders and hair. He held me up, slamming inside me with no reservations whatsoever. He left kisses up and down my neck, my face, my lips. He was everywhere, his grasp on my thighs tightened, as my back pressed hard into the tree. With each thrust, the leaves rained down around us, and my breathing became short gasps.

When his kisses stopped, and he looked at me, and all I could do was grin... maybe I was delirious, or just plain giddy, but I couldn't take my eyes off him. I wanted him more. I wanted to feel more of him, over and over again.

"Oh no you don't," he said as he sped up, and my head bent back in joy, "I'm getting off, not you."

All too soon he came, leaving me only half way there.

"Damn you," I hissed.

"Oh, I'm just getting started."

DAY 7

LEVI

"I might have gone a little overboard," I said, looking around at the broken objects in her room.

"You think?" she asked, as she picked up the broken lamp.

"In my defense, the distance from your front door, to your bed, is far too long."

"In the week you've been here, the distance hasn't changed!"

"And how many times did we actually make it to your bed?" I asked, and she just rolled her eyes.

Exactly.

I grabbed the broom and helped her clean up the mess we—I—had made. The damage, equaling both her bedside lamps, a picture frame, an alarm clock, the wall paper over her bed which was torn, and one of her bed legs, now wobbly.

"You aren't going to let me pay for any of this, are you?"

"You're going to try and find a way to pay for it, aren't you?" she countered already knowing where my mind was going.

I was already thinking of ordering the things and having it shipped to her. "As long as we're on the same page."

"You order it, and I'll return it."

"You return it, and I'll order it again."

"Why are you so damn stubborn?"

"Said the queen of stubbornness," he grinned.

She sighed, "Fine. I will pick out the things, and you can order them for me."

"You can't pick out the cheapest things," I told her, knowing full well she would probably go to the thrift store.

"Levi, you aren't you supposed to meet me halfway here? This is a compromise. I'm letting you replace the things, and I get to choose what they will be."

"It's a great compromise, with the exception of what you're choosing. For it to be a true compromise, you have to let me buy you something of equal or better value, than what I broke."

She shook her hands at me like she was trying to reach for my neck. "This is why people hate lawyers!" she screamed in frustration.

"I know, right?"

"I need to get myself some breakfast, before you drive me insane," she muttered, taking my hand as she led me out of the room.

Today was the last day, and instead of heading over to my place, we decided late last night—or rather early this morning—to finish off the day here.

Watching her make breakfast for the last time, I felt the urge to ask for more time… but I didn't want to be *that guy*.

We'd made a deal, and she didn't look like she was backing out of it, and neither should I…

"What's wrong?"

"Nothing. Just thinking about how much that lamp cost," I lied.

"You're ridiculous," she laughed, handing me a plate.

"Thank you. Do you have coffee?" I asked, as I scanned the countertop for the coffee machine.

"Sorry, I don't drink coffee."

"What?" I asked, as I searched for the coffee maker. Sure enough, there was none. "How'd I not notice this before?"

"You're a coffee person?"

"I was a coffee addict, but now that I think of it, I don't remember having a cup all week."

What the hell? I had had a cup of coffee at least once a day since I was in high school.

"Surprise! This was really just a one-week rehab for you Levi Black. Your family was worried about your addiction, and called me in to help," she joked, handing me a glass of orange juice.

"If my family's turned me in, who's going to help them? Because I know the addiction's hereditary," I chuckled, as I accepted the glass.

"The family package is extra," she said, and I coughed up my drink trying not laugh.

"Ah... stop."

She laughed along with me, and I was at peace with her once again. Grabbing our plates, we moved into the living room, taking our place on the couch, which usually consisted of her sitting in-between my legs.

I'm not sure why, but neither of us spoke after that. We kissed every so often, but it never got too heavy. She rested against me and read to me, I in turn, played the guitar for her, and then we ended up in each other's arms again... without clothes on. We just held each other for hours, talking when we had to, and kissing when there just weren't any words.

And just like that, the day was over. The spell was broken, and reality came creeping back into our lives. As if to prove it, my phone never stopped vibrating, as Betty's preprogrammed messages started to invade my inbox.

"You're popular," she said, standing up, and I wanted to pull her back down on top of me.

"I officially start work again today," I told her looking up at the clock; it was one minute past midnight.

"Then I guess you should be going."

"Yeah." I stood, grabbing my bag.

We said nothing as we headed over to the door, and part of me hoped that she wouldn't open it, but she did.

"It was great meeting you, Thea."

Great didn't even begin to cover it.

"Likewise. This week was amazing," she nodded. "Bye."

"Bye."

I kissed her one last time before turning around.

Just keep walking Levi. Just keep walking.

But I didn't listen to myself. Instead I turned back just as she closed the door…

It was over.

I would most likely never see her again. This week was nothing like I had thought it would be. I never meant to share anything about myself, or even get to know her. It was just supposed to be sex. So why didn't it feel like that?

Just keep walking Levi.

THEA

When he left, I slid to the ground and drew my knees to my chest. I wanted to ask him to stay. I didn't want to open the damn door. But if did, then I would be that girl who couldn't let go, and I rather let him go than risk him thinking that I was *that girl*.

"I'm pitiful, aren't I, Shadow?" I whispered to my cat, as she came to lay on my lap.

This must have been how Cinderella felt after the clock struck midnight and all the magic went away. This had been the best week of my life, and now, it was over.

PART TWO

PRESENT

13

LEVI

Class began, and I walked in to find her seat empty. I could hear the remaining students whispering amongst themselves that they had successfully wiped her name off the board. It would take more than one missed class to derail her status, or was I just being nice because I'd fucked up so badly? I wasn't really sure anymore.

The image that I had created in my mind of Margaret Cunning had shattered before my very eyes at Thea's revelation. Just thinking of her made me sick. What kind of woman does something so despicable to her children?

"To me, she is The Shark because she eats her young," Thea's voice rang out in my mind again and again.

It was like that one horror movie that I couldn't get out of my head, no matter how many comedies I watched afterward.

The class droned on without anything significant happening. Usually I would be pressing them harder, trying to get reactions out of them. However, today, I felt like I was the one off my game. They couldn't tell, to them I was being an even bigger dick than ever, but I knew it wasn't because of anything they had done. I was pissed off at myself.

Truthfully, I had no idea how I managed to make it without dismissing class early, but I didn't linger any longer than I had to.

∽

"Have a good evening, Sir," my driver said to me as I stepped out of the car. I only ever used him when going to see clients or heading to the city.

"Thank you, see you tomorrow evening."

"Very well, Sir."

Reaching into my pocket, I grabbed my keys, heading towards the stairway of my townhouse, when I stopped short. There she was, sitting on the third stair, waiting for me.

"Hi," she stood up, "I know it's late, but can I come in?"

Unsure of what to say, or how to react, and somewhat afraid that I would once again stick my foot into my mouth, I nodded and opened the door for the both of us. Once inside, she didn't move from the doorway.

"I just wanted to say I'm sorry," she said, rubbing her hands together. It was an action I knew she did when she was nervous. "It was completely wrong of me to explode at you like that, not to mention inappropriate. My mother— she was superstar lawyer, it would make sense that you would talk about her in class. My feelings should not—"

"Stop," I said. I couldn't take her apologizing to me. I cupped the side of her cheek, and took pleasure in the fact that she still leaned into it. "I'm sorry. I should have warned you."

"How could you have? Why should you have? You did what you—"

"I did what I wanted to do, without caring how it would have hurt or affected you. I didn't have to bring up Margaret this early in the year, I only did it because of how you reacted to the mere mention of her, and the fact that Tristan told me how much you hated her.

"I did it because I wanted to know more about you, and so I pushed you when I shouldn't have. I'm the one who should be apologizing to you, I'm the one who's sorry," I said before she could interrupt me.

Her head dropped, along with my heart. "You're an ass."

"I know."

"You didn't have to follow me."

"I know."

"Don't look at me like I'm damaged," she whispered, not meeting my gaze.

Lifting her chin her up, I forced her to look at me. "I'm not."

"You're thinking it."

"I definitely am not," I said softly, as I ran my thumb over her bottom lip.

She's so close to me...

"I should go."

"Okay."

Neither of us moved.

If she kissed me now, she would become a student who knowingly seduced her professor, and if I kissed her now, I would become a professor who preyed on my student. Either way, we were both screwed, so fuck it.

Leaning down, I closed the gap between us. In that moment, everything I had been suppressing for the last month came rushing back to me. Dropping my bag, I picked her up, and her legs snaked themselves around me. She molded herself to my body, and her hands gripped on to my hair, as our tongues collided with each other.

I had no idea how we even managed to make it to the bedroom. When we got to the bed, she broke away only long enough for me to pull off her sweater and throw it into the corner. She swept my jacket of my shoulders, and pulled my tie from my neck in one fluid motion. She ripped my shirt off just as I had done to her on our second night.

"So sexy," I muttered, kissing her stomach, as I pulled off her jeans.

I eagerly trailed my kisses downward, pausing only long enough to pull her underwear down with my teeth. My hand was already moving in to tease her. Her back arched up, as I rubbed my fingers against her already wet folds. My tongue followed suit as I licked her, once, slowly.

"Stop… stop playing with me," she protested, as she rocked against my tongue and fingers.

She was right. I didn't want to play, I just wanted to have her. She rubbed herself against me and I couldn't help but grin.

"Eager?" I asked, taking it from her.

"Aren't you? Or has someone else been getting you off now?"

Grabbing her wrist, I pinned her down underneath me. "Don't even joke like that."

"Who says—?"

I kissed her, silencing her before she said anything else crazy. She moaned into my mouth as soon as I entered her.

Goddamn.

I couldn't think straight. I had missed this. I had missed being in her so badly, I didn't have enough self-control to make love. So instead, I fucked her hard, keeping her pinned down beneath me. Her breasts bounced uncontrollably as my bed shook to the rhythm of our bodies. This wasn't slow or passionate; that's not what either of us wanted or needed.

"Levi!"

I loved how she always, no matter what, called my name when she came.

Seeing the look on her face, I couldn't stop myself. I grunted out as I came. Exhausted, I fell onto her chest, and she wrapped her arms around me. I stayed like that for as long as I could, savoring the moment, and the feel of her, as I listened to her heartbeat slowly return to normal.

This moment was just like the last day of our week together, only now, we both knew that this was something different. This was something more than just lust.

That week we had no idea if we would ever see each other again, let alone become so entwined in each other's lives. We were a mystery to each other then, but now, now we should have known better. Or at the very least, I should have known better, but I just couldn't care enough.

When she tried to get up, I rolled over, trying to give her the space that she needed. But watching her reach for her bra was too much.

"Don't go," I finally said. "Stay the night."

"I can't."

"Why?"

She turned back and glared at me, "You know why."

"I do, but stay anyway."

"Levi, please don't make this harder for me…"

"For you? This isn't just hard for—"

She turned, moving on top of me, and kissed me quickly. "I've told you most of my story, I'm just going to finish it now so that you can understand."

All I could do was nod.

"My father is at Northern Correctional."

I cringed. It was one of the worst maximum-security state prisons in the state of Connecticut.

"You know the Savannah Van Allen case?" she continued.

I sat up suddenly, my eyes widening in understanding. "You father is Ben Walton?"

She nodded. "Yes. My father is Ben Walton, and he's currently on death row for the rape and murder of the Boston socialite, Savannah Van Allen. My mother was supposed to represent him. I was just a child at a time, and my sister wasn't even a year old. But

I remember it all. The day Savannah Van Allen was murdered, my father took my sister and I to the Woodstock Fair. There were photos to prove it. My mother knew, she could have had the case thrown out. But then she found out that he was planning to leave her for Savannah. So, in a fit of rage, she handed off his case to a friend, burned all the photos we took that day, and took my sister and I out of town."

Margaret Cunning was the devil.

"He's been in prison now for almost two decades, and *my mother* only confessed to this three months ago. I'm in law school right now because every damn lawyer I went to didn't believe me, didn't have time or they didn't want to touch his case. My grandmother has been paying some scumbag lawyer for appeals, and he's just barely doing anything. At this point, I'm not even sure if he went to law school. So, I'm all my dad has left, and I have to be the best damn lawyer I can, so that I can get him out before it's too late. So now you understand why I can't stay here with you. I need you to teach me, and you can't do that while you're screwing me at the same time."

She got off of me, and gathered the rest of her clothes, while I sat there and trying to restart my brain.

"Thea."

She didn't turn back, instead she kept getting dressed.

"Thea."

Grabbing my jeans, I followed her down the stairs.

"I'm sorry I missed class today Professor Black, it won't happen again," she called over her shoulder as she tried to open the door.

I slammed it shut.

"You have a horrible habit of running away from me."

"It's called self-preservation."

"It's called bullshit. Look at me."

"No."

"Thea, look at me!"

She still didn't move.

Damn her stubbornness!

"Hear me out, and then I'll let you leave."

"Fine."

She turned back and I kissed her. She kissed me back for a split second before pushing me away. "That's what you wanted to say?"

"Yes and no. I understand that this is complicated, and messy, and just all around fucked up. But I also know that you feel the same way about me, as I feel about you, no matter how much you try to deny it."

"Really? So tell me Professor, how do I feel?" she snapped, crossing her arms.

"Confused. Frustrated. Happy. Pissed off and turned on, all at the same time."

"That could be anyone—"

"Not done yet." I pressed my finger on her lips. "You feel all of that, but most of all, you feel like there is no one else on the planet that will make you feel as alive as you are with me. You know it."

"That's a bold statement."

"I'm a bold person, can't you tell?"

"Maybe it's okay for you, but it isn't for me. Anything you give in class, I will feel like I haven't really earned it. Anything you take away, I'll feel like it's out of spite. No matter what, I'll still feel that way if we do this."

"Then let's not label this. Let's just—"

"Keep fucking each other?" she finished.

I held back my anger. "I hate when you say it like that! You make it sound so dirty."

"But isn't that what we're doing? Isn't that what you want?" she snapped back.

"No. No it isn't actually. I want to go on a date—dates— with you. I want us to get to know each other."

She still wouldn't give in.

"If anyone found out, I would be finished. You're *the* Levi Black, you'd be fine, but me—"

"Then no one will find out, and even if someone did see us, I'm lawyer, I will lie through my teeth. I've taken former top students out before anyway, we'll just need to bring case files with us as an alibi."

She dropped her head, allowing her hair to fall forward, masking her face. "Let me think about it."

There was nothing more that I could say or do. I'd stated my case, and it was time to let the juror deliberate. Stepping back, I allowed her enough room to open the door.

This could be my first loss, I thought bitterly to myself, as I watched her walk away.

THEA

I wasn't sure what was racing faster; my mind, or my heart. He was the smoothest talking man I had ever met.

Do not consider his offer, I told myself as I entered my house. *You only said that you would to get out of the there...*

"What in the hell?" I yelled, as I walked in on Selene, who sat on the couch smoking a joint, whilst some shirtless stranger was preoccupied with kissing her neck.

They jumped apart quickly as I entered.

"Get out!" I sneered at him, and he grabbed his belt, shirt, and hat.

"Selene—" he said, turning to her.

"Now!" I screamed, before he could get another word out.

"Really, Thea? Aren't you being a little hypocritical?" she glared up at me, putting her shirt back on.

My hand twitched.

"First of all Selene, I've never ever brought a man home while you were living with me. Secondly, I'm twenty-three, I graduated both high school *and* college. You, on the other hand, are a sixteen-year-old, trying to get a C in trigonometry. We are nowhere near the same level."

Moving over to the couch, I again fought the urge to literally slap some sense into her.

"Weed now?" I asked, as I picked up the joint.

"It's like, totally not even a drug now," she argued.

"Oh yeah? Would you like me to call up a nice police officer, and ask if he can verify that for me? Oh and you're like *totally* grounded now," I told her, mocking her tone.

Her mouth dropped open. "Thea!" she shouted, outraged.

"Don't you dare raise your voice at me! First the nose ring, then the failing grades, now the boys and drugs? Who are you? Because my baby sister is smarter than this."

"Some of us want to have fun and live! Fun? Have you heard of it?" she screamed at me.

"This is not the way you have fun!"

"Maybe not for you. I don't even know if you have fun bone in your body. All you do is study and study, until your brain feels like exploding, then you get drunk, and sleep with some random guy. Well you're just living it up, aren't you?"

"What's wrong with you?" I asked her.

"Nothing is wrong!"

"Bullshit." I was doing my best to stay calm.

"We're just different people."

She walked toward the door but I stepped in front of her blocking her path.

"I swear to God Selene, I will tackle you to the ground before I let you walk out that door to go do something even more stupid."

"Whatever, by tomorrow he's probably going to tell everyone my sister is a weirdo," she replied, heading towards her room.

"If you try and climb out your window, I will know, and I will find you and embarrass you wherever you go," I warned her.

She slammed her door.

Sighing, I fell onto the couch before I remembered what they had just been doing. With a grunt of disgust, I stood back up and headed to the kitchen in search of the disinfecting wipes.

Teenagers are just awesome.

But I also knew that she was going through a lot more internally.

14

LEVI

"Run brother, run as fast as you can," Bethan said to me, as she came out of our parents' home in her dark blue, midnight-evening gown. Her stomach protruded like a beach ball under a blanket. Tristan came up beside her and helped her down the stairs. He was dressed in his best suit, the one I had bought for him last Christmas.

"Didn't the party just start?" I asked, amused as they tried to make their escape.

She shook her head at me, messing up her dark curls. "I just couldn't deal with it anymore, Levi. When mom brought out the pianist, I had to get out of there."

I nodded. These events took a lot out Bethan. She—well, *we*—both felt like as though we were on display for all of the elite members of Boston to ogle at. However, because of my profession, and my frequent dealings with the media and general public, I was better at faking my interest than she was.

"You used your pregnancy, didn't you?"

She grinned, but bent over quickly as another couple walked around us, and into the house.

"Hey, this belly is good for something other than hiding my toes," she winked, grabbing on to Tristan's hand.

How he managed put up with her, I would never know.

"Sorry, to leave you alone with them," Tristan said, though I wasn't sure he was as sorry as he claimed to be.

"It's fine, I know where they hide the good stuff."

"I miss drinking," Bethan pouted.

"Okay, time to go home," Tristan said, leading her down the stairs.

For a brief moment, I wished that Thea were with me, but I pushed that thought out of my mind as I headed inside. Sure enough, it was just as bad as Bethan had made it sound.

It always felt as though I had jumped back into the 1920s for my parents' parties with the white marble floors, the grand chandelier, and the crystal glasses. Everyone here was a *somebody*, and they dressed to prove it. Thousand dollar suits and gowns, Rolexes on the wrist of every man in sight, and diamonds and pearls adorning the necks, ears, wrists and hands of every woman present. This was the Black Family Party.

"Thank you," I said directly to the server's face as he handed me a glass. He nodded, somewhat dazed.

Happens every time.

They usually spent the entire night being waved off and ignored by all attending patrons. Whenever someone actually said something to them, it shocked them out of their minds, like I had just ripped off their invisible cloak.

"Levi!" my mother called out to me.

She was dressed in a red floor-length gown, and had the same green eyes as mine, with light, grey-brown hair that stopped at her shoulders. She kissed my cheeks and smiled. "I'm so happy you're here. Did you manage to see Bethan? She just left."

"Yes," I said with a smile, "I caught her on her way out. You look beautiful."

"Thank you, honey."

She wiped her lipstick off my cheek.

"She's marked you too, I see," my father said, as he came up behind her. "Glad you could make it, son."

"I had an option?" I replied, earning myself a stern look from my mother.

My father stood toe to toe with me, with salt and paper hair, and brown eyes. He used to hate parties like this one until he retired. He was the former district attorney, before becoming a judge, and now he was the man who threw parties to talk about his past glory days. I felt bad for him sometimes.

"Come with me, I have someone I want you to meet," my mother said as she pulled me into the dining room where the rest of her guests were.

"Mom, slow down or you're going to trip over your dress."

Why was she such in a hurry?

She hushed me, and led me over to the bar where a pretty brunette with bright blue eyes, wearing all black, stood.

"Sharpay, this is my handsome son, Levi. Levi, this is Sharpay London. Her mother and I were pledge sisters in college. They just recently moved to Boston." She introduced us with the widest cat-like grin on her face. "Oh, I'll be right back, you father is calling me," she said, as she beat a hasty retreat.

"Wow, she is not subtle at all," I whispered to myself.

I should have known.

Why didn't I listen to Bethan? Why didn't I run when I had the chance?

The last time my mother had set me up with a woman, I ended up marrying her. And just look at how well *that* worked out!

"She's actually much better than my mother who practically dragged me here by my hair," Sharpay laughed.

There was no denying that she was pretty. Some may even say beautiful. But she wasn't the one I wanted.

"I'm sorry about this, I thought I had made it clear to her that I wasn't available."

Obviously we needed to have the I-don't-need-my-mother-to-pick-out-dates-for-me conversation again.

"Oh, you're seeing someone?"

She looked disappointed. Didn't she just claim that she was dragged here almost against her will?

"No," I said, then I reconsidered, "Yes— It's very complicated right now."

"It seems like it. She must be one lucky girl to catch *the* Levi Black."

"It seems like someone knew more about this set up than she let on."

She shrugged. "You can't blame a girl for trying right? I saw you in the Time magazine article. When my mother talked about this party, I figured why not. So, tell me, how complicated is complicated?"

"I'm not sure, but it's worth sticking out."

She opened her purse and handed me her card— *Dr. Sharpay London,* it read.

"If ever you're bored, or in need of a physical, call me." She walked off smoothly.

She was good. Had I met her two months ago, this conversation may have gone a lot differently.

Turning to the bartender, I handed him her card. He raised an eyebrow at me, but took it anyway.

"Bourbon," I said to him, and he poured me a glass.

Downing it, I moved through the crowd, painfully aware that my mother was very likely somewhere searching for me. Making my way up the stairs, I headed towards my old bedroom.

Resting on the bed, I pulled out my phone and saw that there was not one, but *two* missed calls from Thea.

"Pick up," I whispered, hitting redial.

"Didn't you listen to my message?" she answered.

"You left a message?" I looked at my screen and saw the little voicemail icon in the corner, "No, I just called you back."

"I called you by mistake, but I didn't want you to get the wrong idea, so I called again and left a message."

"Thank you?" I laughed.

"You were supposed to listen to your voicemail," she chided.

"I'm sorry," I told her.

"Well yeah, so I'll just hang up—"

"What are you doing right now?"

"It's not sexy."

"Tell me anyway," I grinned.

"I'm trying to get a cigarette burn out of my couch."

"You're right, that was not sexy. Since when did you smoke?"

"I don't! My sister is just… she's just going through a phase."

"Is she all right?"

She sighed. "Levi, what are you doing?"

"I'm talking to you—"

"You're a strait-laced, respectable teacher, and a hot-shot lawyer. You can have any woman you want—"

"You're right," I told her. "In fact, no less than ten minutes ago, a pretty doctor was hitting on me."

"Well aren't you Mr. Lucky." She was annoyed; I could hear it in her voice.

"But I turned her down, because I meant what I said. I'm not going to make it if I spend the semester, let alone the full academic year, trying to avoid you, or deny the fact I want to be with you. I tried, and it drove me crazy."

She was silent.

"If I wasn't your professor, and I had called you on the day after our week was over, and asked you out on a date, would you have gone out with me?"

"Yes," she said whispered, "but it's more complicated than that."

"So what?"

More silence.

"So I can't. I just can't. I'm sorry."

And just like that, she was gone.

If that was her answer, fine.

Getting up, I head back downstairs. My mother called me over in the corner of the room, but instead, I simply waved her away before heading towards the window.

"It seems like things just got a lot less complicated," I whispered into Sharpay's ear with my hand on her back.

She grinned, and I ignored the little voice in my head. The voice of reason. The voice of warning.

THEA

Part of me wanted to call him back, but I just couldn't bring myself to do it. I came back to Boston and entered law school with one goal in mind, and since I met him, I found that I had allowed myself to be distracted, and I had lost sight of my goal.

No matter how much I wanted to, I couldn't put everything on the line for a guy I barely knew. I needed to get back on track, I needed to stop daydreaming and get back to reality. My family needed me, and that superseded all else. It also meant I was going to have to deal with Selene.

She should be trying to sneak back in any time now.

"Shit," I heard her hiss as she stubbed her toes against the table.

"Would you like some ice for that?" I asked her, turning on the light.

"Jesus Christ!" she jumped back, grabbing her chest in fright.

She was a mess, her skirt was on backwards, her make-up was streaked and ruined, and her hair was a complete mess.

"That grounding thing wasn't serious, right?" she asked as she went into the kitchen, and grabbed herself a box of cereal.

"I un-enrolled you from school," I told her.

"Seriously? Right on!" She jumped onto the couch in front of me.

I stared at her for a moment, then I took a deep breath before I reached for the ticket on the coffee table.

"Where are we going?"

"We're not going anywhere. *You're* going back to Maryland," I told her. "I've already called Grams."

"What?"

"You can't stay here—"

"You're kicking me out? Are you fucking serious right now?! Just because I went out a couple times—"

"I'm not kicking you out Selene, you can come back whenever you want, you just can't *live* here."

She looked like I had just stabbed her. "I don't... I don't understand? Is because of that guy? 'Cause I mean, I don't mind if he comes over—"

"There is no guy."

"Then why are you shipping me off?!" she demanded.

"Because you're drowning here Selene!" I yelled getting up. "It was wrong of me to allow you to come here. It was wrong, and selfish, and I'm so sorry. You can't stay, because if you do, you will destroy yourself. This house, this city, it's blackening your rainbow. You don't laugh, you shake at night. You can't stand to be here, and that's okay. So go home Selene."

She glared at me through her tears, and it reminded me of when I came back to get her the first time.

"We don't leave each other," she said.

"I'm not leaving you Selene. I'm going to finish law school, I'm going to get Dad out, and then I'm coming home. I promise I'll work my ass off, but I can only do that if I know that you're okay, and you were okay back home."

Her lips shook, and she broke down as she crawled into my arms.

"I'm so sorry," she cried. "I thought— I thought I could do it—"

"You are the most beautiful, funny, creative, intelligent little sister a girl could have. You mean the world to me, and so much more. You shouldn't be sorry for anything. I'm sorry for not doing this sooner," I whispered to her.

Starting tomorrow, everything was going to change. I'd always been at the top of my class, I'd always worked for everything I ever wanted. And now, I was going to work ten times harder. I was going to do whatever it took, because I couldn't afford to lose. I couldn't afford to get sidetracked anymore.

"You going to cross over to the dark side, aren't you?" she half joked, and I wished I could tell her I wasn't. "You aren't like her, you know. I'm sorry for what I said before."

"Selene it's fine. Just go pack, all right?"

She nodded and I headed into our mother's office. It was the only place I hadn't dared to touch, or even enter. It was like her shrine, and going in made me feel uneasy, but I needed to stop holding back.

Levi had said I should use anything I could to my advantage. My mother was an advantage. I hated using her to get ahead, it made me feel dirty, but I know that that was how I got my scholarship in the first place. When I went in for my interview the dean spent the first five minutes talking about how great my mother was, and how she was one of the building blocks on which Harvard was built.

My mother had a folder for every person who owed her favor, she was just that type of woman; everything came at a price. Now that she was dead, I guessed that everything, just like this house, had passed on to me.

So I was going to call in a favor.

In the back of my mind, I heard the small voice telling me not to do it. Getting any more involved with my mother would be like opening Pandora's Box, but I made the call anyway.

"Hi, my name is Thea Cunning, daughter of Margaret Cunning…"

15

LEVI

*B*EEP.
　　　BEEP.
BEEP.

I smacked my alarm with the flat of my hand, but no matter how many times I crushed the snooze button, it wouldn't shut off.

"I think it's your phone," someone said.

Peeking through only one of my eyes, I saw...

Shit, what was her name again?

"Your phone." She pointed.

Nodding, I sat up, reaching for my phone. "Black."

"Ah, hi. I know this is weird, and you don't know me—"

"You have five seconds before I hang up."

"I'm Selene... Thea's sister?"

I froze for a moment before sitting up. I wasn't sure what to say or think, and the woman who was currently picking her clothes up off of my bedroom floor was not helping the situation.

"Hello?"

"I'm here. How did you get this number?"

"You were the only number in her phone I didn't know, so I figured you're the guy she's been seeing?"

"We aren't—you really shouldn't have called me."

"Look can we meet for like five minutes? Please? It's important. I know you don't know me, and you have no reason to trust me, but I just wanted to talk to you about my sister. You're the first guy to last this long, so I think you care about her. If I'm wrong you can hang up—"

"Fine. Where do you want to meet?"

This family was going to be the death of me.

"Downtown. Do you know where Mico's Coffee shop is?"

"Yeah. I'll be there in thirty minutes."

"Thanks," she said before hanging up.

"Is that your girlfriend?" The brunette... *Sharpay?*... Sharpay London, asked.

It slowly started to come back to me.

"No," I said as I got out of bed.

I was surprised to find that I was still fully dressed in my clothes from the night before.

"Just in case you forgot, we didn't do it," she stated, stepping into her heels.

"We didn't?"

Why couldn't I remember anything?

"You told me that things were less complicated, then we laughed, we drank, and you invited me back here, where we drank some more. I practically threw myself at you, and everything was going great, until you suddenly stopped, pushed me away, and rejected me, right before you passed out," she said with an edge in her voice. "Next time you bring a woman to your place, have the courtesy to do something about it, or else it's just embarrassing."

She grabbed her purse and left without another word, leaving me sitting in bed, dazed and confused.

God I'm a fucking mess, I thought, pulling off my shirt.

I needed to get my life back together.

∼

ENTERING the small green and white coffee shop, I glanced around until I saw a girl, dressed in all black, with a beanie and headphones on, who resembled Thea.

"Selene?" I waved my hand in front of her face.

"Oh, hi," she said, taking of her headphones. "Please, sit," she said motioning to the chair in front of her. "Sorry, I got tired of watching the door like some love sick school girl. People were staring."

"How long have you been here?" I asked taking a seat.

"About an hour." She shrugged like it was nothing. "I was already here when I called you."

"Why *did* you call me?"

"Can I get a name first? I just keep calling you *blue and white stripes* in my head."

"What?"

She smiled, and it sort of looked like Thea's. "The boxers you left at the house," she said as if it were obvious. "They had blue and white stripes."

"This is certainly one way to start a conversation. I'm Levi Black. I'm guessing your sister hasn't spoken much about me?"

Not that I cared.

"No. But don't take it personally, it's just who she is. She tricks people into thinking she is opening up about herself because she rants about the most random things, but she never *really* talks about herself," she said, taking a sip of her coffee.

"Selene, I'm a little confused as to why you called me."

"Because I'm leaving town," she replied and I waited for her to go on. "She's sending me back to Maryland to stay with our grandmother. She's studying law because—"

"Because of your father, I know."

Her eyes widened in surprise.

"Yeah. I'm sorry for calling you out here, and I don't even

know if you're really that close to her, but I just had to ask *someone* to look out for her a little, and you seem to be the only person she knows, or the only person she cares to know."

"Your sister is a big girl Selene, she doesn't need someone—"

"No, she does." She dropped her head, gripping on to her coffee. "She's one of those people that will give up everything for people without caring or noticing what happens to her.

"When she caught me trying to sneak back into my room, she said that there was no one in her life, and that she only cared about making sure dad and I were okay. She was sad. For the first time since I came here, she was sad."

I didn't think that I was supposed to hearing any of this.

"Maybe because you're moving away—" I started.

"You really don't want to accept that it's you, do you?"

"She rejected me," I said, calling over the waitress. "She rejected me not even twenty-four hours ago. I'm sorry if I'm a little skeptical of Thea's feelings… if she has them at all." I turned to meet the gaze of the waitress who looked decidedly unimpressed with her life. "Coffee, black, please," I told the waitress, before turning back to Selene.

"Fine, then let me make it clear." She sat up. "We are black rainbows."

"That's not clear at all."

"When we were younger, our grandmother used to say that everyone was born with all the colors of the rainbow, and depending on the people around us, our colors either brightened or darkened. Thea and I are black rainbows… every once in a while we get brighter, but we always end up black again. People don't stay around us long. Especially after they realize the life we've had, they slowly withdrew themselves from our lives because they feel uncomfortable or they don't know what to say."

"Again, *she* pushed *me* away."

"Self-preservation. It's how she works. But when she's pushing you away, that just means she wants you to hold on tighter."

"That would make me a stalker."

She shook her head. "It's different for us. The moment she starts to get happy, she finds a dozen reasons to run away, when, in all honesty, she's just afraid of one thing; that if you really tried to get know her, the good, the bad and the awful, you'll walk away. She likes you, and that probably scares the hell out of her."

"How do you know?"

"Because I'm scared of all the same things."

I shook my head, as I accepted the coffee the waitress gave to me, and took a deep breath.

"So what you're saying is that I should keep chasing after her like a dog?"

I couldn't do it. My pride just wouldn't let me do it.

"What I'm saying is, if you can't handle her, all of her, then walk away now and never contact her again. You're just going to hurt her, and she's all alone here, living in Margaret's house, because we can't afford to live anywhere else in the city. She walks around like nothing hurts her, but there's only so much a person can take before they snap."

"You said she was happy? How do you know?"

"She hummed. She danced to 80s music, and stole my guitar... all in the same week. She's never been as happy as she was that last week of summer, and she was doing well, until I saw her face last night. I couldn't just leave without seeing you first."

"And now that you've met me?"

"I'll save my judgments for a later date, so be sure to stick around for that," she said, smiling.

"What am I supposed to do?"

"Be there long enough, and she'll come to you. Until then, just watch out for her, okay? I can't be there for her, so if you can… if you want…"

She shrugged and struggled to find the words to say.

I nodded. "I got it. You really watch out for her."

"We're all the family we've got left... you should see the things she does for me."

She stood up, digging in her bag for change.

"I got it."

"Thanks." She smiled. "Oh and we never, ever, *ever* had this conversation. She would kill me—she'd kill *us*."

I nodded, and with that, she left.

After spending a week with her, and watching her in class, Thea was an open book to me. She wore all her emotions on her face, and even when she was trying not to, I could still read her as plain as day. The problem was that she was a city surrounded by walls; you could see it from a distance, but there was no front gate and no way to get in.

It was obvious that Selene had no idea that I was her sister's professor, and I wondered what she would think of the situation then. I wasn't just her sister's lover, and I legitimately couldn't stay away from her until the term ended.

I need something stronger than coffee.

THEA

"Well look who decided to come back to class," Atticus called from the classroom door. "And here I thought dethroning you was going to be hard. I was all prepared last class too."

Walking up to him, I smiled wide before I pulled out the notice. "Atticus Michael Logan, born March 27th, to Mary-Ann and *Governor* Jacob Logan of Greenville, South Carolina. You have two older sisters, and three younger brothers. You favorite team is the Dallas cowboys, and wait—"

He grabbed at me, and pulled me from the doorway, and away from his buddies, but that didn't stop me.

"Now this can't be right," I said in my best southern accent, "but it says here, that you're a registered Republican and yet you've been donating to Democrats. You must have broken your poor mama's heart. Oh no, that can't be right either, here you are, posing with your father, Governor Rick Perry and Senator Ted Cruz, aren't they Republicans? You're a closet Democrat, aren't you? You put so much effort in hiding to help your father's campaign. I hear he dreams of being the president one day. It would be a shame if your family found out, or worse yet, if other people found out that you're just a fraud who's trying to rattle people's cages so that you can swoop in for the kill."

He snatched the papers from me, and sat back in his chair. His face was almost purple. He was positively seething with rage and he looked about ready to kill me.

"What. Do. You. Want?" he sneered.

"Aim your gun at someone else," I snapped. "All *he* wants are twelve people, there are fifteen of us here. Help me bring them down. Once we do that, you've already secured yourself as one of the chosen twelve. What happens after, well, we'll cross that bridge when we get to it."

"And here I thought you were all about helping people, and doing the right thing," he sucked his teeth.

"But I am. I'm doing the right thing, for me."

"Fine. So tell me, how did you get your hands on this information?"

One down, one to go.

"I know a guy and he's good with computers," I said as we headed into one of our other classes. Levi—*Professor Black's*–class, was to be our last class that day. The class we had now was a total snore. Our professor looked like he hadn't practiced law since the Great Depression.

He took a seat beside me, and leaned back into his chair. "So who else are you planning to bring into your little clubhouse?"

I noticed that his accent didn't stand out as much now.

"What makes you think anyone else is invited?"

"Oh?" he asked. "And I guess that I'm just that special?"

"Don't flatter yourself, you'll find out when we get to Black's class."

He shifted, looking me over again.

"What?"

"What happened to you? One moment you were all smiles and rainbows, and now, you're like a black hole."

"Does that make it hard for you to work with me?"

"No, I'm just wondering where I'd have to go to blacken my soul."

I didn't reply.

∽

KNEELING, I helped her pick up all her books, whilst others just walked by.

"Vivian Vega, right?" I asked her, knowing full well I was right. She was the one who *loved* my mother, and was basically a walking encyclopedia of cases.

"What do you want?" she asked, as she pushed her glasses back up her nose, tilting her head to the side.

"Nothing much, I just want you to stop trying to make a fool out me in class. Not only is it annoying to be constantly interrupted by you, but it's borderline ridiculous. You aren't going to upstage me with just facts. You and I are the only girls left, we should work together."

"It sounds like you're scared," she said, her eyes narrowing. "I'm fine on my own. With the way Professor Black keeps hounding you for missing class, I doubt you'll make it to the end of the week, so on that note, I'm going to have to reject your fake *sisterhood* offer."

"Whatever you say Little Butterfly," I called out to her as she tried to walk away.

She stopped and slowly turned to look at me, her eyes were wide.

"What did you call me?"

"Little Butterfly. That's your name, right?"

She dragged me by the hand, pulling me into the girls' bathroom. She checked under all the stalls before looking to me.

"Where did you hear that name?"

"You and I both know the answer to that."

For a fleeting moment, the look in her eyes made me feel a twinge of remorse, then I reminded myself of my purpose, and I knew that if the tables were turned, she would hang me out to dry. Despite her conservative appearance, she was a woman willing to do anything to get to the top.

"So you're blackmailing me now?"

"No. I'm going to ask again for your support, and you will either decide to get rid of me quickly, because I know that you've been stripping your way through law school, or you're going to realize that having me for an enemy serves to your disadvantage. I would never use something like that against you, and I respect the fact that you want this that badly. Be in my corner, and I will be in yours. Like I said, we're the last women standing, and do you really think that those asshats are going to have your back if they ever find out? Believe me, you *want* to be on my team."

I had her by the balls, figuratively speaking, and there was nothing left for me to say. I headed back to the classroom, thrilled that my plan was going my way, so far.

Vivian Vega was a first generation Puerto Rican. Her mother worked as a seamstress, and her father was a taxi driver. She was the first in her family to graduate from college, and get into law school... Harvard Law School at that. The only problem was, she couldn't afford the cost of the institution, and financial aid only covered about half of her tuition. So with no viable alternative, she got a job working at strip club two hours away, just to make ends meet.

"Well?" Atticus asked as I took a seat next to him. Levi—

Professor Black –would be here any second, and I knew that she wouldn't risk being late.

"Wait for it," I told him, and right on cue, she came in and sat down to my left.

Atticus snickered, leaning over me to shake her hand. "Atticus Logan, what's she got on you?"

"Vivian Vega, and none of your damn business."

"Let the games begin," Atticus whispered as Levi—*Professor Black* I had to keep reminding myself—entered the room.

I hated the fact that just the sight of him made my heart slam against my chest. I hadn't seen or heard from him since last week Friday. It had only been three days, and yet, it felt like forever.

I half expected him to walk up to the board and erase my name, but he didn't. Instead, he dropped a folder onto his desk, and turned back to us. He tilted his head to the side and that's when I noticed the small red mark on his neck. His collar obscured most of it, and no one else seemed to notice it, but I did.

It could be a bug bite.

"I've recently taken up another case of interest," Lev— *Professor Black* said, and Vivian passed me her notebook. Atticus leaned in as well, reading over the news clipping.

How had she known?

"Mariah Nash," Atticus called out, before Professor Black could.

"Age 29, charged with first degree murder of her husband, Senator Tyler Nash. Age: 66. Paramedics were called to the Nash family home on July 27th after receiving a 911 call. He was pronounced dead at the scene," I added.

"Mrs. Nash was charged the following Saturday at 9:09am. Last night you officially took on her case," Vivian finished off.

Lev— Professor Black's eyebrow raised, before he looked at the rest of the students— "It seems an alliance has been formed. Congratulations, Mr. Logan, Ms. Vega, and Ms. Cunning, you are now on this case. The rest of you will remain here with another professor, until I get back. You're dismissed for the day. Hopefully by the time you all see me again, you too will have stepped up your game."

I couldn't help it, I fist pumped into the air.

"So lame," Logan whispered.

"I second that," Vivian added.

"Shut up."

"Logan. Vega. Cunning. Why aren't you walking?" Levi—*Urgh! Professor Black! Professor Black! Professor Black!*—called to us.

Following him, we walked quickly, trying to match his pace. He was walking as though his feet were on fire.

"Logan, Cunning, you both remember the Archibald Case?" he asked, as his car pulled up. "This is nothing like that, and one of you will need a cab."

The moment he said it, I was in motion, and I gingerly stepped into the back seat. Following my lead as fast as she could, Vivian hoped into the front seat.

"You lose," Professor Black said to Atticus, before stepping inside the car and taking his seat next to me.

"Ms. Vega, tell me, how did this alliance come to be?"

Damn it.

I sunk into the chair looking anywhere but his face. It had taken all my courage just to get in the car.

"She blackmailed us," Vivian said simply.

Apparently I was too soft.

16

THEA

By the time we reached the office, Atticus was already there. Levi— Professor Black, *screw it, I was just going to call him Levi or else I was going to go crazy,* was as cold as ever in the car. When Vivian stated that I had blackmailed them, he just looked down at his phone, not saying a word.

"Your coffee, sir," Atticus said, handing him a cup as we all entered the elevator.

"Stop kissing my ass Mr. Logan, or you'll get stuck there," Levi replied, taking the cup from him and drinking. He had to stop himself from spitting it out. "What is this?"

"Coffee?"

"This is not coffee!" he snapped, handing it back to Atticus.

Vivian and I held our breaths, biting our lips to keep from laughing.

"Nice," I whispered to him, as we got off the elevator.

It was the first time we had been up here since the Archibald case, and I was finally able to take it all in. On the wall to my right, written in bold, black, glass letters was Levi's name. Within the building, there was a buzz of activity, as countless associates moved about from one end to another.

At that moment, Tristan came out, dressed sharply in a three-piece suit, and handed him a newspaper.

"Where is she?" he asked.

"Raymond just brought her into the conference room."

They both ignored us as they walked down the hallway, and we wordlessly followed. Once again, it was like we were invisible. Anyone that saw Levi coming, either turned away, or kept their head down and walked past him as fast as they could. But even that wasn't fast enough.

"You, with the coffee stain, go home until you figure out where your mouth is." Levi pointed to a man halfway down the hall.

Jeez.

"Does she look like she did it?" he asked us at the door of the conference room.

I could see the woman; she was Hispanic, with long dark hair, and red-rimmed eyes. She was dressed in all black, and even had a small lace veil stemming from her hat, as if she needed to prove to the world she was mourning her husband.

"No," Atticus answered.

Vivian nodded, "Yes."

And then his green eyes fell on me.

"I'm not sure."

"Get sure then. Same rules as the Archibald case," he said as he opened the door.

"What are the rules?" Vivian whispered, as we entered.

"Sit down, shut up, and don't make him look bad," I said rushing to the corner.

Raymond, his associate, came forward and whispered something into his ear, but Levi didn't even flinch, he just stared at her.

There was silence and she shifted under his gaze... I understood exactly how that felt.

"Are you Mr. Black?" she sniffed rubbing her nose with her tissue.

Silence.

"Umm…" she shifted again.

"He's blacking her out," Atticus muttered beside me.

"What?" I leaned in.

"What he's doing, they call it 'Levi's blackout', because he just zones out for a moment before his big move," Vivian finished for him, whipping off her glasses.

How did I not know that?

"You killed your husband." He came out and said it. "What I want to know is why. You signed a prenuptial agreement, so it's not like you were going to get any of the money."

"I did not kill my husband! I loved—"

"You're lying! You can lie to your children, the press, to yourself if you very well choose, but you will not lie to me in my office."

"You're supposed to be my lawyer!" she screeched at him.

"And I'm trying to defend you. So, why did you kill your husband?"

"I did *not*—"

"You killed your husband."

"No."

"You. Killed. Your. Husband."

"NO!"

"You can scream all you want, but I don't believe a word coming out of your mouth. A cocktail waitress who's been married three times already—marries a nice, rich, old man."

"You just said it wasn't about the money, I signed a pre-nup!"

"Then why did you kill him?"

"I did not kill my husband!"

"Liar."

She stood up. "Fuck you."

He turned to Tristan,. "We can work with this."

What?

"I don't understand," the woman said as she slowly fell back into her chair.

"The prosecution won't come at you like that Mrs. Nash, it's not like what you see on *Law and Order*. We may want to put you on the stand," he told her.

"So you believe me?" she asked hopefully.

"It doesn't matter whether I believe you or not, I just needed to make sure you that you didn't crack under pressure—"

"It matters to me!" she hollered at him, jumping to her feet again. "I can't have a lawyer who doesn't believe in me. If that's the case, I'll have to find someone else."

"And you will go to prison," he said simply. "My fee doubles when you're in prison... *if* I choose to take on this case again."

"Does this look like a joke to you?"

"No, but you're the one clowning around. Your husband is dead, and your stepchildren want your head on stick. You *don't* need a lawyer that believes in you. You need one that can win. So my question to you, Mrs. Nash, is; do you want to win? Do you want to stay out of prison?"

Once again she sat back down. "I didn't kill my husband, and I don't like you. But I would like to stay out of prison."

"Good choice," he told her. "My associates will brief you on what I want you to do, and say, until the trial," he said to her, nodding towards Raymond, before taking his leave.

"I want to be him," Atticus whispered.

The world can't handle two Levi Blacks.

"She's guilty," Vivian whispered, more to herself than to us.

"One of you, go get us some coffee," Raymond pointed at us. "We'll be here for a while."

No one moved, so I took the initiative and headed out, even though I had no idea where I was going. Asking someone seemed like a given, but the look they were all giving me...

"Don't mind them, they're taking a trip down memory lane," Tristan said as he appeared beside me, causing me to jump.

"A trip down memory lane?" I glanced back at a few of the people who had gathered to laugh at something as I walked by.

"Break time already?" he asked them, and they rushed back to where they were supposed to be. "At one time, they were like you, under the thumb of the great Professor, Levi Black."

"Aren't they still?"

"Yeah, but they get paid to put up with him. Coffee is over there."

I paused in the middle of the hall, my arms crossed. "Why are you helping me?"

"Can't I just be nice?" He grinned and his brown eyes seemed to light up.

"No."

"Fine, you know my secret."

I thought for a second before smiling. "You mean your eyeliner-wearing alter ego."

"We were short staffed that night. My wife owns the bar," he glowered at me.

I turned my back to him and began to prepare the coffee.

"Don't worry, I won't say anything."

"Why thank you—"

"But that comes a price," I cut him off before he could finish praising me.

"A price?"

"Help me impress Levi with this case."

His eyebrow raised. "Impress?"

"Every year, he chooses one student right? The top of the top in his class. I helped with one case and got my name on the board. Help me with this one too, so I can stay on the board."

"And here I thought you were swimming with sharks, when in actuality, you're the one circling in for the kill."

Just like my mother.

"I got to get this coffee back. Bye *hon*," I said, using the name he had called me at the bar.

He stood watching me with a slight smile lingering on his lips as I walked away.

LEVI

"Your *student* just blackmailed me," Tristan said as he came into my office and took a seat on the chair in front of my desk.

"Apparently, that's her new thing," I told him.

In seventy-two hours she had managed to become a whole new person. She was bolder, and a lot colder. Was this what Selene had been worried about?

"She got you too?" he asked with a frown.

I snorted. "She wouldn't dare. Plus doing that would look worse on her. She isn't stupid."

"So what's going on between you two?"

Pinching the bridge of my nose, I leaned back on my chair. "I don't know. Why do I even care?"

"You like her."

It wasn't a question, but I still nodded. "I like her. I like her a little too much."

"Are you pursuing her?"

Was I?

"I pursued her, and she rejected me because she wants to be a good lawyer."

"Which makes you like her more."

"Are you getting paid for this time? If so, I really should dock your pay."

I didn't need people reading my thoughts or feelings for me.

"You truly are as black hearted as they say, taking money away from your soon-to-be niece's father. I wonder if she will have a cousin soon though. You and Thea—"

"Get out!"

"Hit a nerve there, didn't I?" he mocked, his tone rising. "Let's hope she doesn't see that mark on your neck... unless she already knows it's there."

I threw a pen at his head. "It's a bug bite."

"*Sure,*" he grinned, moving to the door where I suddenly remembered what he first said.

"What did she blackmail you for?"

He smirked. "She asked me to help her impress you by helping you win this case. Apparently she wants to keep her name on the board. She reminds me of her mother."

That made me cringe.

"They say *The Shark* kept a written record of all the favors ever owed to her, along with a few details she had on some high profile people, just in case she ever needed help from them. She used it to *persuade* them to help her."

I didn't say anything, and he took it as his cue to leave.

I liked her and I wanted to be with her again. I could admit to that. What I couldn't admit was that I wanted to chase after her.

I just wasn't sure how to balance all the sides of me; the professor, the lawyer, the guy under all of that... the guy that just wanted to be in bed with her again.

"We have a problem," Raymond said bursting in.

I was already on my feet walking.

"What type of a problem?"

"The video was just *leaked* about our client."

From the way he sounded, I could tell that he didn't believe this was just a coincidence.

As we entered the conference room, I noticed that everyone's eyes were glued to the screen.

"I hate that *BEEP*. I hate that whole in entire *BEEP* family!" A drunken Mariah Nash slurred into camera on the news. "Do you know how much *BEEP* I have to deal with in that *BEEP* family. And his kids, his *BEEP* kids. They're selfish, money hungry little monsters. How am I supposed to smile for the cameras when one of them is druggie, and the other a sex addict; I mean really, he's done the entire house staff *and* the neighbors too. But at least someone is having sex. That *BEEP* couldn't get it up if he was *BEEP* upside down. I want to take a bat to all their heads!"

Raymond turned off the television, all of their eyes turned to me as if I was supposed to have some type of rationale to this level of absurdity.

"I..." Mrs. Nash opened her mouth, but I held my hand up indicating that I didn't want to hear it, and that she shouldn't even bother.

"All of you, go home, talk to no one, we will start over in the morning," I said to them.

"Mr. Black!" Mrs. Nash called out. "Please—"

I could feel the vein in my head throbbing. "I said; go home, talk to no one, we will start over tomorrow."

Even I was shocked at how calm I was being, but in all honestly what could I do? If I yelled at her, she might go home, get drunk, and then make another video.

Shit, she really could do that, I thought, stopping at my office.

"I'm having Raymond and one other associate babysit her," Tristan said, walking up.

"Good to know you're useful."

"That hurts, man." He held his heart.

Rolling my eyes, I headed to my office couch to lay back down.

"You can go home too Betty, I'm not taking any calls," I called, closing my eyes.

"Are you sure—"

"Goodnight Betty."

I didn't bother opening my eyes.

I simply laid there, not moving. I never took a simple case... never.

I truly am a masochist.

∼

It was midnight by the time I woke up. Washing and drying my face in the bathroom, I noticed only two lights were left on in all of the offices; the conference room, and my office.

Idiots left the lights on.

Cracking my neck as I walked over, I froze when I saw her sitting on the floor of the conference room. Her hair was pulled back into a loose ponytail, and she sat flipping through the case files in front of her. She bobbed her head to whatever music she was listening to on her mp3 player, completely unaware of me, or of how beautiful she looked.

I loved it when she wore skirts. I enjoyed staring at her perfectly smooth, long legs. It made me remember how good it felt when they were wrapped around me.

When she turned to reach for another document, she finally noticed me and jumped.

"Jesus Christ, you scared me. I thought everyone went home!"

"So did I, especially since I was the one who gave the instruction," I replied, entering the room as she stood up.

She moved away from me, as though she were afraid that I would touch her. Her instincts were right because I wanted to. But instead, I took a seat.

"I just wanted to get as familiar with the case as possible," she said softly, as she shifted from one leg to the other.

It was so damn distracting.

"I could have sworn I saw you packing up your stuff when I said to leave."

"I did," she smiled, "I even got on the elevator and rode down with everyone, and then I waited an hour at the coffee shop so that Vivian and Atticus didn't stay as well."

"You wanted to be alone with me that badly?" I joked.

A man could dream right?

"No!" she said, a little too quickly for my liking. "I mean no, I thought that everyone was gone, I had to bribe the janitor to stay. Vivian already knew about this case, and Atticus is a fast learner, I just wanted a leg up, and since we can't take the files out of the office..."

She picked up a few of the files and placed them back into their respective boxes.

"You really want this."

"I thought I already made that clear?" She frowned.

"You did," I nodded. "I just haven't seen this side of you yet. It's interesting."

"We weren't together that long, so you don't really know me."

"If you say so."

She shot daggers at me with her eyes.

"What are you going to do about this case?" she changed the subject.

I shrugged. "I don't know, maybe look for some sort of plea deal. The woman shot herself in the foot."

"You're lying."

"What?"

She sat down across from me folding her hands on the table. "You're lying," she repeated. "You're excited. Sure you're pissed off that she did something so stupid, but you're excited that the stakes are higher now. No one can figure out how you can possibly win at this point, which means that when you do, it will be like *'the great Levi Black has struck again!'* It's one of the ways you get off."

"One of the ways," I said, as I looked her up and down again, and noticed that her top three buttons were undone giving me a slight peek at her teal laced bra.

"It looks like someone is helping you with that too." She pointed to my neck, clearly annoyed.

"It's a bug bite," I told her dryly.

"Okay, I believe that."

"You should, because I've never lied to you," I said, and she froze. I could tell that she was getting ready to run. "Except for what you just pointed out, I *do* get off on winning impossible cases."

She relaxed. "So how are you going to win this one?"

"Jury selection."

"Jury selection," she repeated slowly, relaxing into her chair as she thought about it. "But I can't think of any group that would like her. Women are going to look at her like she's a gold digger. Older men are going to take offense to that video, younger guys will just think it funny. Jury selection won't be easy."

"Nothing will be easy, but everyone has prejudices or pet peeves, sometimes it's even hidden from themselves. A twitch at the mention of drugs, or money, or *something*. If that family is as fucked up as I think they are, all we have to do is show that they are no better than our client."

"We don't have to make her likable," she said with a fire in her eyes. "We have to make the Nash family despicable!" she stood up, clearly excited now.

"Exactly how hard can that really be?" I rose as well. "Pack up and head home, the next few weeks will be brutal."

"I know." She didn't look up at me.

Opening the door, I stopped. Turning back to her I said, "Don't feel bad about using your mother's book."

She dropped the papers in her hands, "What?"

Reaching down, I helped her pick them up. "Your mother's book of favors—"

"How did you know about that?"

"Tristan was an intern for your mother, remember? Besides, that book is like myth in law circles. You shouldn't feel bad for using it. And I know you did, because there is no way that you were able to dig up enough dirt on the two contending top students in one weekend by yourself. Whatever it was, it had to be big enough to get them to stop trying to go after your spot. Private detective?"

"Hacker," she whispered, hanging her head low.

"Like I said, don't be ashamed for using it. If anyone else had what you do, believe me, they would be using it a lot more often."

"That's because they didn't know what type of person she really was—"

"It doesn't matter. Using her name, or things, or living in her house, does not mean that you accept her or that you are becoming her," I whispered, as I cupped her face in my hand, and lifted her head to meet my gaze. "It means that you're strong enough to not let her name get in your way, and to use what you have to your advantage. That's a testament to *your* strength, and it has nothing to do with her."

Letting her go, I wanted to walk away and end things on a high note, but I couldn't. I wasn't done yet.

Holding on to her waist, I pulled her to me and I brought my lips to hers. She didn't even try to push me away. Instead, she leaned into me, her arms wrapping around my neck. Grabbing onto her, I picked her up and placed her onto the table.

Kissing her like this was sinful, the way her legs wrapped around me, and the way her breasts pushed themselves against my chest drove me mad. I never wanted to stop kissing her, but I had to… breathing had never been so annoying.

"We aren't done Thea. *'So I can't. I just can't. I'm sorry.'* " I repeated the very words she said to me that night on the phone. "That isn't enough to push me away. Especially when your body still reacts like this every time I touch it."

To illustrate my point, I slipped my hand between her thighs and softly stroked the length of them. She shivered, and tried to turn her head away from me. But I forced her to look me in the eye. She bit her lower lip, trying to keep from moaning, even as she ground her hips against my hand.

"You don't look like a woman trying to run from me," I said kissing her lips softly as I played with her entrance.

"Ah!" she gasped, grabbing on to my arm.

"And you definitely don't sound like a woman trying to run from me."

I kissed her lips, then her cheek, and finally, I lightly licked the edge of her ear and gently sucked on her earlobe. She shivered against me, as her flesh broke out into goose bumps.

"So I must assume that you aren't really running from me," I told her, "which is good to know, because I wasn't planning on letting you go anyway. Like I said," I broke away from her and took a step back as I licked my fingers clean, "we aren't done. So when you're ready to get serious again, let me know, or else, I'll just keep playing with you."

Walking out, I fought with my inner desire to take her right then and there on that table. But I couldn't, at least not now. I was going to reel her in, nice and slow.

I'm going to need a lot of fucking cold showers.

THEA

*T*wo months. It had been two months since that night in his office, and four months since I had met Levi Black. Four months since my world, and my life, had been turned upside down. In class, he was Professor Black, and after that night in the office, he was especially brutally in the classroom—we were now down to fourteen— but the moment I found myself alone with him—no matter how hard I tried I always ended up alone with him— in elevators, stairwells, cars— he always transformed back into just Levi. Just Levi was sexy, and passionate and... he was driving me insane.

When he said it wasn't over, he'd meant it. If we were left alone in his town car, his hands found their way between my legs. When I wore pants, he smirked at the change and he would blatantly kiss me while his driver turned up the radio. The second his lips would touch mine, my mind would go blank, and before I realized it, the top button of my pants would be undone. What was worse was I was enjoying it. I enjoyed seeing how he would get to me. It excited me in ways I didn't understand. My head kept telling me to stop but I didn't want to.

In elevators, he would push the stop button, and push me up against the wall, kissing me as if it were the last time he was ever going to kiss anyone. I would cling to him wanting more than to just a kiss. He did the same thing whenever we were in stairwells; he'd drive me back into a wall and kiss me fiercely and passionately. He'd even take it as far as trailing kisses down my neck, and gently biting the tops of my breasts, before backing away with a smile. That wasn't enough for me.

I didn't *want* to stop him. It turned me on each and every time, and every time he'd let me go, I'd realize that I wanted him more. But he never took it further than passionate kiss, or light teasing, and somehow that made it far worse than if we were actually having sex. His kisses, his touches, they weren't enough.

When I'd sent Selene back to Maryland, I was proud of myself. I was proud that I had put away my lust and selfishness to do what I'd come here to do. But now, it was like I was going back on the promise I'd made to myself.

I just needed to reject him. I needed to be clear and straightforward. *I needed for him to not touch me.*

"So, this will be the end of the line for two of you," he said, as he stood at the front of the class. "Whoever gets the lowest scores on the winter final, will be out. I would congratulate whoever you are right now for making it this far, but losing is nothing to congratulate anyone on."

He walked around his desk and sat down. Taking out his red pen, he began to grade our exams. After spending three hours taking the damn thing, we were all exhausted and eager to leave, however, we needed to know whether or not we'd made it to the final twelve.

Vivian handed me some popcorn and I shook you my head at her. Atticus however, reached over and grabbed a handful.

"Six shots it's the guy in the bow-tie," Atticus said, and the guy turned back and glared at him.

Atticus shrugged and continued eating his popcorn.

"Ten it's scarf guy," Vivian whispered, "the one with the '80s earring."

"Does anyone know anyone's names?" I looked between them.

"No," they both said.

"Why bother if he just kicks them out anyway? Can you remember any of the faces that have been kicked out of this class so far?" Vivian questioned.

"Once the twelve are set, I'll learn the other nine names." Atticus said, already counting us in.

They were so confident, and yet my hands were shaking.

Vivian looked towards me. "Why are you so stressed?"

"Why aren't you? Am I the only one that thought the test was hard?"

They looked at each other for a moment before they both got up and sat at the end of the row… away from me.

Assholes.

"Funny," I said but they pretended that they couldn't see me. "Fine, I hope you both fail."

"Do you hear something Vivian?"

"I'm not sure, but it sounds like the soft, snowy cries of doubt, Atticus."

The soft, snowy cries of doubt?

"That doesn't even make sense," I snapped at them.

"Shh!" Bow-tie guy turned to us.

"Seriously, have you been here all semester?" I asked him, causing Vivian and Atticus to erupt into a fit of laughter.

They stopped the moment Levi looked up though. His green eyes scanned the classroom and everyone stopped breathing. Then, he looked back down, and continued grading.

The bastard was doing it on purpose!

Even so, I enjoyed watching him. His dark hair was slightly

mussed, mostly from the good luck make out session we'd had on the stairwell right before we got to class.

I'm supposed to be rejecting him. But instead, here I was, daydreaming about how good it felt to be pinned against him, and how sexy he was with his glasses on. It was like I was under his control.

Once again when he looked up, we all froze. He got up, grabbed the eraser and began to erase my information.

"Oh shit," Atticus said, sounding as though he were on the other end of the earth, or at least that was what it sounded like because of the way my heart was pounding against my chest and temples.

I watched in horror as he slowly erased my family, undergraduate degree, race, and finally my age, before stopping right under my name. Dropping the eraser, he grabbed the chalk and began writing the names of the other students in the class.

"Son of a bitch," I gasped, easing back into the chair.

"And just when we thought we had finally gotten rid of you," Atticus sighed, taking the seat to my right.

"She's like Arnold Schwarzenegger, she keeps coming back, even when you don't want her to," Vivian added, taking a seat to my left.

"Thanks guys," I said with sarcasm.

"Come on bow-tie guy." Atticus pumped his fist waiting to see if the guy would get up and leave as Levi wrote only twelve names on the board.

Sure enough, bow tie did his walk of shame.

"Yes!" he cheered, and the pour guy looked like he wanted to strangle him. "Maybe next year?"

"Scarf guy is… gone." Vivian high-fived him and turned to me.

Rolling my eyes, I high-fived her.

"You're both horrible people."

"Sure, and how did we become your allies again? Good thing we're friends now," Atticus countered.

But in all honesty, I wasn't sure if they were my friends. They were people I spent a lot of time with, but I wasn't sure if that made us *friends*.

"Ladies and gentlemen, congratulations. You are now a part of 'the twelve disciples'," he said.

Why I do I feel like the pope is sneezing or something?

"From now on, we'll no longer be holding sessions in this room. Instead, all of my classes will be held at my office. You will be learning first-hand what it means to be a criminal lawyer."

He began to gather up his things, and the moment we—Atticus, Vivian and I— noticed, we were on our feet.

"Neither I, nor my associates, have the time to catch you up to speed. And as you know, I am currently working on the Nash Case with three of your classmates. Luckily, they've managed to keep their seats, because it would have been rather awkward for you all otherwise—Why aren't you walking?" he barked.

As we all turned to see what who he was talking to, we saw that all other nine students were still in their seats. Atticus' eyes widened and he jerked his head in a 'come along, hurry up' gesture. The nine students all rose and rushed out of the classroom to follow us.

"Things will be happening quickly," he continued. "If you can't show up, don't come back. If you think you will be celebrating Christmas with your family, look to your left and then your right; shake hands with who you see, because that's who your new family is. You will do what you're asked, when you're asked, and go where you are needed. Every day is Judgment Day. Being part of the twelve is not a free ride. Your real work starts now."

He waited for no one and was already in his town car.

"If you aren't at the office before he is, he *will* smite you," I said to them, as Vivian hailed a taxi for us three.

"See you there," Atticus said as we took a seat inside.

I turned to see them rushing for taxis of their own, but it was rush hour, and it was virtually impossible to hail one down. Which is why we not only spilt one, but we had him on speed dial.

"I kind of understand why his associates treat us like crap now. It's kind of fun when you're the one dishing it out," Vivian said.

And she was right. It *was* kind of fun, but we all knew it was only going to last the duration of our cab ride.

The Nash case was set for the week before Christmas, then there would be a short break before Levi would be back in court.

Where had the year gone?

LEVI

"A juror was tweeting during selection? Are you fucking kidding me? Which one?"

"Juror number four," Tristan answered.

"Damn it."

Good God, this case was driving me insane.

"Who's replacing juror number four?"

They just looked around at each other before dashing for their notes. How the hell could I win a case with these idiots?!

"Who's replacing juror number four?" I yelled.

"Deborah Padovano," Thea said, as she walked in holding two trays of coffee.

"You, get up and take the coffee," I pointed at one of my associates, and then to her, "You, sit down and talk, since no one else here seems to know a goddamn thing."

They switched, and she rushed to the seat, grabbing one file from the stack in front us, and handed it to me.

"Deborah Padovano, age 72, her husband died six years ago of a heart attack and she never remarried, nor has any kids," she recited off the top of her head.

"Where does she work?"

"She owns a small bakery and I think she might be good for us — you— this case," she corrected herself.

"Why?" Tristan asked her, leaning forward.

"Her husband lost their entire life savings on a scam, forcing them to go back to work. He had a heart attack six months later, and she now owns her own bakery with the money she gained from his life insurance. I'm not saying she killed the man, nor am I saying that she was sad to see him go. There are thousands of women all across the country that hate their husbands. All we need is one, right?"

"Stay seated," I said to her. "Everyone else, I want to know every horrible thing that Mr. Nash has ever done in his life, and I want it before the end of the day."

"You, come with me," I called to her.

She hesitated for a moment, then followed me out of the conference room.

"What do you need, Mr. Black?"

She walked with space between us as we headed to my office.

Betty gave me a look, the wrinkles under her eyes standing out more as I held the door open for Thea.

"Hold my calls for an hour."

"Yes sir," she said, with a hint of attitude.

"Is something wrong, Betty?"

"No sir," she replied, as she pretended to type away on her computer.

"Are you sure?" I pushed.

She sighed, pushing herself away from her desk and rising. She turned to face me. "Now that you've mentioned it, how long have I been working for you?"

"Eight years, give or take."

"I understand that you're busy being the Great Levi Black and all, but you would think for my years of dedication at the very least you could—"

Walking over to her desk, I pulled open the bottom drawer, reached all the way into the back of it and placed the pretty blue box on her desk.

I grinned, "Go on?"

"You're a horrible young man," she laughed as she lifted the lid and examined the contents of the box.

Her eyes lit up and a smile broke out across her face as she removed the tickets to her favorite performance of *Swan Lake*.

"You also have a dinner for two at Chateau La Rue, for anytime you want."

"Levi—" she replied.

"Happy Birthday Betty."

"Thank you."

Nodding, I turned back to the other woman in my life. She stood at the window that overlooked all of Boston.

"Enjoying the view?"

"You just had to go and do something sweet," she whispered, even though I saw the corners of her mouth turn up. I stepped behind her. "What do you need, Mr. Black?"

"You," I casually replied, "but since that isn't on the table right now, I'll have to settle with this." I handed her the case file.

She stepped away from me, and I reached for my guitar before taking a seat in my chair.

"I don't understand."

"Tell me how you would lead this case," I replied, strumming the strings on the neck of my guitar.

"You're kidding?"

"Figuratively of course. I like you, but I'm not willing to leave a woman's future in your hands just yet. You kept your name on the board, which means you're still the head of the pack. The deal is, if you do that, I'll personally train you, and this is a training exercise. Now how would you run the case?"

"I would need to read—"

"You've been looking over the case for the last two months. If you still need to read anything, then you're dreaming if you think you can be a lawyer."

She glared, throwing the file onto my desk and crossed her arms.

"I wouldn't waste a jury's time trying to make Mrs. Nash look good, because it would be an insult to their intelligence. I would come right out and say it; Mrs. Nash hated her husband. Right off the bat, they might hate Mrs. Nash, but they will trust me because I'm the only one *not* blowing hot air."

"Okay, what next?" I kicked my feet up, tightening the strings before I began playing again.

"Next, I would make it clear that Mrs. Nash was not the only person that hated him. When his daughter takes the stand, I would ask her how it felt to be cut off from the family fortune—"

"Guilty."

"What?"

"I said 'guilty' because if that's how you're going to present this case, that's what the jury will decide."

"You said in class that the best way to get one suspect to walk is by giving the jury another suspect capable of the crime."

"That's true."

"Then how come my verdict is 'guilty'?"

"Because you're throwing softballs," I sighed, closing my eyes to listen to the music. "Your thought process is right, but your approach is weak. Mr. Nash's daughter was cut off. Why? Go for the jugular."

"Isn't that badgering the witness?"

"Not if you do it right. You might hurt her feelings, others will think you're a bitch, but who gives a damn? At the end of the day it's the win that counts. So don't hold back. Lead her into the questions. Let her hang herself. Approach me as if I were her on the stand."

She nodded, and I placed the guitar down, and straightened my posture as I awaited her questions.

"Ms. Nash, was it true that you left your family home a year ago?"

"Yes, I wanted to see the world."

"It wasn't because your father was furious about your drug abuse?"

"No—"

"No, that he was furious? Or no that you don't have a drug addiction?"

I wanted to grin. She was getting it.

"Yes, I had a drug problem, but I was getting better. My dad was helping me over my sickness."

"If someone was helping you, why would you leave?"

Good question.

"I—"

"And if your father was helping you, why would you need to steal over two hundred thousand dollars' worth of jewelry?"

"I never—"

"I will remind you that you are under oath, Ms. Nash, and that lying on the stand is a criminal offense. Did you know that your father called the police to report that the jewelry had been stolen, however he dropped charges when he realized that it was you?"

I stopped for a moment, in awe of her, and slightly turned on, before remembering something much more important at the moment.

"Wait, do we have proof of that?" I asked, breaking character.

"Not necessarily."

"What does that mean?"

"Mr. Nash kept an inventory of all their jewelry. When I was looking through it, I saw that almost two hundred thousand dollars' worth of it went missing the same time his daughter did. So I called the police department, stating that I was one of Mrs. Nash's lawyers, and I asked if there was a report filed for the missing jewelry. They said that an initial call had been placed, but a couple hours later, Mr. Nash called them back and informed them that he had found it. However, according to his records, there was no further indication that it was ever found."

"And you're saying this now?" it didn't solve the case, but it did make our case stronger.

"There was no paper trail—"

"It doesn't matter. If we can use it to rattle the defense and the witness, it might as well be written in stone."

"Oh."

It was things like this that reminded me that she was still a student, and she had a lot to learn. But once she graduated, she was going to be a force to be reckoned with.

"Okay, start over again." I said, listening to her explain how she would take down the witness.

I could watch her like this forever.

THEA

"You shouldn't be calling me," I said, as I placed a bowl of water down for Shadow.

She got one lick in, before jumping at the thunder outside.

"What if it's work related?" he asked.

His voice over the phone gave me shivers. I'm not sure what it was, but having him speak directly into my ear was... sexy.

"Is it work related?" I asked him, already suspecting that it wasn't.

"It depends on your definition of work."

I wanted to laugh. "Levi, you have to be in court again in the morning."

"Come over."

"Yeah, that's not happening," I said, sitting on my couch.

"Then I'll come over to your place."

"Don't you dare," I warned him.

He sighed, "You're making this so much more complicated than it needs to be."

"That's my line!"

"Ouch. That was my ear."

Crap.

"Sorry, you just bug me sometimes."

"Only sometimes?"

So annoying.

He went silent for a moment and so did I.

"You're going to kill it tomorrow," I whispered.

"I know."

"Why must you be so cocky?"

"I'm from Boston," he replied. "It's part of our swag."

I couldn't help but laugh. "Oh my god you are—"

"I'm what?"

I sighed, as I grabbed my pillow and hugged it to my chest. "You really don't know when to give up."

"Why in the hell would I give up? I'm enjoying it, and so are you."

"I am not."

"Liar."

I could feel his smirk over the phone.

"Come over. We can have dinner, watch a movie, and talk like grown-ups."

I pinched my cheeks to keep from smiling.

"Like grown-ups?"

"Whenever we're alone, I only have a few minutes, sometimes seconds. We never really have the chance to just talk, so instead, I end up jumping you like some horny teenager. As fun as that is, I still would love to get to know you more."

"If there's anyone who knows me outside of my family, it's you Levi. You need to stop digging, because you're only going to find more things you hate about me than you like."

Shit. It just spilled out of my mouth.

"I have to go," I said, panicked that I had said too much.

Hanging up, I threw the phone to the other end of the couch, before placing my pillow over my face.

What's wrong with me?

I could hear the phone ringing, but I couldn't bring myself to answer it. Rolling onto my side, I watched the rain beat against the windows. I could feel my phone at my feet and I wanted to call him. Everything felt better when I was talking to him. I was just a chicken. Why couldn't I be... more woman-like?

When my phone vibrated again I snatched it quickly.

"Hello?"

"Jeez, what's the point of having a phone if you never answer it?" Selene hollered into my ear.

Pulling the phone away I understood what Levi meant. *Ouch.*

"Sorry, I thought you were someone else. Is everything okay? Is Grams ok—"

"Everyone's fine. I just missed you. And I was wondering, can you come home for Christmas?"

"Selene I would—"

"It's okay if you can't. Seriously though, I just met someone—"

"Wait, what?" I squealed.

I jumped up suddenly, scaring Shadow off the chair.

"Selene? My baby sister? She met someone?"

"Hey, don't make me sound like I'm emotionally stunted or something!" she chided.

"No. No." I slowly sat back down. "I'm surprised, good surprised, and happy for you... as long as you're okay."

"I'm fine," she said. "He's good guy, Grams likes him. But she told him he has to get the stamp of approval from you, so that's why I was calling. He's been asking to meet you for weeks now."

She'd left two months ago.

"Weeks? So long have you been seeing him?"

And why was I just hearing about it now?

"We started talking before I left for Boston, but then we lost contact when I got there. And when I came back, we kind of hit it off when again."

Again? Why was I just hearing about it now?

"What's his name?"

"No way I'm telling you that! You're gonna go Facebook stalk him or something, and I want you to meet him in person, *before* you judge him."

"I won't judge him," I said, and even I didn't sound convinced by that. "Much," I added to avoid completely lying to my sister.

"Is that her?" I heard a deep voice ask in the background.

"Selene, it's eleven o'clock."

"Grams is here, and he's leaving."

"Wait, can I at least talk to her?" the guy asked.

"We'll see you whenever you're free and can come down to visit. Good luck with everything. Love you. Bye."

She didn't even let me get a word in before she hung up. Looking through my phone I noticed that all my missed calls were from her. Levi had never even called me back after I hung up on him.

Why did that bug me? Why am I like this!

Getting up, I grabbed my rain boots and my jacket as I headed out.

"Pray for me Shadow."

LEVI

"I'm coming!" I hollered, as I dried my hair off with my towel. Opening the door, I found that my late night caller was the very last person I expected to see.

"Thea?"

I moved aside, letting her in. She took her boots off at the door, before stepping further inside.

"And of course, you're not wearing a shirt," she sighed, heading into my kitchen.

"Be happy I have clothes on at all."

She took two glasses out from the top of the cabinet, and grabbed a bottle of wine from the chiller. Pulling a few drawers open, she searched for what I could only assume was the bottle opener.

"You moved it," she frowned, turning to me.

"Yes, in the four months since you been here, I've moved my bottle opener," I said as I reached into one of the cabinets to get it for her.

"You sound annoyed."

"You hung up on me, remember?"

"You never called back," she said, pouring the wine into her glass.

Sighing, I tried not to get pissed off with her. "I don't want to play these games with you Thea. You can't keep protecting your heart by acting like you don't have one. Why. Are. You. Here?"

"My little sister has a boyfriend," she smiled but it didn't reach her eyes. "I was rolling around on my couch with my pillow to my chest, like a little kid, beating myself up over how much I enjoyed talking to you. Meanwhile, my younger sister is in a stable and mature relationship. Her boyfriend wants to meet me, but I have no idea why, because I am not the mature one in that relationship, either.

"I like you, but I'm a mess Levi. I really am. Some days, I don't even know how I get out of bed. You should walk away because I will likely fuck your life up. Trust me, it's what I do, and I don't want to do it to you."

She finished off the rest of her wine.

"I don't answer to you," I said to her. "You can't make choices for me. If I want to be with you, then I'll try to be with you. The only other person who has control over this is you. So are you in or out?"

She shook her head and reached for the wine bottle when I

stopped her. If we were going to have this conversation, we were going to have it sober.

"Look at me." Of course she didn't. "Thea."

She sighed, looking up, and I cupped her cheek.

"You are not a black rainbow. I see every one of your colors. You may have been one once, but you sure as hell aren't one now."

She gaped at me in shock. "How did you—"

"The day after you rejected me— the first time— your sister called me up and asked to meet with me. She was worried about you being here alone, and I think she just wanted to see me in person."

She sighed, leaning on my counter. "She really is the mature one."

"I think she takes after you."

They had been each other's support systems growing up, and so they always tried their best to remain strong for each other.

"Are you staying the night?" I asked her.

She swallowed, gripping on to her glass.

"We're on winter break right now, and at the moment, I'm not your professor. So, are you staying the night?"

"I am. And I'm going to act like a grown-up."

I smiled, pulling out my cell phone. "Then we're going to need dinner."

THEA

I sat on his lap on the living room floor, changed out of my wet clothes and into one of his cotton shirts. We were both eating Chinese and listening to the thunderstorm outside. After being apart for so long, I was expecting it to be awkward, but it was as if we had picked up right where we had left off.

He stroked my thigh with one hand, while flipping through the emails on his phone with the other.

"A penny for your thoughts?" he asked as he caught me staring.

"Only a penny? What type of girl do you think I am?"

He snickered, kissing my shoulder. "Don't overthink it."

"I'm not."

He gave me a look.

"Okay, I am," I admitted. "But I can't help it. It's like nothing's happened and we're back to week one again."

"I don't mind week one."

"Neither do I, but you know so much about me, and I feel like I know nothing about you."

"Ask me something then."

I thought for a moment.

"Why did you become a lawyer?"

I tried in vain to pick up my rice with my chopsticks as I awaited his answer. After about three tries, I gave up, and took the spoon out of the bag on his coffee table.

He grinned at me, using his with ease to pick up a dumpling.

"No one likes a show off," I told him with a grin.

"I'll teach you." He reached for my spoon, but I backed away.

"You're avoiding the question, Mr. Black."

"I hate that question because I never have an answer for it. I don't know why I became a lawyer. My father was one, and I was good at it, so I just stuck with it." He shrugged.

"That's weird, I was expecting something a little more… inspiring," I said, once again not using a filter.

"It's fine."

"Surely you wouldn't have stuck with it for so long if you didn't like it?"

"Oh no, I love it *now*. But back then, I had no idea what I wanted to do with my life. I kind of just followed the path that had been laid out for me. Luckily, it all worked out and I found my calling.

"Court is like a giant chess game to me. Skill and strategy, confined by a set of laws. It's one of the reasons why I could never be a district attorney, they're shackled to the law. On the outside, there are loopholes and tricks. The harder the case, the better the game."

He grew more and more animated the longer he talked about it. His entire face lit up, and he seemed... really happy.

"And helping people is nice too," he added quickly, and I laughed.

"No judgment."

"No judgment," he whispered again. His eyes went to my lips for a split second before he looked away. "Next question, Ms. Cunning."

"What are your parents like?"

He already knew all about mine... if you could call those people parents. I hated one, and I hadn't seen the other in years.

"Thea?"

"Sorry, I was just thinking. What did you say?"

"I didn't say anything, you just looked like you were getting carried away by whatever thoughts were in your head."

How did he know me so well?

"Your parents?" I asked him again.

"My mother was a ballerina, until she got hurt during her last run of Swan Lake. She now has her own studio, and teaches girls from six and up. And like I said, my father was a lawyer until he retired. They're both Boston socialites now, and they're still madly in love too. On New Year's day, my dad always moves all the furniture around the house and allows my mom to basically put on her own show for him," he said with a laugh, shaking his head at the thought of them.

"They sound great."

"They are. My mom's a little pushy, but now that my sister's had her baby, she's distracted with being a grandmother."

"Your sister, Bethan?" I asked, hoping that I had gotten her name right. "Tristan's wife?"

"Yeah, she had a little girl last month."

"You all are like the *All American family.* It's cute," I said, with a dreamy smile.

I could even picture them on their holiday time Hallmark cards. Shifting in his lap, I noticed the clock.

"Levi! It's two a.m., you need to rest, you have court in a few hours!"

"Okay," he said as he lifted me up into his arms, and began walking towards the stairs.

"What are you doing?"

"The only way I'm going to rest is if you're in my arms tonight," he said.

He was able to turn off the lights before taking me up.

"The food..."

"We'll deal with it in the morning," he said as he dropped me on the center of his bed.

"No sex. If you're off your game tomorrow, I won't forgive myself."

He sighed, and I could tell he was tired.

Sitting up, I ran my hands over his jaw. "I'm not going anywhere, and think of it this way; you get a prize after kicking ass tomorrow."

He turned and kissed my palm. "If I can't have you tonight, at least take off your shirt so I can feel you against me."

With the look in his eyes, how could I say no?

Pulling off the shirt, I turned so he could unclasp my bra. When he did, his hands travelled down my spine as he kissed parts of back.

"Levi," I gasped, when he grabbed my breast.

"I've missed you," he said, as he kissed my spine one last time.

Getting up, he went into the bathroom, and a few seconds later I heard the shower turn on.

"Oh God," I moaned, letting out the breath I was holding back into his pillows. Turning on my side, I breathed in the scent of them. It smelt like him.

What the—?

On his bedside table, there was a copy of *The Great Gatsby*. Sitting up, I reached for it. He had underlined my favorite quote, as if he already knew what it was.

Hearing the shower turn off, I put book back down, crawled under the sheets, and pretended to be asleep. I could hearing him walking around the room for a moment, before I heard the click of the light switch and felt the mattress shift. His arms wrapped around me, pulling me closer to him. He was naked, and he was cold, but I didn't say anything. I simply pressed my body against him, allowing my breasts and hands to rest against his bare chest, as my legs entwined with his.

I had never felt more comfortable in all my life.

In the back of my mind, I kept thinking of that Gatsby quote; "You see, I usually find myself among strangers because I drift here and there trying to forget the sad things that happened to me."

But I wasn't drifting anymore. Because of Levi, I had found a place to rest.

"I've missed you too," I whispered into the darkness.

THEA

Thea,
I know you wanted me to wake you up, but you looked so peaceful that I just I couldn't. You're technically on break, enjoy it. I'll be back soon to collect my prize. Until then, my place is your place. Breakfast is in the microwave.
Yours,
Levi.

Crawling out of bed, I was disappointed that I couldn't be in court with him right now, especially after I had worked so hard on this case. But between all of his associates, and the media, there was simply not enough room inside that courtroom to fit all of us. We were students, so of course they had left us out of it.

Grabbing my shirt up off the ground, I put it on and headed downstairs.

"Levi," I groaned, noticing that he had cleaned up the mess *and* made breakfast before going to court.

On the microwave he left another note:

Slightly burned French toast with bacon and no coffee. Still weird, but whatever.

Levi.

He had remembered everything, but then again, I knew how he liked his breakfast too. Hearing my phone ring, I grabbed the glass of orange juice he'd left for me, before heading into the living room.

Reaching under the couch, I grabbed my phone.

"Hello?"

"Are you watching?" Vivian asked me.

"Give me a second." I searched for the remote.

"How are you not watching this already?" Atticus snapped.

I hadn't realized they were both on the phone.

"I overslept."

"You overslept? I'm not buying that—"

"Shh!" Vivian hushed us. "We should so be there, it isn't fair."

"How much work did you even do?" Atticus questioned.

"Well, with Thea coming in like a knight on a white horse all the time, who can do anything?"

"Damn, you somehow tricked us into being your backup singers, Thea."

"I didn't trick anyone. Now, if you'll excuse me, I'm going to watch Professor Black kick ass while I eat my breakfast," I said as I hung up.

As much as I enjoyed their antics, I just didn't have the energy this morning.

When I saw Mr. Nash's daughter take the stand, I jumped onto the couch and turned up the volume.

"*Ms. Nash, is it true that you left your family home a year ago?*"

You son of a bitch, I grinned wildly. He was using my approach.

"*Yes,*" she answered into the microphone.

"*Why?*"

"*I had a drug problem, and I decided to go to rehab.*"

"No you didn't!" I yelled at the television.

"And how did your father feel it about that?"

"Like any father would, he was angry and disappointed. He cut me off."

"So then how did you pay for rehab?"

"I stole some of their jewelry. But I called him later about it, and told I him what it was for."

Damn it, the prosecution was making her go with some version of the truth. Mr. Nash's daughter was the only person we could serve up as with a solid enough motive to want her father dead.

"And you were you there for the whole year?"

"Yes."

"Where was the rehab you attended located?"

"West Seneca."

"And you—"

"Objection your honor; is Ms. Nash on trial here?" the prosecutor asked as he stood up to face the judge.

Levi turned to him and raised his eyebrow. Strangely enough, he looked pleased.

"Your honor, I just want know whether or not Ms. Nash is in the right frame of mind to be on the stand, after years of substance abuse."

"I'll allow it."

"Thank you, your honor. I'm sorry, where did you say your rehab was located Ms. Nash?"

"Seneca Falls."

Wait.

"Seneca Falls or West Seneca Ms. Nash? Those are two different places, about two hours apart."

"I mean West Seneca—"

"But the rehabilitation centers in West Seneca are charity owned and run. Where did you spend the two hundred thousand? Are you sure it wasn't in Seneca Falls?"

"Yes, I meant Seneca Falls, I'm sorry."

"Ms. Nash, you do know that lying on the stand is a criminal offence right?"

He had her.

"Yes."

"Ms. Nash, you couldn't have been in West Seneca, and you couldn't have been in Seneca Falls, because their program only runs for 160 days. So where were you?"

"I—"

"Did you actually go to rehab?"

She faltered, then went red. "I plead the fifth."

Levi went on as though she had actually answered, "So, if you weren't in rehab, then where did the money go?"

"I plead the fifth."

"If you didn't go to rehab, then you didn't get clean. So when you came home to find out your father was going to cut you out of the will as your step mother had asked him to do, were you not upset?"

"Yes," she said with tears in her eyes. "But he never thought about it, until she put it in his head."

"Three weeks later, you found out that your father had been murdered, isn't that right?"

She opened her mouth and then shut again.

"I have no further questions for this witness."

"YES!" I jumped up and down on his couch. When I heard my phone ring I answer it immediately. "Bomb goes the dynamite! Did you see that? Genius! Pure genius!"

"THEA!"

I stopped finally looking at the ID of the caller on the phone's screen. "Selene? Sorry, I thought you were someone else."

"I figured. I'm sorry to bother you, I can call you back later—"

"No, no. It's okay, I'm good, I just got a little worked up over a case."

"Grams, said that another one of Dad's appeals failed today. So I thought I'd write my first letter to him today, and I wanted you to read it. I know you've been writing to him since you found out, and I didn't want him to think that I didn't care or that we aren't paying attention to what's happening to him."

And just like that, my excitement was gone, and I crumbled back onto the couch. I didn't even know one of his appeals failed today. Usually the "lawyer," if I could call him that, spoke to me.

"He won't write back," I said to her. "I know he gets them, he just never writes back. Don't read anything about him on the internet, okay? If you have questions, call me."

There was nothing but hate on the internet when it came to him. Once you dove in, it became a black hole that shredded you on the way out.

"I know. I just want him to have something of mine. Can you read it over for me?"

I didn't want to.

"Sure."

LEVI

I wasn't sure what I was expecting to find when I got back to my place. Half of me figured she would have run home, and the other half of me hoped that she was still in my bed, curled up and naked. However, it was neither of those things.

My living room had been converted into a small office, with files and photos all over the coffee table. She sat with her cat in her lap, and headphones on, flipping through pages upon pages, and highlighting large blocks of text. It reminded me of the night I walked into the conference room to find her still working.

Dropping my things onto the couch, I came up behind her, kissing her neck before taking off her headphones. "I thought I told you to relax. I honestly don't need that much help with the case anymore."

"It's not your case, it's mine," she whispered, looking back up at me. "Well really, it's my dad's case."

I looked around the room at all the boxes stacked around her.

"Did you collect all of this?"

"There wasn't that much to his trial, so I basically started from the bare bones. If I see anything, I send it over to his lawyer, but that's only happened twice. It was useless. I'm sorry about the mess. I promise I'll get it cleaned up before I leave. I just couldn't be at my house right now."

Jesus.

Sitting down next to her, I pulled off my tie. "It's fine, really. I have space, but I'm just confused, why are you looking at this now?"

"My sister called me today, to tell me his appeal fell through again, and that she'd written him a letter," she said, as she handed me her phone to read the hand written note her sister had scanned and emailed to her.

Dear Father, Mr. Walton, Ben, Dad,
I'm just going to skip the introduction. I've written it so many times that I'm almost out of paper. I don't know if you remember me, I'm Selene, your other daughter. I wish I remembered you, because from what Thea can recall, you were pretty cool. She's becoming a lawyer to get you out herself, and believe me, if there is anyone in the world that can do it, it's Thea. She's like a mule; once she puts her foot down, she isn't moving until the jobs done. Believe me, I know this because she's basically raised me all my life. So what I'm trying to say is, we got your back, and I hope that you're doing okay... as okay as you can be at least, given the circumstances. I can't really do anything but cheer Thea on right now, but just know that we haven't forgotten about you, so just keep holding on for us.
See you soon,
Selene.

Putting the phone down on the table, she rested her head into my lap without saying a word. I wasn't sure *what* more there was to say.

"I'm working as fast as I can—"

"You'll kill yourself with this, Thea." I paused, trying to think about the best way to phrase my next question. "Why haven't you asked me? You said you hated the lawyer that's working on it now, so why didn't you come to me?"

"I did, months ago. When I called about it, the person I spoke to, I think it was Raymond, said that you don't handle death row convictions. I called dozens of lawyers and they all said the same thing. When I met you in the bar I had no idea who you were, but during our week together you told me your name and I put two and two together but it didn't matter anymore. I had decided to handle it myself. I would never have thought you were going to be my professor." she confessed keeping her eyes closed.

I hadn't known. All the cases were brought to me by Tristan or Raymond, and from there, we screened the ones that were either the highest profile, or that we were passionate about.

"I also didn't want to drop this on your shoulders. If I did and you didn't believe him, or if we lost, I was scared about what would happen between us. I'm selfish like that. I can't see anything new here, and neither can his lawyer. I would be setting you up to fail. I feel like I need to undo this myself and… I don't know."

"Alright," I said, taking her hand and kissing the back of it, "when you need me, just call on me and I'll be there. But for right now, I have your back."

She sat up, bringing her face close to mine. "You never say, or do, anything that I think you're going to do."

"That's a two way street," I said touching her face. "I want to go out with you."

"Aren't we doing that?"

"No, we aren't. Going out means going to the movies, dinner, games. We can go outside the city if you'd like."

Her eyes went back and forth, as if she were scanning my face for some sign of something.

"Hmmm... outside of the city, that sounds really nice," she said as she tilted her head at me. "And you must already know, but you were amazing today."

She leaned in and kissed me.

"Does that mean I get my prize now?"

She nodded, and stood up. Taking my hand, she pulled me up off the ground, and I let her drag me upstairs, towards the bedroom, where she pushed me onto the bed. She stripped down right in front of me with ease, and when she was naked, she crawled on top of me and began unbuckling my belt. She slid down between my legs, staring directly at me as her fingers found their purchase, and began their magical work. She licked her lips, and bit her bottom lip, and I twitched in her hand.

"Thea..." I couldn't look away from her.

"Yes?" she asked politely, as she stroking me with both hands.

Fuck.

Placing my hands behind me, I tried to hold myself up.

"You're so hard, Mr. Black," she whispered as she stretched upwards to kiss my neck. "Tell me what you'd like me to do."

"Uh...What?" I asked, as my brain was no longer communicating with me.

"Tell me what you want me to do, Mr. Black," she repeated once more with a grin.

She ran her thumb over my head, applying just the right pressure to make any man go insane with pleasure.

I couldn't speak. It had been too long since we'd been like this, and I had almost forgotten what it felt like.

"I'm sorry, I can't wait any longer," I told her, as I grabbed onto her waist and flipped her over. Screw foreplay, I needed her now.

She reached under the pillow, and pulled out a condom. "Then don't."

Fuck me.

Pulling off my clothes as quickly as humanly possible, I heard her giggle and it only made want her more.

"Someone's eager."

"You have no idea," I said as I kissed her.

She had been the cause of one too many cold showers, and she was going to pay.

She clung onto me as I slowly entered her.

"Ah...gah," she moaned, as her nails dug into my back. "More."

Ignoring her, I took my time to enjoy the feel of her. I savored the way she clenched on to me, the feel of her breasts as they rubbed against me, the way she shook with need, and the sweet taste of her full lips. I loved every moment of it.

Reaching up, she held on to my jaw, forcing me to look at her. "Stop being selfish and fuck me."

"You're my prize, remember?" I asked, as I gently bit down on the tip of her thumb, before letting her hands go.

Pushing against me with all of her strength, she forced us to roll over until she sat on top of me.

"If you don't take your prize, someone else will steal it," she said, as she lifted herself up the length of me, before sliding back down. She did it slowly, teasing me and it was a pleasure that was almost too intense to bear.

"Jesus Christ," I hissed, holding on to her as she rode me. I couldn't help it, each time she came down, I'd thrust my hips upwards, driving myself into her with full force, trying to match her pace.

Wrapping my arms around her, I hugged her to me and held onto her tightly… months of teasing, and frustration. We let go of it all, grunting and gripping onto each other like our lives depended on it.

"Levi!" she cried out, as she threw her head back and arched her back.

Her fingers dug into my skin and she clenched her eyes shut. I could feel her spasm around the length of me, and as she reached her peak. The sweat from my hair stung as they dripped into my eyes and turning her back again, I lifted one of her legs onto my shoulder, enabling me to go deeper than I ever thought possible. Biting on to my own lips.

"Oh... my... God," her voice shook.

"God has nothing to do with this," I told her, as I grabbed her breasts, and trapped her nipples between my fingers. I applied enough pressure to make her moan and squirm under me, then, I leaned forward and took one of her nipples into my mouth as I flicked its raised head back and forth with my tongue.

"Levi... sooo... good," she groaned.

I can't hold back.

Kissing the skin of her neck, I grunted inaudibly, holding her firmly against me as I came.

She held me in her arms as we both gasped and panted.

"Why did I say 'no' to you again?" she asked.

"You had a brief moment of insanity, but I forgive you," I whispered back, as I planted kisses along her breasts.

I rolled off of her and lay at her side.

"If everyone had sex like that, the world would be a much better place," she sighed happily, and I laughed.

"I couldn't agree more. We should pray for them or something."

She laughed, curling up against me, and I couldn't imagine any other place for her to be than in my arms.

I was in deep, and I was never getting out.

∼

HALF ASLEEP, I reached out for her. But there was nothing there. Opening my eyes, I touched her side of the bed, as if doing so would make her magically appear, but she was gone. The spot where she lay was still warm though. I rolled over to look at my clock.

2:23 a.m.

Sitting up, I grabbed my boxers, wincing at the pain in my shoulder. Moving to the mirror, I noticed the black and blue bruises, and the red scratch marks that her nails had made.

"Holy shit," I whispered, turning around so that I could see the full extent of the damage. *I didn't even remember her scratching at me so much...* Regardless, I wore it like a badge of honor as I walked down the stairs.

Sure enough, there she was, packing up all of her work, dressed in nothing but a shirt, *my shirt*. I smiled.

"Baby, come back to bed."

She jumped, startled to find me standing there, or maybe her shock was because of the name I'd called her. *Baby.* It sounded so natural, so easy, so...right.

"Give me a second," she said, and continued to pack away the files. "If I leave these out, you're going to wake up before me and clean up everything again. Tomorrow is the closing arguments—"

Picking her up, I threw her over my shoulder.

"Levi!"

"I can't sleep, and I have a big day in court tomorrow. I need you in bed," I said with finality, as I carried her back to my room. Placing her on the bed, I slid out of my boxers and crawled in beside her.

"I heard a lot of 'I's' in that sentence," she whispered, as she pressed her back to my chest and allowed me to wrap my arm around her.

She smelled like wild flowers and her skin felt so warm against my skin.

"*You* need sleep too," I muttered, my eyes closing. "When will you get it? I don't just *want* you at my side, I *need* you."

I love you.

THEA

I've never been wanted by anyone, the way Levi wanted me. It was odd to me. I didn't understand it, and yet, I was stupidly happy whenever I was around him. I couldn't explain it, I just felt... free.

No one outside my family knew about my secrets except for him. I had made the mistake of opening up to a few people in high school, but that blew up in my face. A few weeks later, people started whispering, and the rumors started to fly. My teachers grew worried, and it even went as far as the counselors requesting to meet with me every day. But the thing was, I had already gone through therapy. My grandmother had spent thousands on Selene and I, just so we could talk to complete strangers about how we felt, or how we perceived the world around us. But sometimes we couldn't even speak. We just weren't mentally ready to traverse down that particular lane of our memories. I didn't know what to say to them, and that had only made things worse.

After six years of being forced to talk to people, I swore that I would never bring it up again with anyone... until I meet Levi. From the first day I met him, my world kept changing.

"What's wrong?" Levi asked, as he came up behind me, catching my gaze in the mirror's reflection.

"Nothing. Where are we going again?" I asked, turning back around.

"We're celebrating with a weekend date," he announced with a smile.

He grabbed both my bag and his, and carried all our things downstairs. He of course, had won the case, and all the news programs were running on repeat about how the great Levi Black had done it again. He had made it look so easy that no one seemed to remember the predictions of Mrs. Nash's case. However, some people were livid that Mr. Nash's murder was still unsolved.

"You're getting lost in your thoughts again," he remarked, as he handed me my hat and scarf.

"I was thinking about the case—"

"No," he held up his hand. "We've spent months thinking about the case. Now is the time to forget that we ever had any—" He stopped and patted his pockets, "Where's my wallet?"

"In the kitchen, which reminds me..." I headed to the kitchen while he trailed behind me. Opening the fridge and the cupboards, I began grabbing apples, chips, water, and whatever else could fit into my bag.

"What are you doing?"

"You said it would take us an hour or two to get there, right?"

"And you're going to get that hungry? I'm not judging you, but—"

"No! It's for the both of us, have you seen the snow outside? If we get stuck somewhere—"

He laughed at me. "You watch the weather channel a little too much."

Ignoring him, I grabbed the rest of the stuff and threw it into a bag, then I turned and handed him his wallet. He just grinned at me and the child in me took over. Twisting my face, I stuck out my tongue at him and began to walk towards the front door.

"Did you just—"

"I thought we were in a hurry, Mr. Black?" I was already at the door, putting on my winter jacket and snow boots.

"You don't want to get a few blankets too?"

That was actually a good idea. I turned and started towards the linen closet, but he intervened and grabbed my free hand. "On second thought, there are plenty other ways to stay warm," he said with a wicked grin. "Come on Thea, let's go."

Shadow stared at us as we closed the door on her, and I sort of felt bad.

"Tristan and Bethan will take care of her," he reassured me.

He'd done it again.

"Will you please stop reading my mind; it's disconcerting."

"It's not my fault that you're so easy to read," he pouted, as he opened the door to his black Audi for me.

In all of our time together, this was only the second time I had been in his car and by the time we got in, we were both trembling. His hand rested on my thigh, and his fingers gently traced intricate patterns onto my jeans.

"Are you sure it was alright to miss spending Christmas with your family?" I asked, as we drove past the Christmas decorations.

It was already December 29th, the realization shocked me. This entire year had passed by in an eventful blur, and in less than three days, it would be a new year…

He turned up the heat in the car. "I could ask you the same thing."

True.

"My family aren't big Christmas people. We sit around in our pajamas stuffing our faces and watching reruns of all the classic Christmas movies."

"That sounds amazing," he laughed.

"I'm serious, didn't your mother throw a huge party?"

He had spent the day with me instead.

"She did, and I opted out. The Blacks' family Christmas parties are more of a show than an actual family get-together. The great thing about having a high profile case, which we shall not discuss, is the fact that no one expects you to do anything. How's Selene?"

"She's a bag of mushy-gushy feelings. Apparently she spent the day at her boyfriend's place… wearing a *bright-colored* dress. My grandmother can't use a cell phone to save her life, but she somehow managed to take a picture and send it to me. It was green, and she looked stunning."

I closed my eyes and rested my head against the headrest. My baby sister was in love, and it suited her.

"You're happy," he stated, and I turned to look at him.

He leaned back into his seat, and kept one hand on the steering wheel, and the other on my thigh. His five o'clock shadow looked like it was now on its ninth hour, because he had been "too tired" to bother with it. I noticed he was wearing the watch I got him for Christmas, which was ridiculous when I stopped to think about it, because he had much better ones.

"What?"

"I'm happy." I said simply, as I placed my hand on his and looked out the window.

"So am I," he smiled.

Christmas carols played on the radio, but neither of us was listening. His hand felt like it was burning its way through my jeans and he was actually touching my skin.

"Thea," he said softly, as the car stopped.

Turning back to him, he kissed me, cupping the side of my face. He gently sucked my bottom lip, and I opened my mouth for him in response. He deepened our kiss for only a moment, before the deafening sound of a car horn behind us drew us out of our bubble. Grunting in frustration, he broke away from me. Suddenly the inside of the car felt as though it were a hundred degrees. Taking deep breath, I took off my scarf and turned down the heat by the time he started driving again.

He didn't say anything, he just shifted in his chair and I could see why. At least it wasn't only me.

"Why are we like this?" I laughed.

He smirked as he glanced at me, and then back at the road.

"Good things come too rarely for either of us to question it."

I was a good thing.

LEVI

I still don't know what it was about her that turned me on so much. Yes, she was beautiful, smart, dedicated, loyal, funny, and so fucking sexy…

Well then, maybe I did know.

But it was like everything about her effected me. She didn't even have to do anything. Just watching her paint her nails got me hard. It was the lust between us that had brought us together in the first place, but with time even lust fades. Being married once, I remembered the first few weeks being filled with lust, but after sometime, that faded. We were childhood friends. We hadn't got married because we were passionately in love but because everyone expected it from us. I felt fine around her. It felt like it made sense back then. But looking back on it, we were always better off as friends.

With Thea, everything was so different. I felt like for the first time someone had given me glasses. No longer was the world a blur. I could see so clearly I wondered how I ever lived so blindly before. I was well aware that she was thirteen years younger than me, but even that didn't seem like a good explanation. We were magnets to each other, and once we were close enough, we couldn't help but get stuck together. I was captivated by her.

"Wow," she whispered, as we pulled up to the cabin, "it's beautiful."

Turning off the engine, I sat back and watched as she looked around in amazement.

"Why don't we get stuck in here for a while?"

She nodded, and I reached across her, searching for the lever that would allow her to recline in the seat. We were so close that our noses almost touched, and then I found the lever and pushed back her chair until it was flat. Doing the same to mine, we both lay there gazing at the night sky through the sunroof.

"The stars are so beautiful here. You can never see them like this in the city," she mused.

"There's going to be a meteor shower tonight," I told her, taking her hand in mine.

"Wait," she said as she drew her hand back. Pulling off her gloves, she slipped her warm hand back into my own. We lay like that, each in our own seats, holding hands and gazing at the stars above.

The silence settled and it was comforting. Suddenly a low, gurgling growl echoed through the car, and with a laugh, I turned to her and asked, "Where are those chips again?"

"It doesn't seem so silly now does it?" she chuckled.

Rolling my eyes, I sat up and reached into the backseat, searching for her little bag of munchies.

"Levi!" she gasped, pointing as she caught sight of the tail end of a shooting star.

The sky was still for a moment before one another shot across, and then another until it looked as though it was raining streaks of white light.

"Wow," I murmured, falling back against my seat.

"How many wishes do you think we can get out of this?" she asked, but I couldn't tear my eyes way from the sky.

"How many wishes do you need?"

"Three."

That got my attention, and I turned my head to look at her, but she didn't look away from the sky.

"A penny for your thoughts?" I wanted to know.

"Just this once," she smiled, and closed her eyes. "Wish one; I get my dad out of prison. Wish two; Selene stays happy. Wish three…"

She stopped.

"Wish three?" I prompted.

She wouldn't look at me, but she squeezed my hand. "Wish three is that I stay with you."

There was a lump in my throat, and I squeezed her hand as I looked back up at the sky.

"Star light, star bright, the many stars I see tonight, I wish I may, I wish I might, keep this girl for the rest of my life."

She was silent for a second before throwing me the chips.

I looked at them, and then at her, before we both broke out into a fit of laughter.

THEA

Shifting over onto my side, I watched as he slept… which was kind of creepy, yet dazzling all the same.

"You're staring," he said, not bothering to open his eyes as he burrowed his head deeper into the pillow.

"Sorry—"

"Just ask whatever it is you want to ask."

I sat up and I tried to lift the sheets with me, but he just pulled them back down. I tried again, and again, he pulled them back down.

"Levi."

"My eyes are closed, you don't need to cover up."

"Firstly, why does it matter if you can't see me? And secondly, I'm covering up because I'm cold."

He reached up, placed his hand on my breast and lightly flicked my nipple. "You are cold."

Pushing his hand away, I took the sheets, and this time, he didn't stop me.

"What's your question?"

"What *do* people do up here in the middle of nowhere?"

With a smile, he opened his eyes and looked at me. His eyes were wicked and his expression mischievous as he took me into his arms and kissed my neck.

"Not that," I giggled—because apparently I was a giggler now—as he kissed my neck.

He laughed along with me, and sat up against the headboard, fully awake now. "We do whatever we want to do. We can walk into town, or the forest. We came here a lot when I was younger, with my father, so I know all the trails. You brought your ice skates with you, right?"

"I *brought* them. Yes. Do I know how to use them? *No*."

"How can you not know how to ice skate? You're from Boston."

"Well, I spent most of my life in Maryland. People there hate ice; we don't dance on it."

"I could have sworn the youngest American athlete to compete in the Olympics for ice skating was from Maryland."

He was such a know-it-all, and the smug look on his face—why did it make me want to smile too?

"How do you know that?"

"I read," he said, as he stood up.

I followed the lines of his body until he snapped his fingers. "I'm up here."

"I have no idea what you're talking about."

"Don't lie, you were checking me out!"

"I need to get dressed," I said, as I grabbed some clothing and headed into the bathroom.

As I closed the door behind me, I leaned against it and I found myself looking up at the wood paneling that made up the ceiling.

Everything was so rustic, and yet it still managed to have a contemporary feel to it.

After getting out of the car, he gave me a tour of the cabin, which took a total of about ten seconds. It was small and cozy, with a stone fireplace and an old fashioned stove. He had said that it was technically his father's cabin; however, his father had given it to him simply because Levi had loved the place so much.

He and his father had initially purchased it to get away from the women of the house. They would come up here to just get away from it all and just do manly things such as hunting or fishing— though, according to Levi, he was horrible at it. He claimed that he didn't have the patience, but if Levi didn't have the patience for something, I'm not sure how anyone did.

Levi said that he came here to "escape" the madness of the city, and I could understand why. It was like being on your own little island.

"Take your time, the lake will still be frozen whenever you decide to come out," he teased, as he stood outside the bathroom door.

On second thought, he only had patience when he wanted to.

"I'm done," I said, opening the door.

He looked me up and I grinned.

"Who's checking out who now?"

"Come on," he grumbled, handing me my jacket before taking both of our skates.

Taking my hand, we walked out back into the fresh snow. It was amazing; the ice formed on the tips of trees, and the deer that stopped to stare at us before jumping back into the forest. It felt as though I were in a Disney movie.

It was a short walk from the cabin to the lake, and the moment I saw it, I wanted to turn right back around, but he was already changing his shoes.

I sat down on the log, and reluctantly slipped into my ice skates.

"This doesn't look safe," I said, wobbling as I tried to stand up.

"It will be fine, I promise."

He took my hands and backed up onto the ice.

"Levi."

He let go, glided back, and jumped right onto the ice.

"What are you doing?"

"If it can hold me, it can hold you," he said as he skated back to me.

"Okay, what about me, plus you?"

He picked me up this time, taking me with him into the center of the lake.

"Don't—"

He jumped and I shut my eyes.

"We're still alive," he snickered.

He put me down, and my legs wobbled and slid apart, forcing me to grab onto him once more.

"Yep, this is not going to work."

"Thea Cunning, quitting? Blasphemy," he joked. "Come on, just hold on to me, and we'll take it slow."

"Where did you learn to skate?" I asked, trying to distract myself as we started moving once more.

"Hockey. The only time I ever got on the ice was to make sure someone else fell off."

That's reassuring!

"Aren't you supposed to be more focused on scoring, instead of knocking people over?"

"We were little boys, it was fun knocking the guys around like we saw on TV. I lost my first tooth that way too."

Why didn't any of this surprise me?

"You're doing it again," he said to me.

"What?"

"Look down, you aren't wobbling anymore. You were just over thinking it."

Sure enough, my legs were straight.

I grinned. "Yeah. I guess you were right."

"So, can I let go?"

"No!" I shrieked, as I grabbed onto him in a panic.

My legs slid forward and slipped out beneath me, and as I fell onto the ice, I dragged him down with me.

"Ah!" he grunted, laying in a crumpled pile with me on top. "Thea, Thea, Thea."

"Sorry."

"I'm going to have to let go, or you will never learn," he said solemnly, as he stared up at me.

"Worse comes to worse, you'll be stuck holding on to me forever."

He thought about for a moment before kissing my nose. "Good point."

Yeah, I didn't mind that either.

21

LEVI

I was so damn sore.

Note to self: never teach anyone to ice skate ever again.

"Levi, you can't miss New Year's Eve too," my mother declared over the phone, and I stepped out of the room, closing the door behind me.

"Mom, I'm busy."

"With what? Your case is over. Congratulations by the way, since you didn't even bother to call home. This family has never missed a New Year's Eve together, and I'm not having it now."

"Mom—"

"Please," she pleaded softly, and I ran my hands through my hair in frustration.

Going meant I had to leave Thea, and I didn't want to, especially not at the start of the New Year. I had planned for us to be in bed, wrapped up in each other's arms when the countdown began, not at a party.

"Son." all of sudden my father voice was in my ear.

"Seriously? She gave the phone to you? What am I, twelve?"

"Who is she?" he asked, and I froze.

"What?"

"You've never missed a family New Year's, not even when you had upcoming cases. There can only be one reason. So, who's the lucky lady?"

I wanted to tell him, just not yet.

"Dad, give the phone back to mom."

"Fine. Fine. But you can't keep her a secret forever, your mom will sniff her out."

"There is no lady. I'm taking my students out."

What the hell? Was that the best I could do?

"Really?" my mother asked, as she took back the phone. "That's great hon, bring them along, I would love to meet them all."

"Mom—" I whined.

"Make sure you let them know it's a masquerade ball."

And with that, she hung up.

"God damn it!" I shouted to the dead line.

"Is everything alright?" Thea asked, rubbing her eyes as she came into the living room.

"I somehow managed to invite the entire class to my mother's New Year's Eve party."

Moving into the kitchen, I searched for something to drink. I listened as her feet marched against the floor, rushing towards me.

"Tell me you're joking!"

"I wish!"

I poured the wine she brought.

"Why?"

"My mother wanted me to come home. I lied and told her that I would be spending time with my students. Next thing I know, she invited everyone. Which means that I need to write an email to the class, and you need a dress," I said as I poured her a glass.

She didn't say anything, and I could see her mind turning a thousand miles a minute.

"The place will be packed and everyone will be drinking. No one will be thinking about us…" I said, trying to reassure her and alleviate any anxiety that was surely building.

"Actually, I wasn't worried about that," she replied, seeming as shocked as I was by her own revelation. "I was just thinking that I would be meeting your parents, but your point is more important—"

"No. I like where your thoughts are going," I said, moving in closer to her.

She tried to look away from me, but I wouldn't let her.

"You're starting to think like my—"

"Don't say it. If you say it you will jinx it," she said, eyes wide.

"Girlfriend," I finished with a grin.

She sighed, dropping her head on my chest in mock distress. "You said it."

"I did," I admitted as I held on to her, "and I want to stay here longer, but we have to get back before everything closes. You need a dress and a mask."

"A mask?" She looked up and frowned.

"The party is really more like a masquerade ball."

She rolled her eyes, and kissed my lips before breaking away from me and heading back to the bedroom. "I'm going to go pack. You should hurry up and write that email. But then again, no matter when you write it, we will all jump to your beck and call."

She was the only one I wanted to jump at my call.

*Focus...*I thought to myself, taking out my phone and opening my email. It was short and quick.

To The Twelve Disciples, tomorrow, at nine o'clock, you are to be at 193 Commonwealth Ave for my last act of kindness for the semester.

Professor Levi Black.

Note: It's a masquerade.

Thea read from the door of the bedroom. "Your last act of kindness?"

"Too much?"

"This thing we're doing—"

"Dating?" I teased.

"That. It makes emails like this seem non-threatening, you know that right?" She frowned.

"Believe me, once classes start again, Ms. Cunning, you will not be saying that. I can keep the two parts of me separate." I said it with a serious tone, trying my best to sound menacing, despite the fact that I couldn't help but touch her now.

My hands traced the side of her curves from her hips to her chest.

"How?" she asked.

I had finally figured out why it was that I didn't treat her any differently when we were in class.

"Because I want to make you the best damn lawyer I possibly can. Which means I will be pushing you at every turn. You'll want to take my head off, I might even hurt your feelings, but at the end of the day, if it helps you to become a better lawyer, then it's worth it to me."

"Thank you—"

"You don't have to thank me, just prepare yourself," I replied, picking her up and taking her into the bedroom.

"For class or for—"

Kissing her, I unbuttoned her jeans.

∼

WE HAD both taken a hot bath and she crawled into bed before I could even stop her. The snow was coming down too hard for us to leave just yet any way. The moment I got into bed with her, I noticed how tightly she clung on to me. She was different. We were different. But we were also living in a bubble. What would happen when we got back to the real world, and class started? I was afraid that she would run away again.

Tomorrow would be our first test to see if we could actually do this. Could we really be together? I was well aware of the consequences, but when I weighed them against the alternative of letting her go, the risks far outweighed a life without her.

Reaching for my phone, I texted Bethan.

"Thea is going to need a dress for the New Year's ball."

I didn't even have time to put down the phone before she replied.

"You're bringing your student/girlfriend? Welcome to the dark side, brother."

"I invited all of my students, and who said she was my girlfriend?"

She was, but Bethan, with her big mouth, didn't need to know that.

"So you always help your female students shop for dresses when they've been invited to our parents' party? Is that like a special side gig professors do?"

"Bethan, can you help or not?"

"Fine. But first, I get to meet her."

"No."

Thea was not going to go for that.

"So how do you expect me to get her a dress if I don't even know what she looks like? What size she is, or even what styles she likes?"

"Her favorite color is teal."

Moments later, my phone's ringtone echoed within our tiny cabin space.

"Urgh," Thea groaned in her sleep, turning away from me.

I answered the phone before it could ring a second time. Getting up, I went to the window and whispered into the phone, "I texted you instead of calling for a reason Bethan."

"I need to meet her," she whined. "Tristan already knows her, and you obviously care about her. I need to get to meet her before you act like she's just some normal student at the party. Why are you being all weird about it?"

"I'll talk to her about it, okay?" I wasn't sure why I was being "weird." I was just worried about how Thea would react. She was still a flight risk.

"Talk quickly..." she said, then trailed off as a tiny, shrill cry rang out in the background. "Shit, I woke her up."

She hung up on me as her daughter's cry reached full volume.

Shaking my head, I turned back to the bed, only to find Thea sitting up, glaring at me. I laughed at the look on her face.

"What's more important than sleep?" she demanded.

"Sorry. I was trying to get you a dress."

Her face softened, even though she pretended that she was still mad with me.

"You didn't need to do that. I'm sure I would be able to find something nice for myself. I have a few dresses back home that should be okay."

"Would you happen to have any dress made by Giorgio Armani, Stefano Gabbana, or Prada and Miu Miu?"

She looked at me as if I had lost my mind.

"I have a Prada clutch?" she said slowly.

"At the risk of sounding like a materialistic ass—"

"A Black Family party is for *high society folk*. Right."

She shook her head looking somewhat dazed and amused.

"My sister, Bethan knows people. She can help, and at times she can even prove to be useful." I laughed in an attempt to lighten the mood for the bomb I was just about to drop on her. "She just wants to meet you first," I said, and waited for her reaction.

"Okay," she replied, laying back down.

"Okay?" I blinked.

"Okay. I'm going to meet your family anyway. I'd rather not do it in my dress from Macy's. Plus, if I meet them separately, it won't feel overwhelming and I won't panic."

"There's no need to panic. Bethan is loving the fact that we're together. Her big brother is finally breaking his own rules on life."

She didn't look like she believed me.

"You'll be fine," I smiled.

THEA

"I am *not* fine," I said to him as we drove to his sister's condo.

We hadn't been able to leave the cabin until the following afternoon. The pipes had frozen over, which left us with ice cold water to shower with. To top it all off, I didn't have anything nice to wear. Just jeans, and a bright yellow sweater—which made me look like Big Bird. And to make matters even worse, we had been stuck in traffic for three hours, before we were finally able to get into the city, all because fallen trees had blocked the roadways at various points.

"I'm a mess. Please drop me off at my place so that I can change... *please*..." I pleaded.

"There's no time," he replied.

He didn't seem to get it.

"The party isn't for another five hours, there's still plenty of time."

He looked to me like he couldn't believe I had said that.

"How long does it take you to pick out an outfit in the morning? You change at least three times. On top of that, you flatiron your hair, and always manage to do one side of your make 'wrong' so that you have to end up redoing it. Let's not forget about your jewelry and accessories which is basically just you being frustrated with the fact that it doesn't match your outfit—"

"Okay, I get it. Excuse me for wanting to look nice."

"I'm not complaining, but my point is that we just don't have time for you to go home to change, so that you can meet my sister only for you to pick out a new outfit and change again. The issue really is that we *only* have five hours. Besides," I chuckled, "Bethan is the last person who will care. After all she wore black slacks and a cardigan to prom. Also, we're already here."

I looked up at the condo building, as he pulled up to the front doors and handed his keys to the valet.

All I could think about as he held open the door of the building for me was— *Am I making a mistake?* What was she going to think about me? Levi kept saying that there was no need to worry, but I couldn't help it. What did we look like from the outside? After all, I had met her husband because I'd wanted to get drunk at a bar... *her bar.* And now, I was sleeping/dating a man, who happened to thirteen years older than me, oh, and I was also his student. I couldn't even tell her that I had a job other than interning at Levi's office.

After college I had gotten a job, teaching English in a middle school. I had wanted to help Selene pay for college when her time came, amongst other things. But after finding out about our father, I decided that I would use that money to pay for law school. And truthfully, that money wouldn't have gotten me anywhere, it was the scholarship that had saved my life. Because of it, I didn't need to continue working and I could just focus on school.

"She's having a panic attack," Levi said to the woman, as she opened the door.

"You should be, you guys are late!" She looked at me and frowned.

Her eyes were the same green as Levi's and her hair was just as dark. The resemblance between them was almost uncanny.

"There was traffic Beth," Levi said, as she made space to let us in.

"Beth-*an*. It's just two extra letters, you don't have to abbreviate it," she snapped at him. "And, you haven't been answering any of my calls."

"Why would I bother answering you, if I knew that we would be having this argument anyways? Besides, Beth, Bethan, Bethany, does it matter?"

"Just because you're named after jeans, doesn't mean you have to take it out on the rest of us with normal names."

"Ha!" I snickered out loud. They both turned to stare at me and

I quickly shut my mouth. "It was kind of funny," I shrugged and smiled.

She grinned. "See? Not nervous anymore."

Levi smirked as well, and they did a little fist bump.

"Annoying, isn't it?" Tristan sighed, as he bounced a big-cheeked little girl in his arms. "They play fight like that all the time."

Bethan walked over, wiping the drool off her daughter's cheek. "We used to do it at parties when we were younger so that our parents would send us to our rooms early. Sorry about the place, it's a little bit of a mess," she said, motioning around the room. "This little one doesn't give anyone a break."

"Er—It's nice to meet you, I'm Thea."

"You ready to go?" Tristan asked as he nodded to Levi.

"Go?" I turned to him.

He nodded, "Tristan, Little Bellamy, and I, are heading out to give you both time to get ready. If you need me for anything, call."

"Don't worry, everything will be fine, you guys get going," Bethan said, as she pulled me to her side before I could say another word.

He came over to me and kissed my cheek.

"Aww…" Tristan and Bethan said at the same time, and he glared at them.

"Bye," he whispered to me.

"Bye."

Neither of us moved.

"Seriously? This isn't the Titani; you'll see each other again," Bethan said to us.

Levi finally managed to break away from me, and headed to the door, with Tristan and Bellamy in tow.

"Anything she says about me is a half-truth," he added before Tristan pushed him out.

"Jeez, I've never seen him so attached to anyone," she said as she exhaled deeply. Turning to me, she stretched out her hand and smiled warmly. "It's so nice to officially meet you Thea. I hope we haven't freaked you out too much."

"No. It's... you're so lively, it's nice."

"Some people say crazy, but thank you. Would you like some wine?"

Yes.

"No, I'd rather not get buzzed before the party tonight."

"Oh, then we're completely different. I can only get through these things if I'm buzzed." She grabbed a bottle from her kitchen before walking towards the back of her condo. "The dresses are back here," she called.

The whole living room floor was covered with toys and baby items, but once we got to the hallway, I finally began to see how nice her place was. She had framed records of everything from the Beatles, to Led Zeppelin on her walls like photographs.

"Nice music," I said when we stopped at the door.

"Thanks, I'm sort of a fanatic... here we are, the room of dresses past," she said as she opened the door to a bedroom now doubling as a closet full of beautiful gowns.

Not just any dresses... dresses that I could not even fathom buying. When Levi had asked if I had any Armani or Gabbana dresses laying around, I thought he was crazy. I even later Googled how much those gown would cost and the cheapest one was almost four thousand dollars? Who would have those just 'laying around'?

Apparently his little sister.

"My mother bought me dresses all year round before I got married in the hopes of classing me up. I just don't have the heart to tell her that I've never worn any of them. Thank God you have boobs, or none of these would fit."

These look like they cost much more than four thousand dollars...

"Bethan I can't—"

"Levi said you'd be difficult," she sighed. "He also said to remind you that have no other choice and to say..." She pulled out her phone from her pocket, "...would you really want to miss an event where all of your classmates will be trying to make a name for themselves?"

"Levi," I sighed, pinching the bridge of my nose, a habit that I had only recently acquired from a *certain someone*.

"He's in love, it's kind of cute," she laughed and my eyes widened at the word... unfortunately, she noticed. "Oh, you guys haven't dropped the L word yet."

I was going to have to get better at controlling my facial expressions.

"No did he say—"

"No, I just guessed. He's just really happy. I don't remember him being like this with his ex-wife. Which is why I just *had* to meet you."

"And?"

What did she think so far?

"If you aren't serious, don't stay," she said earnestly as she stood directly in front of me. "You're beautiful, smart enough to get into Harvard Law, and earn his respect. He wouldn't keep you as a student just because he was attracted to you. He's serious about that sort of thing.

"Tristan told me he tried putting you through the wringer and you still fought to make it. So you're strong to boot. Levi doesn't have a chance in hell. He will stay with you to the end of time and back, it's just the type of guy he is... until he gets hurt."

"Like with his ex-wife."

She nodded. "He wasn't perfect, no guy really is. But what she did to him crushed him. So, if you aren't serious... if you can't fight for him as much as he'd fight for you, then please end it before he gets in any deeper."

"I'm in deep too," I muttered, the back of my throat dry. "I've been with a lot of guys. More than I'm proud of, really. Black, white, it doesn't matter. They come, we have a good time, they go, and I move on. But with Levi, it's like I'm rooted to the ground, and those roots grow stronger and deeper with each passing day.

"I don't know what will happen in the future, but I want to fight for him. Which is why I need a dress, because even if your parents don't yet know that we're together, I still want to make a good first impression. I want them to like me."

She grabbed a dress off one of the many racks. "Then let's get started. When you walk into the room, no one will be able to forget you."

I liked her.

22

LEVI

Checking my watch for what had to be the tenth time that night, I found myself unable to contain my excitement. It was 9:30 p.m. All of my students were here, with the exception of Thea. Apparently, she had to go home for something and would take a taxi.

Five hours is more than enough, my ass.

She took forever in the morning. I could make a full breakfast, write a few emails and be on my second cup of coffee by the time she came downstairs. Yes, she looked beautiful, and yes I appreciated the amount of effort she put into beautifying herself for me, but some days it annoyed me to no end.

But then again, if she was perfect, that would tick me off more.

"You look tense," Tristan said as he came over to me with a glass of champagne.

In his other hand, he held the handle for his sliver masquerade mask. Bethan was off making the rounds with their daughter.

"I'm fine."

"She'll be here soon, just focus on the other ones. Look at them, they even have business cards!" He laughed.

"What could possibly be on it?" I wondered. "They don't even work anywhere."

I chuckled, watching as Atticus Logan excitedly spoke to my father, and the rest of the old men. He wore a red masquerade mask that only covered his eyes, but even from here, I could tell it was him. The men all laughed along with him, nodding in earnest at whatever tale he was spinning.

"You've made their year with this," he said to me as his gaze followed the other students who were doing their best to socialize and connect with future bosses… *as Thea should have been doing*. My eyes narrowed and I checked my watch again. Anyone who was anyone was here, even the mayor.

"It's the least I can do for them, with all the crap that I'll be throwing at them next week."

If they didn't hate me now, come next week that would change fast.

"She's here," he said looking at the entrance, and my head whipped back.

"Wow."

It was the only word that my mind could form.

She wore a fitted, off-white ball grown, with gold lacing. Her mask matched her dress perfectly, and with each slow step forward, I wanted to take one towards her. I found myself doing just that when Tristan grabbed onto my arm.

"You can't just go up to her. She isn't your date, she's your student," he reminded me.

She searched through the crowd and I wondered if she could find me. I needed her to know that I at least saw her.

Come on, I thought as she searched through the crowd, until finally, her eyes caught mine. Her lips turned up in to a smile, and I winked at her before mouthing; *You look beautiful.*

I wanted to watch her forever, but just as I had noticed her, so did the rest of her classmates, Mr. Logan being the first one. I knew they were allies... friends now, but it still bothered me how familiar they were with each other, and how she could laugh with him so easily.

"Careful now, your jealousy is showing," Tristan snickered, before taking a sip of his drink.

"I don't know what you're talking about."

"Levi, my boy!" My father called out over the music, and I could tell that the liquor had gotten to him already. He came over along with a few of his buddies and put his arm around me.

Oh no.

"Ladies and Gentleman," he called out, then waited as the music slowly as the volume of the music slowly died down. "Ladies and Gentleman, I will proudly proclaim that my son, Levi Roman Black, is the best goddamn criminal attorney in the state of Massachusetts. And furthermore, to the sons-of bitches that I know will need his help later on... you're welcome."

They all cheered and laughed, raising their glass to me. My father turned to me and shook my hand before being pulled into the craziness of the night.

"Well that was cute," Dr. Sharpay London, smiled with a glass to her lips. She was, as always, dressed to kill, in a blood red gown and black mask.

"Long time no see," I greeted her.

"Too long," she whispered. "Dance with me."

It wasn't a question.

She took my hand, dragging me to the center of the room.

"Sharpay..."

"It's the least you can do, after leading me on, and letting me go," she smiled as we waltzed.

"Forgive me," I said to her, as I searched the dance floor for Thea. But it seemed as though more people had joined us on the floor, and I couldn't find her through the dense crowd.

"Not until you take me out on a proper date."

"I'm sorry, I can't," I said looking back at her. "I'm sort of seeing someone."

"The *it's complicated* girl?" she asked with a certain degree of annoyance in her voice. I spun her outwards and brought her back to me. "I thought you ended it."

"More like a dramatic pause."

Where was she?

"Is she the one you're looking for?"

"No," I said quickly, a little too quickly in fact.

Finally, I spotted Thea standing in a group talking to the rest of her classmates. I could allow myself to get closer to her now that other students were around.

"Sharpay you are an attractive and successful woman. I'm sure any man would be more than happy to be with you—"

"Just not you."

"Sorry."

But the truth was that I wasn't really sorry.

As the song came to an end, I turned away from her and headed towards the corner of the house. The closer I got, the better I could hear their conversation even without seeing their faces.

"How much do think this place is worth?"

"Ten million, easy."

"Does it matter? None of us are making that any time soon." Her voice reached my ears.

"Easy for you to say, you're law royalty, I bet you grew up going to parties just like these. Just look at that dress. What's your zip code?"

"I'm glad to hear that you're all inspired," I cut in before she could respond, and they all turned and backed away like I was Freddy Krueger.

"You're scaring them, sweetheart," my mother said, as she joined my side and looked them all over. "Though I do wonder," she mused, "if they're so intimidated by you, then they're probably no good at work."

I grinned inwardly, as I caught on to what she was doing. "They're by far the worst class I've ever had."

"Oh my!" she said with a fake gasp, but behind her mask, I knew she was smiling.

"We're only as good as our teacher," Thea spoke up, and they looked to her like she was insane.

"We must be pretty damn good then," Atticus added.

"Oh we're pretty badass," Vivian said, and Thea raised both of her hands and high fived her comrade without even looking; it was almost as though they had planned it.

"Well congratulations to you three for having back bone," my mother smiled, "Levi, show them no mercy—"

"Mercy? Professor Black? Ma'am, I'm sorry, but none of us know what you're talking about," Thea said, and a few of them fought back laughs.

I hadn't noticed until now that with the exception of Vivian, she was the only female, and with her standing in the middle, throwing back everything we dished out to her, she looked like a queen.

"What's your name?" my mother asked.

"Thea Cunning."

"Wait," my mother looked her over. "Would you by any chance happen to be the daughter of Margaret Cunning?"

Shit.

It looked as if someone had shot her through the heart. The pride, the joy, and everything she had been moments ago, shrank at the mention of her mother's name. However, she didn't drop her head; instead, she forced a smile.

"Yes, ma'am, I am. Did you know my mother?" she asked politely, not at all fazed.

No one else could see it, but the Thea from earlier has disappeared. The person smiling in front of us now was so foreign to me.

"Oh my goodness. It's a small world. I had the pleasure of meeting your mother many times. She was a wonderful woman, and a brilliant lawyer. I'm so sorry to hear about her passing earlier on this year."

"Mother, why don't you go—"

"Honey!" she ignored me, calling over my father, "One of Levi's students is Margaret Cunning's daughter."

Fuck.

"Thank God I'm out of the game," he said as he came over. "The Cunning genes *and* mentoring from my son? The world doesn't stand a chance! Your mother was a force to be reckoned with in court. I never won a single case against her." He shook her hand, and it might as well have been a knife, but she accepted it graciously. "I can see it now… you look just like her. You'll make a damned good lawyer."

"Don't give her too much praise. Ms. Cunning has to work her way up just like the rest of them, and she's been slacking. Mr. Logan here has been on her heels since day one, and at the moment he's a fine contender for the top place in the class," I said as I tried to change the direction of the conversation.

Fortunately, it worked.

They all started talking animatedly… except for Thea. She took a step back, allowing the group to crowd in and surround my father, until she stood outside of the circle. No one seemed to notice or mind. She looked up to me and her eyes were dull. She gave me a fake smile, trying to convince me that she was okay, then she turned and walked away, disappearing into the crowd.

I had to wait a moment, laughing along at jokes I didn't even hear, and nodding at comments I couldn't care less about, before finally excusing myself.

Following the direction she went in, I tried to not draw any attention to myself as I went up the stairs. I saw the tail end of her dress disappear around the corner as she went into one of the bathrooms.

Before the door could close completely, I slipped in behind her. She kicked off her shoes as she reached the vanity, and she was trying her best to breathe slowly.

"Breathe," I said to her, pulling her into my arms, "just keep breathing."

"I'm fine," she stated forcefully, standing straight once again.

"You're lying." I kissed the side of her shoulder. "You can pretend for everyone else, but do not do it to me."

I joined her side and together we sunk to the floor. I pulled her unto my lap, and her dress billowed out around us, providing us with our own private island of sorts. She rested her head on my chest and I ran my hand up and down her back.

"I did this to myself Levi. I knew who she was. I knew that I would run into people that would sing her praises. I stepped into her world; I'm following in her footsteps. I have to accept that. I can't just break down when people say her name or talk about how great of a person she was.

"Sometimes I think I should just come out and say it, tell them who she really was. But if I did that, then I truly would be a disgrace; the daughter of a convict and an abusive mother... who wants to be known like that? I suffer because I'm too much of a coward to tell the truth. So I have to accept it. I thought I had done so well too. I could even force a smile, but I couldn't force myself to stay," she whispered. "I don't want to be the girl that always crumbles, the one that always needs to be saved, especially in a life I chose for myself. I won't."

"What's the point of being with someone if they can't save you every once in a while?"

She shook her head. "I've never saved you."

She really had no idea what she meant to me.

"You save me just by being here. I was miserable before you, and I didn't even know it. That's how deluded I was. The last four months have been the best of my life. And in," I paused and checked my watch and my eyes went wide, "six seconds, I hope this New Year lives up to it."

She looked up at me and kissed me.

"Five," I counted.

Kiss.

"Four."

Kiss.

"Three,"

Kiss.

"Two."

Kiss.

"Happy New Year."

"Happy New Year," she whispered back, and I closed the gap between us as the fireworks exploded right outside the window.

She broke away to look at them. As she gathered her dress in her hands, she crawled further into my lap and nuzzled my neck. "We have the best spot in the house."

"Yes we do."

THEA

We had spent almost an hour in there, just watching the fireworks display, and after that, just talking. Interestingly enough, I couldn't even remember what we talked about. All I remembered was how heavy my heart felt when he decided that we needed to get back.

Grabbing my shoes, he held the door open as I walked out.

"Oh my God," I heard a short gasp to the left of us.

There stood Vivian, in her navy blue dress. Her eyes shot to me, then to Levi before she took off running back down the stairs.

"Shit."

I dropped my shoes, hiked the length of my skirt up and ran after her. I could hear Levi calling out to me, but I didn't care. I needed to stop her. Everyone was either to drunk, or too tired to notice us as we ran right past them and out the front door. I shivered at the cold of the pavement under my heels, but I didn't stop running after her down Commonwealth Avenue.

"Vivian wait!" I yelled, when she reached the curb.

She turned around and spat with all the hate in the world directed at me, "Stay away from me!"

"Vivian—"

"You make me sick!" she screamed. "I do what I have to do because I don't I have any choice. My parents aren't fancy, high-powered lawyers. I didn't go to some Ivy League school. *This* is my shot. *This* is my moment to make something out of myself and help my family. So I strip. I dance half naked in front of men so I can go school, and I hate myself for it.

"This whole time I've been kicking myself whenever I'm near you because I wanted to be like you. I thought to myself, 'Wow, here is a woman, a colored woman at that, who is at the top of her game, who is doing it the right way'. Low and behold, you're screwing our professor! And you don't even need to! Usted es repugnante!"

"Are you done?" I asked her, as she stood on the corner shaking with rage. She looked away without saying a word.

"When I found out what you do to put yourself through school, I never once thought less of you, and I never once thought of you as disgusting. You can judge me all you want, but you don't know me. The ideal you had in *your* head of me is not something that I have to live up to. You can think whatever you want about me, I'm still going to be me."

I turned around to leave when she called out again.

"I'll tell the dean. I'll get him fired. There are other professors and you will be out in—"

"No you won't, but if you're that stupid, go ahead and try. But first, let me run down the scenarios for you. If it goes the way you're hoping, I will be shamed out of school, and Professor Black will most likely stop teaching, or stop teaching our class. But he will still be a great lawyer. You, on the other hand, will lose your big chance to better yourself because we all know that he's the best way to move up and learn. Option two, and this is because you've pissed me off, *the* Levi Black and *the* daughter of Margaret Cunning vs. a stripper. We will destroy you. If you want to come after me, that's fine. If you want to hate me, go right ahead. But you will not obliterate everything that man has built for himself. I won't let you."

I felt bad for having to do that to her. She was right to be angry with me, but it was my turn to save Levi, even in this tiny way.

Maybe I was just like my mother… willing to do whatever it took to further my own goals and happiness, even if it meant hurting other people.

The thought made me sick.

23

THEA

"So... Is anyone going to clue me in as to what the hell is going on?" Atticus asked, looking between Vivian and I who now worked on opposite sides of the office. It had been a week since that night, and we still hadn't spoken a word to each other. We did our work, pretended the other wasn't there, and then went home.

She didn't answer him, and neither did I.

"Okay then." He leaned back.

Levi had only brought it up to me once and that was the night of the ball.

Are you running?

That was all he wanted to know. It frustrated me how relaxed he was about all of it. However, I wasn't running. I couldn't find the strength to run from him anymore, and I was tired of running.

Now that we were basically living at his office, filing reports, doing coffee runs, or just stapling papers, I once again realized how important he was.

"What's going on?" Atticus asked again, but this time he wasn't talking about us.

Instead, he was looking out the office and at the stream of reporters that were following Betty. I wasn't sure, but I suspected that she either knew, or assumed, that something was going on between Levi and I. Every time I walked past her in the hallway, she would pause, look me over, and smile to herself like she'd heard something funny.

"Didn't you hear? Professor Black won Lawyer of the Year," Raymond said as he leaned against the door.

He looked as sharp as ever in his navy blue suit.

I had read up on Raymond; he was one of Levi's first associates, and the only person who was not of Harvard breeding. Instead, he went to Boston College and had attended one of Levi's seminars. To get an internship, he stood outside every day for three weeks, and handed Levi his morning cup of coffee… in the winter. In his personal reports, it said he only took four days off per year to visit his mother in Jamaica.

"He has an interview going on, so if anyone asks you anything about anything, smile and lie."

"So, if they ask how it feels to spend our evenings filing briefings from three years ago, we should say it's great?" Atticus asked sarcastically, as he pulled out the files he needed to work on next.

"Some people would kill to be where you are. I remember being at the bottom of the food chain. Believe me, it's worth it when you get to sit at the grown-up table." He looked to me, "Now, one of you, get me some coffee."

"Black?" I asked getting up.

"Cream and four sugars… you really should stop volunteering yourself, or you'll be remembered as the coffee girl," he said to me, leaving as he heard his named called by none other than Tristan.

"He's right you know," Atticus replied, and Vivian walked right in front of my face, as if I wasn't even there, grabbed my papers and then moved back to her desk.

"Anyway," Atticus shook his head, "coffee girl can—"

"I hear office gossip when I'm walking around. Plus being seen working is good—"

"Aren't you supposed to be getting me coffee?" Raymond asked me.

"Really? Good, Levi was just asking for it. Hurry up," Tristan said, leading Raymond away.

"You'll get to hear some of the interview," Atticus pointed out.

"Of course," Vivian muttered.

I turned on my heels and left. She wanted to be a child about it, then fine, I could handle her little digs. Entering the break room, I ran straight into Betty, sending her tray of cookies and pretzels everywhere.

"Betty, I'm so sorry," I said as I dropped down and began picking up the mess I had made.

"It's okay, never mind the mess, I'm just going to have to order something for them—"

"I can run out and get it."

"You're a lawyer, not a delivery girl. I got it," she laughed when I stood back up, handing her the tray of broken treats.

She was being nice... no one in this office was nice to any of the "twelve". We all believed that Levi had told them to give us the hardest time possible over the smallest of things. For example, last week Atticus had misplaced someone's cup, and all of sudden it was being treated like a missing person's case.

"I'm not treating you differently," she said.

"I wasn't thinking that," I lied.

"You know that thing that Levi does where he looks into your pretty brown eyes, and all of sudden knows all your thoughts? Yeah, well, I taught him that." She winked, walking around me.

"Why do you always smile when I walk by?"

She paused. Tilting her head to the side, her eyes crinkled as she smiled.

"Do I? I honestly didn't notice. Seeing the way you and he

dance around each other reminds me of the time when I was my husband's secretary. It's like a déjà vu for me. You should forget the coffee and run back now... Raymond always messes with one of you..." she added the last bit, and took her leave.

What?

Dashing out of the room, and back to the conference room I found that both Atticus and Vivian were gone.

What the hell?

"I only count eleven?" someone said from inside Levi's office, and I couldn't see because of the wall the camera crew made spilling out into the hall.

Shit. Think Thea.

I couldn't go in there late without anything, he was going to chew me out in front of everyone.

"You're in trouble," Tristan grinned stepping up right next to me.

"It's your fault. I thought we had a deal. I'm never getting coffee ever again."

"The deal was to help you help Levi win the Nash case."

I hate lawyers.

"I still have the guyliner card."

"It's your word against mine, and you better hurry up before you miss out big. I doubt they will start over because of you." He lifted up a folder. "Then again, this could save your ass."

He was enjoying this.

"What do you want?"

"Babysitting, this Friday."

"Done."

"And Saturday."

Goddamn him.

I snatched the file from him and I read it over quickly to see what was in it.

"Fine," I said, before I took off running full speed towards the office.

"I'm sorry, I'm here," I said, moving through the crowd to where Levi stood at his window with the rest of the students behind him for a photo.

He looked at me and I could just feel the lecture coming.

"I'm so sorry, I wasn't aware we had time for photos, Professor Black. I spotted this and thought you might need it." I handed it to him.

He took it, reading it over. "We will discuss this later."

"I'm so sorry to keep you waiting," I said to the reporters in the room.

"It's fine, we were just testing the lighting anyway. We know the work comes first."

Smiling, I nodded and moved towards the rest of them. Vivian shook her head, sucked her teeth at me, and looked out the window.

"Now, can we get the two females in the middle?" the photographer asked us.

Sure, if you want to capture a murder on camera.

I moved towards the center, as did she.

"Was there even anything in that folder?" she hissed at me under her breath.

"If you have to ask that, you aren't paying attention," I whispered back and smiled as the flash went off.

"Thank you, that's all we need for now."

We all broke apart, leaving the room to give them space. Before I could make it back to my desk, Atticus came up behind me and grabbed my arm, along with Vivian's, and pulled us away from everyone and towards the stairwell.

"What are you doing?" I pulled my arm away from him.

"Whatever this big bad secret is, I want to know now before both of you fuck this up for us," he demanded, looking at the both of us.

Vivian freed her arm and moved as far away from me as she could within the cramped space.

"Fine, I'll start with my secret then; I'm a white, southern, gay, democrat whose father happens to be a Republican Governor," he confessed looking between us.

I didn't say a word, crossing my arms as she did.

"I can wait," he said and leaned back against the door, "but do you really want to be stuck in here much longer?"

"I'm republican, and a stripper, can I go now?" Vivian snapped at him.

His eyes went wide for a moment before he tried to hide it.

"Okay... I didn't see that coming," he replied slowly.

Vivian looked to me, waiting as if to tell me I didn't have the balls to admit my secret... and I didn't.

"And she's sleeping with our professor," she spat out in disgust.

"That I kind of saw coming. No offense," he looked to me and said.

"I worked just as hard for my spot here," I said to her once again.

"Sure you did," she snorted. "If you've done nothing wrong, then why can't you admit it.?"

She pushed Atticus out of the way, taking her exit.

All I could do was sit on the stairs. "If it makes any difference, I was seeing him before I knew he was our professor. I just thought he was a lawyer, I had no idea who he really was until the first day in class..."

"You don't have to explain yourself to me," he said as he took a seat beside me.

"Really? If anything I figured you would be just as pissed off as she is. It feels like you and I are always neck and neck."

"Yeah, but you aren't beating me because you're with him. It would make sense if you put in just the normal amount of effort. But you're always going the extra mile, and if someone else tries to catch to you, you push yourself harder. If you could have just gotten by sleeping with him, then you wouldn't have bothered to dig up any dirt on us."

"Maybe I'm just a horrible person," I huffed looking the other way.

"You're not," he said, and I looked to him. "You knew I was gay, didn't you?"

I didn't say anything.

"I figured as much, but you never brought it up, that day, or ever. You were never going to use it against me? I'm not my political affiliation. Who I vote for does not define me... my sexuality... who I chose to love. That is me, and you didn't trash that. You're not a bad person Thea. I am the last person to judge who should and who shouldn't be together because society says so."

I sighed, "Damn it, now I have to call you my friend."

We both laughed.

"Don't worry about Vivian, she'll get over it."

"Are you sure?" I asked, because I really didn't see that happening.

He shrugged, "Well you women are hard on your own sex for some reason."

Before I could reply, the stairwell opened. Levi looked between us for a moment, with his eyes hard, and his lips pressed into a fine line. Atticus stood quickly, but I froze under his glare.

"You, my office *now*," he said as he pointed to me. Then he walked out without another word.

Shit.

"This would be a good time to use your magic to not get me fired," Atticus almost begged as I headed out.

Levi walked swiftly with his fists balled at his side, and his whole back was tensed.

"Levi, you have a call—"

"Hold it," he snapped, cutting off Betty and stepping in his office. She looked to me wide eyed.

This right here was the problem with being romantically involved with your boss.

"You wanted to speak to me, sir?" I asked, with my back straight.

"Are you sure you're not busy?" he snapped throwing the file I had given him earlier onto the desk before grabbing his guitar in the corner and taking a seat. "If I knew the workload was so light around here, I would have only picked six students."

"And Atticus and I would still be one of them," I shot back.

I hadn't done a damn thing wrong, and I was not going to let him make feel like I had.

"Professor Black, I'm sure you're only interested because we were stupidly discussing something private during your time, and for that, I am truly sorry. However, I would like to make it clear, once again, that I am serious about my position here and my intention to learn from the best. There is nothing, not even a little bit, going on between Mr. Logan and myself. I'm not that stupid, nor that cruel, to be doing anything in your stairwell with you twenty feet away."

He strummed the strings, not saying anything as his fingers worked over the neck of the guitar.

"Is there anything else, Sir?"

"That file, where did you get it? Honestly," he asked, calmer now.

"I traded babysitting Bellamy for Tristan on Friday and Saturday for it. It's just a mistake on your brief for the bar association tomorrow, right? Nothing big."

"Even little mistakes look bad. I'll be sure to thank Tristan then. That will be all," he said as he resumed playing.

Nodding, I turned to leave when I heard him whisper.

"There's nothing there? Not even a little bit?"

I turned to face him, my expression softening as my heart broke at his tone. "It's not even possible. I'm head over heels for someone and Atticus... well, I'm not his type."

I didn't think I could be with anyone else now anyway.

He didn't reply, and he didn't need to.

. . .

LEVI

When I got back to my place, she was curled up on my couch, watching the news and eating a bowl of cereal. She looked up at me briefly, but didn't say anything. Her cat, Shadow, sat at the door, her brown tail swaying back and forth as she looked up at me as if to ask me what I had done.

Petting her head a little, I dropped my stuff at the door and went into the kitchen. Grabbing a bowl of kettle corn, and a beer from the fridge, I took off my shoes and sat down next to her. The thing I both loved and hated about Thea, was the fact that she couldn't help but speak her mind. With each bite I took, I could tell in the corner of my eye that she was getting more and more ticked off with me.

"Can you pass me the remote?" I asked her.

"No. You are an ass," she snapped. "An ass who does not trust me."

I sighed. "Look I'm sorry. Yes, I'll admit that I was jealous, but can you blame me? Why were you two *alone* in a stairwell... laughing together?"

"God forbid."

I sighed, "You both just seem very close. Since day one, you both click. He's not bad looking, and he's closer to your age—"

She laughed. "Says the guy who was dancing all up on a pretty brunette?"

"What?"

"On New Year's, at your parents' masquerade ball, you and that woman in red, you danced with her. And she was the only woman you danced with all night, I might add, but you don't see me yelling at you."

It took me a moment to follow.

"Are you sure you weren't just saving it for this moment? She's a family friend and she dragged me out to dance. I spent the whole time trying to think of how to get closer to you."

"It was because of Vivian. I was with Atticus because he

wanted to know why we weren't speaking to each other, so he dragged us both into the stairwell. Then she left, because she can't stand to be around me for more than ten seconds without trying to bite my head off. And before you ask, yes he knows. Will he talk about it or tell anyone? No he won't. We all have things on each other now, so it's fine. Here's your damned remote," she finished, as she chucked the remote at me.

I placed it, and the kettle corn, on the table alongside my beer. Moving over to her, I kissed her neck.

"I'm sorry," I said again with each kiss until she laid back. Once I was on top of her, I kissed her lips. "I was jealous. I'm a jealous man, I can't help it. I don't ever want to lose you to another man..."

Not ever again.

"I'm not *her*," she whispered as she ran her hands over my cheek. "I've gotten used to reading your face too. I'm not your ex-wife, no one can take me away from you."

Her hands ran down to my chest, slowly pulling off my tie.

"How many times do I have to prove it you?"

She never looked away from my eyes as she up unbuttoned my shirt.

Her beauty, her passion, her intelligence, the look in her eyes, the way she challenged me.

Everything she was, affected me.

"I'm unconditionally in love with you."

24

LEVI

I'm an idiot.
My Thea, God bless her, was a runner by nature. The moment she got spooked, she had a tendency of throwing up walls, and last night I must have scared the hell out of her. I hadn't meant to tell her that I loved her out loud. I couldn't help but think it, and before I could stop myself, it was spilling out of my mouth... we made love, but she never once said it back, and she didn't bring it up again.

∼

"THIS IS A BAD IDEA," Bethan said in a panic, as Tristan held her back from taking their daughter out of Thea's arms.

"What if she wakes up at night and she doesn't see me?"

"She will cry, go back to sleep, and see you again in the morning," Tristan sighed, placing Bellamy's bags on the floor. "She has everything she could possibly need. It's just one night, she'll be okay sweetheart," he reassured Bethan.

She shook her head, and took Bellamy back into her arms. Tristan groaned, shaking his head at her. "I'll be in the car."

I understood his frustration. Since Bellamy's birth, Bethan had never let her out of her sight for more than a few hours. She had kind of put everyone else on the back burner. But I also understood Bethan's reasons; they had tried for years to have a child of their own and had suffered numerous miscarriages. While pregnant, she didn't want to get her hopes up and she had often complained or ignored the life growing inside her because she was worried about losing it. Now that she had a healthy little girl right in front of her, being apart was almost more than she could bear.

"Bethan," I said, but I wasn't sure what to say to her.

"Bethan," Thea said softly, moving closer to them both, "I basically raised my baby sister. I never went anywhere without her. I went to a high school right across the street from her elementary school. I get it, and I promise to send you pictures during the night. But I think you both need a break before you crack."

She sighed, kissing Bellamy's head before handing her over to Thea.

"Thank you."

"No problem, she's so quiet, we'll be fine," Thea said as she rocked her.

"I'll be here as well, so go before Tristan writes a big speech in the car," I said, taking her hand and leading her to the door.

"Okay, if you—"

"We got it, we'll be fine. Goodbye," I cut her off, as I ushered her though the front door.

Tristan mouthed *thank you*, as he held open the passenger side door for her. Waving at them, I closed the door before leaning back against it. Inside, Thea sat on the floor, and placed Bellamy in her bright pink princess bouncy chair.

"You always know what to say," I said to her, as I crouched down beside them.

She smiled, still staring at Bellamy, "Most moms— good moms — just want to know that their kids are safe. It makes me happy to see how much Bethan loves her. After we were born, my mother kind of just left us in the care of our father. He was writer, so he stayed at home while she was out making a name for herself... sorry, that was depressing—"

"Don't be, you can talk to me about anything." I kissed the side of her head and stood back up again. "What do you want to eat?"

"I'm fine right now. I need to study anyway, but thank you," she said, grabbing a few books out of her bag and dropping onto the couch. I noticed that she didn't look at me once.

"Oh, right, you have other classes. How are they?"

I'm so lame. I'm trying to start conversation with my girlfriend, because I said the damn "L" word.

"Compared to yours? Not nearly as stressful."

Still no eye contact.

"Even Professor Noland? She gives out papers like Christmas gifts."

She shrugged. "Yeah, but honestly if you regurgitate everything she says in class in your paper, you'll be fine. It's like she doesn't even notice it's her own words."

I wanted to shake the living daylights out of her. I could accept the fact that she wasn't ready. What I couldn't accept was the wall she was rebuilding right before my eyes. Bellamy threw her toy across the floor, and only then did I see her face as she handed it back to her.

"I thought you wanted to eat?" she asked, flipping through her book again.

"Yeah, I'm going to."

Walking into the kitchen, I dialed the one person in the world who I knew would understand this.

"Selene?" I said softly.

"What's up Levi, how's my sister?"

"I think I broke her," I half joked, pulling the jar of jelly out from the fridge.

"Eww..."

"Not like that! I told her I loved her last night."

"No. No. No," she repeated.

"Yes. Yes. Yes. And now I can't even get her to look me in the eyes."

"There are only three people in this world who have ever said that to her... actually two since I don't know about the first one; but still... only our grandmother and me. And in all these years, she's never said it back to either of us. The best I've ever gotten was a 'me too.'"

Well at least it wasn't just me.

"So basically, I'm screwed?"

"Pretty much. But I'm glad you said it. Just give her a while, she'll reset herself. And it will be like it never happened—oh crap. I have to go Levi, I'm grounded, and if my grandmother sees me on the phone..."

"What did you do?" I asked as I cut my sandwich in half and turned around to wash out a plate.

"I snuck out to see my boyfriend. Don't tell Thea! Promise me you won't, you owe me for all the free sister advice."

"Fine, I won't tell her—"

Turning around, I found Thea standing in the kitchen with Bellamy on her hip hiccupping as she rubbed her back.

"Okay, bye," Selene said before the line went dead.

I said bye back, even though the line was dead.

"She has a bottle of gripe water in her bag, can you hand it to me. It's the clear one," she pointed.

Nodding, I dug through it for a moment before turning around and handing it back to her.

"How do you know how to do all of this? Most twenty-three year olds would hate spending their weekends like this."

Finally, she looked to me and smiled. "My grandmother says I was born at forty and by the time I was ten, I could play bridge with the best of them."

"So that would make you the cougar in this relationship?"

"Is that what I am now?" she asked, holding up Bellamy's bottle, "I can work with it. But can you really keep your body looking young at fit with all of *that*?"

Her eyes glanced at the chips, beer and sandwich combo I had going on my plate.

"Don't even go there."

She laughed, causing Bellamy to wave her tiny hands in excitement. Shaking her hand, Thea looked up at me.

"What?"

"Nothing."

THEA

BUZZ

BUZZ

"Thea, your phone," Levi muttered beside me as he rolled over.

"I'm too tired to move," I groaned.

Bellamy had just went down for the night after refusing to eat. It had taken her a good two hours to realize that her parents weren't around her anymore, and once she did, she lost it and began screaming as loud as her little lungs would let her, for as long as they would let her. I just wanted to sleep, but my phone wouldn't stop vibrating against the bedside table.

BUZZ

BUZZ

"Thea…"

"I'm getting it…" I grumbled, as I sat up and reached for it. The time was 1:53am, which meant it was too late for anyone to be calling for anything.

"What?"

There was silence.

"Selene?" I looked at the caller ID.

"Turn on the news."

"Selene it's two in the morning why are—"

"Thea! Turn on the damn news!"

What the hell is wrong with her?

"Okay, hold on." I got up out of bed, trying not to wake up Bellamy who slept in a makeshift crib next to us.

When I turned on the television I didn't see anything.

"Selene are you sure this isn't local news for you? I don't see anything—"

"They aren't talking about it, but look at the bottom banner, under the Twitter feed."

I searched, watching as the sentence rolled by, still not seeing it anything...

"Selene..." I stopped, and so did every other part of me. I couldn't breathe and soon even standing was too hard. I collapsed onto the ground.

"Thea?" Levi called out to me.

"Thea?"

I heard him, but I didn't see him until he was right in front of my face.

"What's wrong?"

Everything.

"My father tried to commit suicide." I said the words, but I found myself unable to believe them.

My mind was spinning, and all I could think about was getting him out before it was too late.

"I need to get him out. Levi, please, help me get him out."

Collapsing into his lap, I cried, I sobbed, I begged him... and part of me knew that this was going to destroy us. This was the other shoe that had been waiting to drop. And as it fell, it landed on the back of my neck.

25

LEVI

I wasn't sure how to have this conversation, but I needed to tell her the truth. She looked like her entire world had just crumbled all around her... how could I add to her pain.

But if I said nothing...

"I need to tell you something," I began.

When she looked up at me, her face was full of trust, of hope, and I wanted to stop speaking. I didn't want to say it, but I had to.

"Savannah Van Allen was my mother's friend, and she was also my ex-wife's mother."

There it was, the trust disappeared right in front of my eyes, and all I could see instead was rage.

"Thea..." I reached for her, but she smacked my hand away and stood up.

"Why... why didn't you say anything? I told you *months* ago! Why didn't you say anything?"

"I wasn't sure what to say—"

"How about 'Thea for years I thought your father murdered

my wife's mother'!" she screamed at me. "Why am I using past tense? You probably never believed in me from the beginning."

"That's not true!"

"Why else wouldn't you speak up? Why else would you never bring it up, when I talked about him all the time? You never really believed that I could get him out. He was just going to die in prison, and I never would have needed to know."

"I didn't tell you because it doesn't matter to me! I love you, I want you to stay, and I didn't want you to use this as an excuse to run away."

"You loved me and didn't want me to run? Or is it that you weren't sure what to say? Which is the truth? Or do you just say pretty things without thinking about what they actually mean?!"

"I'm telling you because I will help you. I *want* to help you."

"Don't bother. Anyone who hides the truth from me in order to keep me at their side isn't someone I want to be with."

She moved to the door but I grabbed on to her.

"Thea—"

"Let go of me!" she screamed, and wriggled out of my grasp.

I couldn't.

"Don't do this, please. I was wrong not to tell you, I know that. But we aren't running away from each other anyone—"

"There is no *we*. Getting involved with you was a bad idea, I knew it then and I should have trusted myself. I can't trust you, so let go of me Levi, or I will scream until someone calls the police."

She ripped her arm from my grip, not even bothering to grab her coat before slamming the door on her way out. A moment later Bellamy's screams echoed through the house, mirroring my own internal grief and frustrations.

∾

"I HATE YOU," Tristan said, dressed in sweatpants and Red Sox hoodie.

I ignored him and handed Bellamy back to Bethan.

"Where's Thea?" she asked, looking around.

"She left me."

Her eyes widened as she rubbed Bellamy's back. "I'll put her down in the guest room."

Nodding, I let her go, before leading Tristan into my living room, stepping over all of the boxes.

"What's all this?" he said, with a lot less edge to his voice.

"Case files on State of Connecticut vs. Ben Walton on the kidnapping, rape and murder of Savannah Van Allen," I said as I sat back down on the couch and rubbed my eyes.

It was already seven in the morning, and I didn't see myself sleeping anytime soon.

"You're going to need to connect the dots for me here Levi."

"It's one fucked up story," I laughed bitterly. "According to the state of Connecticut, my ex-wife's mother was murdered by my now ex-girlfriend's father."

"Holy shit," Bethan gasped, already back downstairs.

I lifted my empty glass up and tipped it in her direction before finally pouring myself a shot of brandy.

"How many of those have you had?"

"Don't worry," I drank again, "this is my first one. I've been waiting for you guys to come back, and now that you're here, I think I'm just going to go ahead and get drunk… because I'm fucked."

"You're trying to get him out?" Tristan asked, looking at my notes. "Levi, have you lost your damned mind?"

"He didn't do it," I replied, as I finished off my glass and poured another one.

"Levi, I understand you like her—" Bethan began.

"Love. I love her. We're telling all truths today," I cut her off.

She sighed, starting again. "Okay. I get that you *love* her. But she's his daughter. Of course she thinks her father is innocent, but that doesn't make it so."

"That was the very first thing I thought until I started to find out more about Margaret *The Shark* Cunning. Spoiler Alert; she's the devil, and believe me, if I could criminally prosecute her, I would a thousand times over."

"Levi, tell me this isn't just because you love her, and I will back you up one hundred percent. You know I will. So tell me, what do you know that we don't?"

"Ben Walton and Savannah Van Allen were having an affair. When Margaret found out, she, from what I can gather, tampered with evidence and left him out to hang. She confessed to this eight months ago before dying of stage four-lung cancer. That's why Thea's in law school."

They didn't say anything for a moment. Bethan slowly sank onto the couch.

"Is there any proof of this?" Tristan asked, as he reached for my notes.

"Only God knows at this point. Thea has been combing over these files for months. I haven't touched them, because I knew the minute I did, I would have to tell her."

"So you told her?" Bethan questioned.

"Yes, and she walked out."

"And you're still looking into this?" she whispered. "This is Pandora's Box, Levi. The moment you open it, bad shit is going to coming flying out at you from every direction. Mom... Oh my God, Mom will just lose it. Not to mention Odile."

As she sat there staring at me, Tristan spoke up, "But if the man is really innocent, I can't imagine not doing anything just because we will piss a few people off. They should know the truth, and the right people should be jailed for their crimes. That's the point of the justice system." Tristan looked to me. "I've spent my career with you, helping people stay out of prison. Sometimes rightfully so and other times not. I'll support you on this, but there's a great chance we will lose, and lose badly."

"I'm prepared for it."

"You might not get her back either," he added.

That I wasn't as prepared for.

"I'll deal with that."

"Can I just play devil's advocate for one second?" Bethan frowned looking at us both. I just nodded for her to go on. "Aren't you being a little too trusting? Levi, babe, these are your careers, careers you've both spent years, and hundreds of thousands of dollars crafting. I've been here from the beginning. I've seen the shit you've both put yourselves through just to get this far.

"I like Thea, she seems like a really sweet girl, but do any of us really know her? For all we know she could have been planning this for months. She comes into my bar, and just happens to meet and go home with the best criminal attorney in the country? Then, she somehow turns out to be your student, and from what Tristan's told me, she's not afraid of playing the blackmail card. And on top of all this, she drops this bomb and tells you about her father? I know this sucks to hear, I know you really do love her, but what if she's using you? I mean consider the timing of all this... what if—"

"Stop," I whispered, not wanting to hear anymore.

"Levi—"

"No. She isn't that person."

I knew her.

Tristan frowned. "She did blackmail me once just to get what she wanted—"

"No!" I snapped at them both, and they just looked at each other. "Fine, let's say what you're saying is true. Let's say that for months she's been jerking me around, and she's that good of an actress that I fell for it. Nothing changes for me. Even if she admitted it right now, I would be hurt, and so fucking pissed off, but I would still be right here looking through all these files. I would still want to help her even if she betrayed me like that. Thank you for worrying about me Beth, but I've made up my mind."

Tristan sighed, got up, and headed to the kitchen. Before long, he was back with two more glasses and he poured us all a drink.

"Where you go, I go. And when this is done, I am taking the longest fucking vacation of my life," he said, as he handed me my glass.

"Thank you."

THEA

I was half frozen by the time I got to Atticus' place. I couldn't feel my toes, and my fingers felt like they could be snapped off one by one. When he saw me, he didn't crack any jokes and he didn't say anything stupid. Instead, he stepped aside, and held the door open, allowing me to enter his tiny, one bedroom apartment, and crawl up onto his couch.

He placed a thick blanket over me, and left a cup of hot chocolate on the coffee table, for whenever I was ready to drink. He sat down in front of the couch, watching the news in silence.

"That's my dad," I whispered, and he looked between me and the television, at the Asian man speaking.

If I could, I would have laughed.

"No. Down at the bottom of the feed, Ben Walton, the murderer, who tried to kill himself. That's him. That's my dad."

He understood me now. "My dad was a corn farmer before he became a Governor."

"Thank you," I said, as I wiped my eyes.

He wasn't making fun of me, he was simply trying to tell me he that didn't care.

"They say he killed Levi's ex-wife's mother."

From there it all just spilled out of me... everything from when I was a child, to my step father's alleged crimes, to that last moment with Levi, the moment where it felt like he had stabbed me through the heart with a smile.

. . .

LEVI

It was my third time walking past the office. She should have been in there, but she wasn't. I had seen all of my students with the exception of her... Three days; that was the last time I had seen her. Neither she nor her sister had answered any of my calls, and at this point, I didn't even know if she was okay.

"You can stop walking by, she isn't coming in today," Atticus said to me, with his tie over his shoulder as he changed the light bulb.

"So you've spoken to her?"

"Kind of hard not to, what with her crashing at my place and all... I'm already out of cereal," he replied, stepping down from the ladder.

I felt my hand curl into a fist just seeing the smug look on his face and I had to force myself to relax.

He was a student. He needed to learn to not be involved in my personal life.

"What is the percentage of cases that are plea bargained and settled outside of court?" I quizzed him as calmly as possible.

He straightened up quickly; "Less than five percent."

"And this from Levi Black and Associates?"

"Three—No. Three and a half times as many."

"Why?"

He paused trying to think.

Too slow.

"Because a great lawyer isn't afraid of court. Courts are your arena. This was a simple question, Mr. Logan, and not one you will be likely to come across again, especially on your final. You're slipping."

He nodded, and I could see him kicking himself.

Much better.

I only managed to get three feet away before I turned back. I just had to know, I had to ask. "How is she?"

"She is Thea," he replied, "and just so you know, I'm gay. She's the reason that I can tell you that... that I can tell anyone that now. So you don't have to worry about me being around her."

He didn't linger, he just moved on with his work.

"When you're done, Mr. Logan, she might need a friend to check up on her once she sees the news," I said, kicking myself as I walked away.

This is what she'd meant when she said that it was impossible for them to physically be together... his *orientation*...

"Don't even say it, Betty," I told the older woman who sat behind her desk. She pretended to zip her lips, but her eyes were talking... laughing actually.

In my office, I sat at my desk checking my watch.

"You have an hour until the story breaks," Tristan said, as he came in.

"I'm going to meet my mother and let her know in person before then. You coming?"

"To that slaughter? No thank you, I have over a thousand pages of case notes to look through. When will we start assigning people?"

"Tristan, they will try to bury us in paper work and red tape. Believe me when I say we are going to need every last person on this. Once this news breaks, we will feel a backlash like we've never felt before. You can still back out."

"O Captain! My Captain!" was his only reply.

"Wish me luck?"

"From the man who believes you make your own luck?"

Too bad I didn't feel like that man anymore.

THEA

"*Ladies and gentlemen good evening, tonight we have breaking news out of Boston Massachusetts, where top criminal attorney, Levi Black, has now taken on the case of convicted murderer, Ben Walton.*

"*Seventeen years ago, Ben Walton was charged with the kidnapping, rape and murder of Boston socialite Savannah Van Allen... A charge that Mr. Black now wishes to overturn. In a statement to KYLM, Mr. Black says, 'there is no doubt my mind that Ben Walton is an innocent man who did not receive a fair and just trial, as is his constitutional right. This is due to not only the blatant incompetence of the police, who did not follow basic protocol regarding the evidence, and but also his own legal representative. We are calling for a new trial and anyone who wants the truth and see due process done right should not be against this.'"*

My phone rang nonstop, but I just couldn't believe my ears as I listened to the radio. He was still going through with this?

"Hello?" I finally picked up the phone.

"Put the cereal down. Get out of your sweatpants, and get to the office now, this place is about to become a battlefield and it's time for you to serve. This is why you wanted to become a lawyer, right? This is your big moment, so don't be selfish and let your emotions get in the way of helping your dad. That *is* what you want, right?" Atticus yelled into the phone over the ruckus in the background.

"I'm not at your place. I needed to make a stop. I'll be there by in a few hours—"

"Thea, where in the hell could you be going that's more important than this?"

"I'm going to visit my father," I said, hanging up on him just as the police officer and his dog came up to my car window.

I gave him my pass, and he waved me through.

I could feel my heart slamming against my chest as I parked and got out. Over the last couple of months, I had written him over two dozen letters and had never heard anything back. I figured that he didn't want to see me... and I was too scared to go see him.

I had a vague image of the man that was once my father in my head, and I didn't want that image of him to be gone as well. Would he still smell like aftershave? Would he still eat purple skittles with me? It was dumb, and I knew I was holding on to false hope, but it was all I had left. I was being selfish though, not seeing him all these years because I didn't want to lose my happy memories.

"Who are you here to see ma'am?" the guard at the desk asked me.

"Ben Walton. I called."

"Some ID please?"

Handing him my driver's license, he scrolled down a white clipboard his shaking his head at me.

"I've got a Thea Walton on the list. No Cunning. The names have to match. He should have filled out a new visitors sheet for you, this one hasn't been updated in years."

Obviously he never expected me to come either.

"I have an old ID," I said as I opened my wallet and took out the old college ID; the school had messed up and put my old name on it. I had gotten a new one, but couldn't bring myself to throw it out. He took it held up to my face and then looked at my license.

"Step over there, we need to search you," he said, as he handed them back to me.

"Thank you," I replied, as I walked to where he pointed.

"Do you mind if I check for any foreign objects in your hair and on your person?" a woman asked when I stepped up.

She asked, but I don't think it was a question.

Nodding, I turned around. She patted a little hard but I didn't say anything. It felt like a never-ending line of checkpoints before I was finally taken to the visiting room. On TV, I had always seen the glass with the telephones on both sides, but in real life, it looked more like a cage.

The guard signaled for me to sit, and when I did, the door on the opposite side opened. I held my breath as he walked in, his hands, feet and waist chained. He was just as tall as I remembered, with skin as dark as mine, and grey hair. His faced looked hard, like he had taken so many hits to the face that it was almost stone.

I noticed the large white bandage wrapped around his neck, and the method of his suicide attempt became apparent. I held my breath, fighting against the surge of emotions that had welled up within me. He sat down, but they didn't unchain him.

"Who are you?" he asked as soon as he picked up the receiver.

His voice was deep and scratchy and his eyes looked me over emotionlessly.

Wiping a tear from my eye, I tried not to let it bother me. "It's me, Dad. Thea Bear? Remember?"

His eyes widened slightly, but he didn't speak.

"You've been getting my letters right? Selene's too?"

Again silence.

"You haven't written back so…"

"You shouldn't have come here," he said to me, as he hung up the phone.

I slammed my hand against the glass, causing the guards to come forward from their place at the doors.

"Sorry," I said to them quickly, and turned back to him. I motioned for him to pick up the phone again.

He cracked his jaw, as he once more picked up the receiver. "What do you want?"

"I came to see you, it took me two hours to get here—"

"I didn't ask you to."

"Well, you should have!" I snapped at him. "You should have asked us to come. You should have written us back. And you sure as hell shouldn't have done that to yourself. We are family—"

"We are *not* family. You do not know me."

"I know you didn't do it, and I know you are my father. I don't need to know anything else. I don't care about anything else. You're getting out of here."

He shook his head. "How much is this new lawyer costing you? I met him. He looked like something I can't afford. You're all wasting your time and money… I'm tellin' you they do not care. I've acce—"

"If you say 'accepted', I swear to God, I'll lose it. This isn't something you accept, and don't you dare say that to anyone here. Levi is different. This is different. If the money bothers you, then the moment you get out, we'll sue the state and then you can pay it all back. But right now I need you to tell me you didn't do it."

He leaned in. "So you don't believe me after all."

"I do believe you. I just need to know if there's any more fight in you. I'm here, I will walk the line, but I need to know that you're walking it with me, Dad."

He put his hand up against the glass as he looked at me. "I was prepared to die knowing in my soul that I didn't do anything wrong. That I would leave this world an innocent man. The appeals that failed didn't matter no more. Then you and you sister had to go and complicate everything with your letters. It was easier when you didn't speak to me."

"Just because something is easier, doesn't mean it's better. Now is there anything you can tell me that can help us? Please Dad, I need you to just try."

LEVI

"Get out!" she screamed, as tears ran down her face, "I have no idea what possessed you to do this, but until it's over, stay away from me."

"Mom, I know you're angry, but if this man—"

"If? If? You are putting this entire family, not to mention the Van Allen family, through this all over again, and you have the nerve to say 'if'?"

"Fine. He didn't do this, and he does not deserve to be behind bars. The person who killed Savannah does, but not him. How do you not see that? Especially with the way his case was handled!" I yelled back at her.

"Get him out of here," she yelled at my father. "Get him out or I will say something a mother shouldn't. Get him away from me."

"Don't bother, I'll see myself out. Whether you like it or not, I am going through with this case," I called out to her, but she wouldn't look at me.

She held her hands to her face and cried, and in that moment, I hated myself for putting her though this again.

Halfway out the door, my father called to me, "Levi, what are you doing?"

"Getting a man, my client, out of prison," I answered him.

"You've worked so hard all your life. I have seen you build up a career for yourself, and now you're about to blow it all up? No one will touch you after this. I just don't understand."

"An innocent man is in jail… if you don't understand that, I really don't have time to explain it to you," I said, already walking to my car.

LEVI

It had begun; the non-stop phone calls, the press gathering outside, the associates running around with their hair on fire. I needed something to tell them. I had gone over Ben Walton's case at least four times now, and I had never seen such stupidity in all my life. Evidence wasn't bagged, the scene wasn't closed off, and one of the witnesses went missing after her statement, and did not testify… it was just one big clusterfuck.

"Are you ready to give your speech?" Tristan asked, as he came into the conference room.

"Why do I need to give a speech? They're lawyers, and we are going to practice law, it's that simple," I said, even though I had just thought giving a speech.

"So, you have no idea?"

"Not even a little."

"You need a minute?"

"No, bring them in."

This was going to be a long night.

I didn't have to wait long; it seemed like they were all waiting for me to call them in. My associates sat around the dark oak table, while the students gathered near the back.

"Ben Walton, our new client," I said, as I glanced over them.

I placed a picture of Ben Walton and wrote his name on the large window that overlooked all of Boston. Then, I began my 'speech.'

"I was freshman in college when he was convicted. Which means most of you were in still in your preteens, but I'm sure if you've lived in the city, you know about the uproar that the death of Savannah Van Allen caused. As the story goes, Ben Walton kidnapped, raped and stabbed Mrs. Van Allen a total of fourteen times. She was later found in a motel room in Connecticut."

"Witnesses had placed Ben Walton outside of her home the day before, and his DNA was found at the scene of the crime. The case was spun to make Ben Walton seem like an infatuated stalker who preyed on Mrs. Van Allen."

"Makes sense," Raymond spoke up, as he loosened his tie, "but why was he there? Why was his DNA in the motel room?"

"Because they were having an affair," a voice called out from outside the office.

I would have recognized that voice anywhere.

As she walked into room, it felt like she was a whole foot taller. She took of her jacket and gloves, and dropped them onto the chair. She grabbed a folder off the table before making her way over to where I was.

"Is there any proof of that?" Vivian asked, as she rose her hand in the back.

"Yes. Me," she said. Then looking to me, "It's your case, but can I brief them?"

Could I deny her anything at this point?

Nodding, I handed her the marker and took a seat at the head of the table near Tristan.

"Ben Walton is my father," she said, causing them to whisper, as she drew a timeline connecting to the photo on the window.

"Unknown to many people, Ben Walton was once known as the fiction writer, Law Bonnet. He and my mother, Margaret Cunning, never formerly married—"

"Law Bonnet? The writer for the weekly Boston Noble Magazine, how is that possible?" Atticus cut in.

This was the first time that either of us had heard that bit of information.

"To avoid a scandal, the Boston Noble employed a ghost writer to take his place," she said, marking that date further down the timeline before walking back to the beginning.

"Each year the Boston Noble holds a large gala featuring anyone who had been on the cover. That year, Savannah Van Allen was not only on the cover twice, but she attended the gala. That was beginning of their six month affair."

She marked the date on the timeline and turned to look for Savannah's picture on the table. Finding it, I slid it over to her and she tacked it unto the timeline, "However this was never brought up or mentioned by either the prosecution or Ben Walton's own defense."

"Mistake on the line of the defense," I stated out loud, and the students in the back wrote it down quickly.

"On the weekend of Savannah Van Allen's murder, my father took me to the Woodstock Festival… most likely as cover for his affair."

"You were what, probably six or seven at the time? No offense, but that's a little young for you to be considered a credible witness or to provide him with a reliable alibi. Do you even remember that day? The prosecution will destroy you, and say that you either blacked out the memory of the murder, or that you were not aware when it was happening," Vivian pointed out, much to her credit.

It was valid point. Children were horrible witnesses.

"You're right," she said, without even flinching. "For the most part, that day is a blur to me. I remember going to the fair, and I remember seeing the lights on the bridge as we were going back home. However, I wasn't the only person there, so was Savannah Van Allen's daughter."

What? I sat up suddenly.

Taking a photo out of the folder she'd been carrying, she taped it up on to the window. Sure enough, there was my ex-wife, eleven, maybe twelve years old, posing for a picture with her mother at the fair.

"Where did you get this?" I whispered. *"How* did you get this?"

"It wasn't the most legal of means, but when I went to see my father, he told me that Savannah had brought her daughter for the same reason he did, as an alibi and a cover up for their affair. I no longer have the pictures of that day, but I figured she had to have kept something."

"So you hacked her computer?" Tristan asked her.

He sounded relieved that he could finally see how this case could come together.

"*I* didn't do anything, but like I said, not the most legal means," she replied, pointing to it. "The prosecution's whole case was built on the fact that my—that Ben Walton, was some kind of love-sick stalker. They painted a picture of a woman who was scared and was being held captive by a monster. But does she look that way to you? No one ever spoke to Odile Van Allen. People wanted someone to be convicted, and Ben Walton was the easiest choice."

Tristan leaned in behind me and whispered, "She sounds like she's pleading her case now."

"She is."

Everything she'd done and put herself through was for this.

"Why didn't your mother take this case then?" Raymond asked, "Or at the very least, she could have gotten someone to help with it if she didn't want her name to it."

I looked to her, waiting. If she wanted to do this she was going to have to pull out every damn skeleton out of her closet.

"Because she was spiteful. When I spoke to Ben Walton, he

says she had the evidence to prove that he was innocent, but when she realized it wasn't just an affair, that he'd planned to leave her for Savannah, she became jilted and destroyed the evidence."

"But she told you?" Atticus added pushing her.

"She told me that she wanted him to spend the rest of his life in jail," Thea said dryly. "She passed off the case to a public defendant she knew, and that was the last contact she ever had with him."

She turned to me, and I nodded as I stood up. "As most of you know, keeping a man out of prison is relatively easy. *Getting* a man out is a whole other ball game. And on top of that, this is a death row case. Prepare yourselves to be hit with every roadblock humanly possible. There is no way we can simply exonerate him, but that isn't what we're going after right now. What we need right now, is to get a retrial, and the only way to win this case is through social media and public pressure. We are throwing all of the case information out there."

"But won't that just make it easy for the prosecution to combat everything?" Thea asked me.

"It's the only way," Tristan answered. "If we try going legal route, we will be stuck for months, if not years, behind the legal tape."

Years sounded about right… they would out spend us, and bury us under a mountain of paperwork and technicalities.

"Besides, all the pieces of this are starting to come together… there is more proof out there, we just need to find it. But for now, we will make so much noise that they will have to take notice. You all are in a social media generation, it's your job start blogs, give interviews, tweet to every last celebrity who is against the death penalty, make the people take notice. We might even be granted a miracle and someone who still has photos of that fair may come forward with something we can use. We will be working out of the office, but also be prepared to go to Connecticut when the time comes—"

"Mr. Black," Betty interrupted me with panic in her voice, "your ex-wife, she's here."

"Weren't you married to Odile Van Allen?" Raymond asked with a frown.

A series of gasps echoed through the room.

"I'll be right there," I told Betty ignoring him. "Get to work people."

"Godspeed," Tristan said on my way out.

Yeah, I was going to need the grace of God to make it away from her clutches in one piece. My mother had nothing on the rage that she was going to throw at me. This morning I truly felt bad... I knew how much this tore her apart. We were younger, but she knew. She knew her mother was having an affair and she had said nothing.

No, she had to have said something, and no one listened.

Walking into my office she, with her long dark hair and hazel eyes, turned to me shaking.

"You fucking bastard!" she screamed, charging at me. "Do you hate me this much? I cheated on you, so now you are going to hurt me like this?! This is low, so low, it's disgusting, even for you! Why are you doing this? Why are you doing this?!"

Grabbing her fists, I held her steady. "He didn't do it. But you know that don't you? You were there. They were together. You know that."

"I have no idea what you're talking about. You—I don't even know who you are now!" she yelled, ripping herself away from me.

"That weekend your mother took you to the Woodstock fair—"

"I don't understand why you're doing this! I'm sorry I hurt you. I was way too young to get married—"

"Odile! Listen to me! You were at the Woodstock fair that weekend because your mother—"

"Don't you dare speak about her! You have no right to speak

about her! You knew her. She was a good person, she did not deserve to be murdered by that monster!"

"You were there," I said softly, trying to get through to her.

"I was at home with my older brother that weekend. We ate cherry flavored ice cream but it was horrible so I gave it to—"

"To me," Thea came in, her eyes wide as she stared at her.

She looked dazed, like she was half here, half in her mind.

"That day at the fair, I met you in front of the Ferris wheel. My dad was in line with your mom for ice cream. You didn't like yours, so you gave it to me. But I couldn't hold both mine and yours and I dropped it all over your stockings and shoes. I remember…"

"You're insane! I don't know you. I've never met you in my life. I would have remem—" She broke off suddenly and looked to me, "Is this why you're doing this? For her?" She snorted, "You've always liked your girls young, pretty, and broken. It makes you feel all manly inside when you save us." She turned to face Thea. "Be warned sweetheart, the moment you fix yourself, he will distance himself from you."

"*That* is the reason why we broke up, and the reason I'm on this case is because there is an innocent man on death row!"

"There are innocent men in prison, welcome to America, Levi! Why him! Why now? Save your self-righteous bullshit for someone else!"

"It is because of me," Thea said, "but that doesn't change the fact that my father did not kill your mother," Thea said, as she kept her head up.

"According to the law, he did, and I will make sure that he stays behind bars where he belongs. He's done enough to my family. You want a war Levi? I will bring it to you. Maybe you forgot who the Van Allen family are, but we will remind you." she spat as she pushed past me.

"You can't keep running from the truth Odile. You can't keep lying to yourself! Please." Thea shouted after her.

"Come near me again, and I will sue you for slander and anything else that I can think of. You're all insane!" Odile replied, walking away until she disappeared behind the wall.

When my eyes fell back on Thea, she was holding out an envelope to me.

"What's this—?"

"I can't expect you to do this for free."

She had to be kidding me with this. "I'm not accepting that."

"I knew you were going to say that, which is why I deposited the payment into the company account this afternoon. This is the receipt."

"Thea—"

"I need to get back to work," she said as she turned and walked out.

God damn it!

THEA

"*This* is just another example of the way blacks are treated in America today. How many Ben Walton's are there all over the country? How many trials have been completely butchered by the public defenders who just don't give a damn?!"

"Completely untrue; public defenders are overworked and underpaid, yes, this was by all means handled horribly by the state police and the media. The evidence should have been handled properly, and no information should have been leaked to media. But to say this is a race issue is wrong. People of all races and ethnicities are all locked up everyday—"

"Preach!" Atticus said, as he lifted his hand up to the sky, drawing my attention away from the debate that was going on most news stations now.

One week, that was all it took for this to become a firestorm issue. No matter what channel I flipped to, there was at least one segment on the Ben Walton case. Levi had an interview with KWNN coming up in the next few minutes, and it was going to be broadcasted globally.

"What? You think just because I'm a Democrat my views on

this would magically change?" he asked, when I sat back down at the conference table. "I *don't* think this is a race based case. I think anyone who had been involved in an affair with her would have suffered the same punishment."

He prepared himself for my comeback, but instead, I nodded my head, "I agree."

"You what?"

"I agree. All the evidence we have points to this being a series of disastrous events."

"The public defender is an alcoholic!" Vivian ran in waving a paper above her head. Tristan came up behind her, and took the paper out of her hands.

"How did you get this?"

"There wasn't much information about the public defender, so I thought I would go down to his office and see if he still worked there. He didn't. He was "let go" six months after the case. Since he wasn't officially fired, there was no write up. However, when he went looking for a new job, his former boss wrote a letter detailing his drunk stupors saying, '*that man* should not be allowed to practice law.'"

"Where is he is now?"

"He died five years ago due to an alcohol-related liver disease."

"How sad. But dead men can't refute evidence. They just gave you this letter?"

"The new boss apparently is sympathetic to this case. She only asks we do not make too many connections between their office and him."

"Keep this up, and we might have to save a spot for you when you graduate," Tristan said as he glanced up at us. "Do you two have anything useful to add, or are you going to keep braiding each other's hair?"

Luckily, we didn't have to answer that question. Levi came on the screen, and I hated the fact that his tie was slightly crooked, and I wanted to be the one to fix it. Its off-green color made his emerald green eyes stand out even more.

I want to touch him again.

Even with everything that was going on, and the fact that my life had changed overnight even more so than I ever would have thought possible, I still longed to touch him.

"Thank you for taking the time to speak to us Mr. Black."

"No, thank you for bring up this case. For so long we've only heard one side to it."

"So. Do you truly believe that Ben Walton is innocent?"

"I do."

"But you were married to Odile Van Allen, were you not? Why would you even consider taking on this case?"

"I was, and my marriage to Odile Van Allen has no bearing on this case. I understand that it must hurt her, but that was never my intention. People have been asking me why would I take this case and it confuses me. There is an innocent man on death row. I know that. I can prove that. I'm not demanding that the state release him, all I'm asking is that they revisit his case.

"The law states that the motion for a new trial can be sought if the correction of an injustice is needed, and when I look at Ben Walton's case, all I see is injustice. Whether or not that injustice has been inflicted upon him because he's black, I don't know, and I don't care... the fact remains; a grave injustice has been done and he is entitled to a legal defiance against the man who sat next to him; he was an alcoholic who was fired six months after Mr. Walton had been convicted. We have in our possession, a letter from his former employer, which states that he shouldn't have been allowed to practice law. To me, this is a perfect explanation as to why he couldn't challenge one single witness."

How did he know that? We'd only just found that information out ourselves!

"Text messages are great, aren't they?" Tristan kicked his feet up. "He's in full fighting form right now."

"If the state truly believes that he is guilty, then granting a new trial should not be a problem. We have tipped our hand. All of our cards on the table. With these types of mistakes, mistakes not even my students would have made, a man's life is on the line, so I ask you here today, how can you turn your eyes from such an injustice? Ben Walton had a life, two beautiful daughters, an amazing career as the chief writer and editor at the Boston Noble, under the pseudonym Law Bonnet—"

"*Law Bonnet was Ben Walton?*" The reporter said in shock.

Law Bonnet was the master of breaking news. He wrote about everything and one from presidents to politicians and called them out, to exposing headline stories. If you wanted to know what people were going to say on the news on Monday, you had to read Law Bonnet on Friday.

"Yes, and the moment Ben Walton was arrested, the Boston Noble hid all ties that connected them to him, and gave the name he had created for himself to a ghost writer. If this had been brought up in court, the Jury would have known that Savannah Van Allen was given not one, but two feature articles that year. The first one was offered to her, and the second one she personally requested. She knew him. She was involved with him. The more you pull on the string, the more evidence there is that falls out of the closet."

"I can't wait to read the Boston Noble in the morning," Atticus snickered to himself.

"They, and Levi Black, are already trending on Twitter," Vivian said as she scrolled through her phone. Looking around, I hadn't noticed how many people had come back into the room just to watch Levi on the screen.

There are people who are moved by the world, and then there were people who moved the world. Levi Black was the latter of the two. He just had that ability. He commanded respect, and people who listened to him would follow him anywhere... myself included.

Tristan stood, rereading whatever was on his phone before speaking. "I hope you all took notes, what he just did was force

Boston Noble to respond, and by doing so they make this case larger. Pack up and go home, we're done."

"What? How are we done?"

"Let me rephrase. Pack up, go home, kiss your partners, and get as much sleep as you possibly can. We've been granted a hearing and we will most likely get a retrial, and then, this stops being easy," he said as he walked out, leaving me speechless as I fell back into my seat.

This was only the first part of it, and already it had taken so much out of me. I needed to be stronger.

LEVI

Grabbing my guitar, I laid on my office couch mindlessly strumming the tightly wound strings. The day seemed to have passed by in a blur of camera lights, interviews and meetings.

"God, no," I groaned at my phone.

"Tough day?"

"Shut up."

Tristan placed a glass of water in front of me like that was supposed to do something for me tonight.

"Water? Seriously?"

"You have an even bigger day tomorrow," he said as he stretched and then collapsed onto my chair. "If you start drinking now, you may never stop."

He was a pain in the ass, but he knew me. "Look in the front pocket of my bag."

"Why?"

"Just do it." I kept on playing.

Reaching in, he pulled the small black card out. He stared at it for a while and dropped it on the table.

"Black, Knox and Associates? I'm finally getting my name on the door... a door that might not even be there when we finish this case."

"Have more confidence. Besides, it's the thought that counts."

"You swore never to be partners with anyone again... the last guy you were partners with slept with your wife."

"Thank you for the reminder, asshole. Luckily, you are married and in love with my *sister*. I trust you. You're a good lawyer, and you've always stood behind me even when I was standing on bullshit. I should have done this a long time ago."

He sighed, leaning back into his chair, "We better win this or I'm going to be pissed off as hell. Not to mention having to deal with you, if Thea never speaks to you again."

"I'm not doing this for her." I wasn't even sure if that was a lie anymore. Maybe I had spent so much time convincing others of my reasons that I was starting to convince myself. "This has become so much bigger than just her and I—"

"So what you're saying is, you won't go see her in the conference room?"

"What?" I sat up, and he grinned.

I pretended that I didn't care anymore and lay back down. I glanced at my watch.

1:00 a.m.

"Someone should tell her she doesn't get extra credit for being here at this ungodly hour," I said.

"I'm not her teacher," Tristan cracked.

"Odile told me that I purposely look for women who are broken and too young for me," I told him.

And when I thought about it she was right. So what did that say about the type of man I was?

"Bullshit."

"She has a point—"

"Sure, if you look at it from the dark and cloudy prescriptive of your psychotic ex-wife, but over here on our side of the rainbow, I can see just fine."

What the hell?

"I think you are trying to tell me something, but you're not speaking English."

He rolled his eyes, and leaned towards me, sitting on the very edge of his seat as though he was about to reveal a secret. "For as long as I've known you Levi, you've been attracted to strength. Whether it was cars, homes, cases, women… You don't look for broken people. Everyone is broken to some degree, we all got our own shit to deal with. The difference is how we handle them.

"You liked Odile because even after the death of her mother she stood with her head held high. She spent time volunteering, giving back to the community, studying. The same thing applies to Thea. With a mother like hers, there's no doubt in my mind that she's had one hell of a childhood. She then had to raise her sister. She's worked her ass off in one of the best schools into the country, and upon finding out her father was wrongly accused she didn't break down. She didn't give up. She instead said she wanted to be a lawyer. She is by far one of the strongest people I know, and there's no shame in being attracted to that. Why you've started to listen to the words of your ex-wife now, is beyond me."

"Tristan the wise…" I didn't know what else to say.

"You do know we are going to have to get Odile to testify. She knows something… she has too."

"The question is why isn't she telling us the truth?"

I'd thought about that over a thousand times, and I still didn't have a definitive idea. All I could think of were the worst-case scenarios.

"She could have been angry at her mother for breaking up their family," I said, throwing out the idea.

"She was what, eleven, or twelve? I can understand why she would have been angry, but now, as an adult, to allow a man to stay in prison, when she knows otherwise? She can't possibly have hated her that much."

"Alright, then she blocked it out. Didn't want to remember what had really happened, so she took what was in front of her, placed it in a box and locked it away. She doesn't want to go back to that, so she's pretending?"

He nodded, "Okay. Let's say it's that. She is not the first child to find out that one of her parents is having an affair. Again, Odile is emotionally mature enough to at least know that by now. I can see her telling her father off, or not speaking to her father, but for her to have blocked it all out like that? Things like that tend to happen only when severe trauma is involved…"

I paused, and so did he; our eyes met as we both arrived to the same obvious conclusion.

"The type of trauma that comes from seeing your mother murdered?" I finished for him.

"She saw what happened, but she wasn't killed either? If I was going to kill a socialite, and I knew that her daughter was nearby, I would either kill her child too, or use her for ransom," he stated.

"She knew the killer!" we both said at the same time.

"Or," Tristan paused looking me in the eye.

"Or?" I didn't follow his thoughts.

"Here me out, but what if she did it," he said slowly.

I had to let that sink in, but it just didn't compute for me. "Tristan, she was preteen."

"Exactly! Her mother was using her as a shield to have an affair. That must have set her off. We've seen kids much younger than her do the same thing, it is not that far-fetched. Her mother had cash on her that weekend. She could have changed her clothes, called a taxi, and headed home."

"Tristan she would have to be a sociopath."

He looked at me, not saying anything else.

"Either way," I paused, sickened by the thought of it, "you're going to have to talk to her. She won't listen to a word that comes out of my mouth."

Right now she hated me more than anyone else in the world…

"All of this is useless until we're granted a retrial. I'm going to head home and actually see my wife," he rose up and looked back at me, "When you see Thea, please don't do *it* in the conference room, we still have to work in there."

"I'm not going to see her."

"Sure, and a starving man won't eat if a banquet is laid out before him. I'll see you in a few hours."

He left.

1:15 a.m.

She needs space.

1:32 a.m.

Plus, everything is complicated. I'm her father's lawyer now. But then again, when aren't we complicated?

1:46 a.m.

She better not be here still.

1:57 a.m.

She couldn't still be here.

I got up and placed my guitar down against the chair. Walking out of my office, I could see the light of the conference room on. With each step, I felt my chest tighten and my ears began to ring. I could only see this going badly, and yet, I kept walking until I was almost at the door.

Her back was to me as she stared at the time line on the window. We had filled it in a lot in the past week with pictures and notes. Pretty soon we would no longer be able to see the cityscape that lay behind it.

"Urgh!" she groaned, placing her hands on her head looking from one end to the other and back again.

"Go home," I said, and she jumped.

She didn't turn around.

"As your professor, and the head of this case, go home. You aren't any good to me if you're sleep deprived."

"You're one to talk," she said as she finally looked to me. "I'm just a lowly student. You're the head lawyer, and as the daughter of your client I think you should be getting sleep."

"One moment you're the daughter of a client, next you're

lawyer, or a student, or my girl—my lover. You're a woman with too many damn personas, I can't keep up."

"I am the daughter of a client, a lawyer and a student. I was *once* your girl—your lover. And now, I'm leaving. Goodnight."

She stepped into her shoes and turned to grab her coat, gloves and scarf. But when she came to the doorway, I put my arm out, so that I could block her path and prevent her from leaving.

"Levi, move."

"I can't," I said honestly. "I'm here now because I hate being home without you—"

"Levi, please, don't—"

"You came into my house, drank my wine, and said you were in. You said you were in, and that you were done running. That we were grown-ups. Then, you turned around and took it all back. You left me, and I'm supposed to just sit here and accept that?"

She turned, not meeting my eyes. "You are. Because you did this. You lied to me."

"Then punish me in some other way," I said as I stepped in front of her and forced her to look at me. "I lied, yes. I wasn't sure what to think about the entire situation, and all I knew was that I wanted you. I still want you... and I know that you still want me—"

"Don't speak for me. You don't know what I want."

I kissed her. I kissed her hard, grabbing onto her waist I picked her up... and she kissed me back.

With a sigh, her jaw relaxed and her mouth slowly opened for me.

"When will you realize that what your heart says, and what your mouth says are two entirely different things?" I said as I barely broke away from her.

"I should be the one to decide that."

I kissed her again, biting her bottom lip.

"You are. Each time you kiss me back or stay in my arms or

you look at me with those eyes of yours… you're making the decision to be here. So go through with it; be here in this moment with me Thea."

"Levi, I can't think when you're this close to me," she tried to pull away.

"That's your problem. For once, stop over thinking things, just be here with me," I repeated, as I kissed her forehead, her cheeks, and her nose, then finally her lips.

I didn't kiss her as hard as before. I wanted to see if she would push me away, if she truly wanted this to end. But she didn't. Even as I pushed her back onto the table and ripped her shirt apart, she didn't push me away.

Instead, she pulled me in and her hands slid from my neck to my pants where her nimble fingers unbuckled my belt. I slid my hands along her stocking clad thighs, and I yanked on them until the light, delicate material tore apart in my hands.

"Damn it Levi—ah!" she moaned as I sucked on her neck. She was shaking, and so was I… it had been far too long since we were last like this. Tugging down her bra, I grabbed a hold of her, squeezing both of her nipples.

She leaned back on the table, resting on her elbows as I licked from her neck to her chest.

"Levi," she shivered, "please don't play with me."

I smiled, as my hand travelled between her legs and stopped at her sweet spot. "So what you're saying is, you want me to fuck you… now?"

She didn't speak. Her hand grabbed unto mine, trying to force me to go faster but I wouldn't.

"Levi…"

"Say it. Say you want me to fuck you and I won't stop until you scream my name over and over again."

She bit her lips, her mouth slightly parted, but she didn't speak. Adding another finger I quickened my pace and I watched as her eyes rolled back before I stopped again.

"Goddamn it, Levi!"

"Say it!" I hissed. I couldn't take much more of this. The mere sight of her made me so hard it was painful.

"Fuck me, damn it!"

Thank god.

Releasing my grip on her, I spread her legs wider. I pressed the tip of my head against her and thrust forward.

"Oh... my... God," her voice shook.

All that that came out of my mouth were grunts.

Her moans, her nails digging into me, how tight she felt around me. Laying her out on the table, I fucked her. There was no other word for it, with one hand on her waist and the other in her hair, I held on to her, I used her body as leverage to angle myself, and I slammed into her so hard that the table beneath us began to shift.

"Levi... I... I...!"

I crushed my lips against her mouth and our tongues ran over each other. Her hands grabbed on to my ass pulling me to her.

"Fuck!" she gasped, as she reached her limits, but I wasn't there yet. Lifting her legs onto my shoulders, I went faster, harder... so fucking hard. I couldn't hold back.

"Fuck," I hissed, coming much sooner than I wanted to.

Kissing the space between her breasts, I wrapped my arms around her and pulled her to me.

"Why do I have no self-control when it comes to you?" she whispered.

"Probably for the same reason that I've become so addicted to you."

I'm in love with you.

28

THEA

I was sore and nervous. On the drive into Connecticut, I almost had to pull over twice. I sat in the courtroom, trying my best to remain as still as possible as we waited for the judge to come back. It was enough to drive me crazy. We had been waiting for an hour already. Levi sat next to Tristan at the defense table, and both of them looked as relaxed as humanly possible. I just couldn't understand how they could do it. If we failed here, there would be no appeal, and most likely my father would die in prison. But what could we appeal with? We had already presented all the evidence to the judge. This was it. All the reasons for a new trial had been stated, and they were good reasons… right? Would they be enough? Maybe I should talk to them?

"Everything's going to be fine. They were amazing up there. And one day, we will be too," Vivian whispered, taking a seat next to me in the back.

"Thanks," I said slowly, surprised by the fact that she was talking to me now.

She clasped her hands together. "I quit my job… my *other* job."

I was surprised that she still had time for her *other* job. "That's great."

"I just wanted you to know... and I wanted to say... I wanted to say that I'm sorry. For everything that's happened, and for what I said to you. I'm sorry. You're good lawyer and your personal life shouldn't have been judged; least of all by me. So, I'm sorry."

"That's a lot of sorries in one sentence," I said as I took her hand in my own and squeezed it lightly. "Thank you though, because right now, I feel like I'm going to be sick."

"*Eventually* justice will be served."

"All rise," the bailiff said, and we all stood.

As the judge entered, I tightened my grip on Vivian's hand. I wasn't sure if her other hand on my shoulder was there to comfort me or to free herself from my vice grip. Either way, she didn't say anything. My stomach was like a vast pit of butterflies, and everything in me, my heart, and my mind, were getting sucked in.

"I have looked over this case carefully, and although I do agree with the defense on the troubling extent to which Ben Walton's case was handled I cannot, in good conscience demean a new trial, further adding to the Van Allens' suffering. Therefore, Mr. Black, your motion for a new trial is denied."

He slammed his gavel against its wooden counterpart, and just like that, he was gone.

Denied.

That means no.

That means everything we had done was a waste. It's over, we lose.

We've lost.

"Thea!"

Vivian caught hold of me as I collapsed backwards and into the chair.

I couldn't feel any part of my body any more. Everything hurt on the inside, it was as though my lungs were filling up with water and I was slowly suffocating. My vision was tunneling. I heard people clapping, like this was something to be happy about. This wasn't justice. Justice was an illusion. Hope only caused more pain, and right now, I could no longer move.

We were supposed to win.

Our evidence was good, everything was working in our favor. We had the newspapers, media outlets, activist groups, everyone was behind us, pushing us forward, rooting us on and yet still, we had lost. We lost in with three sentences.

"This isn't over."

I don't know why, but in that brief moment, it didn't feel like I was falling. Turning to him, I hadn't even realized that I was crying until he wiped my tears away.

"Don't give up on this. This is just a setback, albeit a big one, but we can—"

"Thank you Levi." My voice cracked, but I went on anyways. "Thank you for everything you've done for me. But can I get a moment alone? I'll be right out, but I just need a moment."

He looked torn, but he grabbed his things and left. The whole place was empty and I wept. With my hands over my mouth, I wept.

It was only when my throat went dry, and my eyes were swollen, that I stopped. Just like I was when I was younger, I wiped my face with the back of my hands and I reached into my bag for my little bottle of eye drops. Then, I stood up, brushed off my clothes, and walked out of the courtroom, only to see the back of Levi's head as he spoke to the press. I didn't want to see either of them now, not like this.

However, as turned to walk down the stairs, I noticed someone coming up them, towards me. His eyes were dark, almost black, and he glared directly at Levi, enraged. He reached into his jacket and once again my stomach dropped, my ears burned and my heartbeat fastened. It felt as though time itself had slowed down. Everything fell out of my arms as I ran towards him. He looked at me like I was insane and mouthed something, but I couldn't hear anything over deafening explosion of the shot…

BANG

It rang in my ears, then the pain came, and I wasn't running any more.

"Thea! Thea!" Levi screamed down at me.

His eyes were so wide, they looked like they were going to fall out of his head.

Why was it, that no matter how dark everything was becoming, he could give me such clarity? He was like this never ending candle in perpetually dark room.

"Thea! Thea! Say something! Thea!!"

The lights dimmed, then went out.

TRISTAN

"Today, on the front steps of the Connecticut state house, twenty-three year old Thea Cunning, daughter of the recently deceased, legal maverick, Margaret Cunning, and the infamous criminal, Ben Walton, was shot.

"Police were able to capture and detain the shooter. This news comes on the heels of the shocking ruling by Judge Thomas, who denied Mr. Black and his client, Mr. Walton, the right to a new trial, leading many to speculate that this was attempt to silence the young Ms. Cunning and her attempts to free her father. Doctors say her condition is critical—"

Turning down the radio, I tried to get that scene out of my mind. It had all happened so quickly that my hand was still shaking.

One moment Levi and I were sitting in the courtroom, shocked by the judge's ruling, and the next, we were outside speaking to the mob of reporters, trying our best to make sense of what had just happened when out of nowhere, Thea screamed out for Levi, running—no, *jumping* in front of the bullet like she was getting a fucking hug instead.

She flew. I swear to God almighty, she flew when the bullet hit her. She flew back into Levi's arms, and all he could do was stare down at her with a frown, as though he didn't understand what he was seeing, while everyone else ran for cover. He, like a statue, knelt, staring as her blood poured out of her and onto him. Then, the reality of the situation must have caught up to him because he started to shake and scream her name.

His pressed his hands to her stomach, trying to stop her from bleeding out. He called out to her, but she didn't speak. Apparently I had called the police, but I don't remember doing it. Just the sight of Levi, in tears, on his hands and knees with the woman he loved bleeding out in front the court building. The image would be with me forever.

"How is he? How is she? What is going on? Where do we need to go?" Bethan ran out of the house when I got home.

Her parents held on to Bellamy, and I walked to them, taking my daughter out of their hands and pulling her into a hug.

"Tristan," Bethan sobbed, and I pulled her into my arms as well.

They were safe. They were okay… as they should have been, but I just needed to see it… to feel it.

"What happened? We've been trying to contact Levi, but his phone is off. There was a gunshot, and then all cameras turned off," his mother said, as she came up to me.

For some reason the sight of her made me angry… maybe I was angry at the world, but right now, Mrs. Black was the focus of my rage.

"You left him," I said as I handed Bellamy back to Bethan. "He was going up against the world. He told you the truth, he went out to seek justice for *your* friend who was murdered, and to free a man who's been in jail for almost twenty years for a crime he did not commit. And you left him, you both left him out in the cold!

"That family, the Van Allen's that you care so dearly for, I think they just tried to kill your son, and the twenty-three year old who found out ten minutes before that her father was likely going to spend the rest of his life in jail for a crime he never committed, leapt in front of him and took the fucking bullet. Keep turning your face from the shit but that doesn't stop you from smelling bad at the end of the day now does it?"

They looked stunned, but then again, who would dare raise their voice against the Blacks?

"Tristan," Bethan whispered, grabbing on to my sleeve and lightly bouncing Bellamy as she cried, "let's go, we should be at the hospital."

"You go. But be careful. I'm going to go talk to someone," I kissed her and Bellamy's foreheads before walking back to my car.

"Should we go? Should we go too? Will he want us there?" Mr. Black called out to me, and in my bitterness, I turned and shrugged.

"Do whatever you want, Mr. Black, it's what you people do best."

I got into my car, slamming the door as I drove off.

I wasn't done. I had left him alone in the hospital because one: he, in a brief moment of clarity asked for my help, and two: because I needed to see my family. No matter what happened today, he wasn't going to leave her side...

'Thea. Thea! No... please no. Come on—"

I shuddered at the memory in my head; his screams kept repeating, as if he was the one who was dying. Levi rarely asked me to do anything for him. So this I would do. I owed it to him.

Parking across the street, I got out of my car and noticed that the maids were all busy dragging an assortment of bags down to a waiting car.

Odile came out last, with her newborn child strapped into his car seat. Her brown hair was pulled up into a messy bun, and she was dressed in a pair of jeans with sneakers. In all the time that I had known Odile Van Allen, she never wore sneakers outside of the gym.

Leaning against her car, I folded my arms across my chest and waited for her to notice me. When she did, she looked away, pretending as though I wasn't there.

"Levi said when you left the office that day you all but swore to him that the Van Allen's would not take this sitting down. So we waited for the other shoe to drop. We waited and waited but no shoe. Not even a statement out of any of you."

"Go away Tristan," she snapped, trying to put her child in the back seat.

"Then today, in court, a judge took a longer than usual time to deliberate... almost like he *wanted* us all to believe he was truly thinking then matter over. But come on, Judge Thomas? A good lawyer knows the law. A great lawyer knows the judge and I know Judge Thomas. We both do, he was born right here in Boston, and he used to donate to all the Van Allen charities. The man is a quick thinker and an even quicker judge. So tell me Odile, what did you offer him?"

"I did nothing! The loss of your case was by your own doing—"

"Then a man tries to murder Levi. But I know him too. Or at least I thought I did. He used to work on your father's summerhouse as the groundskeeper. I thought I was going crazy, because the Odile I used to know wouldn't try to commit murder."

"Read. My. Lips. I didn't do anything!" she shouted, at me slamming the door to her car before walking over to the driver's side.

"I'm reading them but they're lying to me! What about your father Odile?" I asked, and she stopped. "Since this case started, your father has been in New York, right?"

"Yes," she composed herself

"Are you covering for him again?" I asked as I stepped between her and the driver's door, preventing her from going anywhere.

"Excuse me—"

"I'll skip to the end, since you seem to be in a hurry to leave town. You're covering for him now like you covered for him when he killed your mother—"

"He did not—"

"Now how many times did he make you repeat that chant?" I asked as I walked around the car. "You told him about the affair, didn't you? You called him while you and your mother were at the Woodstock fair, and told him. You told him that your mother was there with someone else—"

"Shut up Tristan! You have no idea what you're talking about!"

"And when he got there, he killed her. Stabbed her... what was it? Fourteen times? That sounds like a crime of passion to me."

"No you're wrong—"

"Who else would you be covering for? Why keep lying for him? He tried to kill Levi today. Your father is a murderer Odile, and you are letting him go!"

"No! It wasn't him! It was—" She froze, her eyes wide.

"Who was it then?"

She walked around me, heading to her son's side as he cried.

"Tristan, leave it alone. Please, just leave all of this alone. Everything was fine—"

"Everything was not fine!" I yelled once more.

She flinched, then began rocking her son back and forth as his crying intensified at my outburst.

Taking a deep breath I tried to calm myself. "If you're scared—"

"I'm not scared," she lied, shaking her head.

"Then say the truth. You are *not* fine. With this hanging over your head and in your heart, nothing is *fine*. Your mother was in love with Ben Walton. Doing this is not what she would have wanted. You lying for the rest of your life to everyone, to yourself, it isn't want she would have wanted."

"Then she shouldn't have embarrassed us like that!" she spat at me. "Right in the open, she was cheating on our father. She wanted to use me as her cover so that she could sleep with him! It's her fault. This is all her fault."

It sounded like she was trying to convince herself.

Wait.

"Embarrassed *us*. *Our* father. You're speaking about two people. Your brother, you called your brother. Cole was what, eighteen? Nineteen? You didn't want to tell your dad, so you called your brother."

Everything was starting to form in my mind.

She didn't answer.

"What happened that night in the motel room Odile?"

She shook her head as she wiped her tears away—."This was done. It was over. Why did you have to bring it—"

"Because this isn't right. You know that. This is blackening you soul. Your smile used to light up rooms, and now you're a walking pit. The brother you think you are protecting is slowly killing you, and you won't be the only one to suffer. That child in your arms, he will suffer worse than anyone, because he will never understand why you are the way you are. Why you will hurt him because you are hurting yourself. So please Odile, tell me, what happened."

She swallowed, still trying to wipe away her tears and with a choked sob, she began.

"She took me to that stupid fair. She said it was just going to be us that weekend, just the girls. But then *he* came, and she thought that I was stupid, that she could just force me to be friends with his daughter, and I wouldn't notice what was going on.

"I was mad at her, and when I saw the pregnancy test in the bathroom that night, I just couldn't take it anymore so I called Cole. I told him everything and he told me not to move, that he would be there soon. I stared at her and I realized that I hated her; I couldn't stand the sight of her, so I went to sit outside. It was cold and she kept telling me to come in, but I told her to leave me alone. Finally Cole arrived, and he told me to stay in the car… I…"

She covered her mouth and finally looked to me. "She screamed once. That was all I heard, but it took Cole so long to come out again, and when he did, he had changed. He threw away the trash, and got into the car with me.

"The whole way home he said how we were a family—we were the Van Allens. He called her a disgrace, and told me what to say. But I didn't realize he had killed her until she was on the news. Everything happened so fast and he said no one was going to talk to me. He told me to stay away, so I did. No one came—"

"You have to testify to this Odile."

She shook her head. "I can't. I just can't. They will crucify me. Everything will fall apart. I can't."

"I'll help you. I will do everything in my power to protect you. But you need to testify because hearing it from you is much better than hearing it from a tape."

I reached into my front pocket and pulled out my phone.

Just like that, she broke down, and I pulled both her, and her crying son, into my arms.

LEVI

"Levi!" Selene yelled as she ran towards me.

I had just called her, didn't I? How did she get here so fast?

Looking up at the clock, I realized that four hours had somehow slipped by. It had taken me some time after... after it had happened to call her. But she was the only person who I knew Thea needed most.

"Have they said anything? Do we know anything? We couldn't get an immediate flight out and they kept saying that she was in critical condition. And—"

"Breathe," a teenage boy, about seventeen or eighteen, said. He had dark brown skin and black eyes. He placed his hand on her back and rubbed it soothingly. I hadn't noticed him until now.

"I'm sure she's fine—"

"She was shot! She is not fine! I don't understand!" I cried.

Never in my whole life had I felt as useless as I did today. I was failing everyone and everything.

"I haven't heard anything yet," I said to her, which only made her cry more.

In the four hours that had passed, I had heard nothing.

"Selene?"

She broke away, wiping her eyes and turned to face a worried, older woman who was making her way towards us with the aid of a cane. She was short, with white hair and dark wrinkled skin. Though she was two generations above, there was no mistaking the resemblance. This was Grandma Cunning.

"No word yet," Selene said and the woman looked to me. "Grams this is Levi Black. He's not just dad's lawyer—"

"Selene, it's fine. It's nice to finally meet you, ma'am."

I extended my hand towards her but she just stared at it and then back to me.

"So you're the one who's dating my granddaughter?"

"N—" I began, but Selene elbowed me.

"Yes. Yes I am."

I couldn't deny how good it sounded to say it out loud.

She nodded, finally shaking my hand and taking a seat.

"Can I get you anything?"

"Don't go outta your way for me son, just sit," she said as she took a deep breath. "You saw it didn't you? You were there."

I didn't want to talk about it. I was trying to block it out. I made no reply.

"You took this case for her?"

"Yes," I told her. There was no point in lying now. "But she made me believe."

She smiled, "Yes. She's a passionate one."

"I know."

"You take a case on for her? So she takes a bullet for you?"

I sat up, blinking as I thought about it. Her on the ground, staring up at me, trying to speak, but before she could her eyes had slipped shut. I thought she had died. Right in front of me, with my hand on her stomach, trying to stop the bleeding. I thought she had died, and I wanted to die alongside of her.

No.

Sniffling, I wiped the corner of my eye and sat back in my chair.

"I don't mean to chastise you, Thea does what she wants. It wasn't your fault. But when she wakes up, you'd better knock some sense into her." She paused and placed her hand over her mouth, and I took her other hand into my own. "You better tell her she can't be jumpin' in front of no bullets just because she's in love with someone. I would yell at her myself, but I know I will end up crying right in the middle of it."

"That would make her feel worse. You should do it." I forced a laugh. "She's going to be fine."

Why didn't I believe myself?

"You better not pull any stunt like this, either of you. You're always following her lead," she pointed to the couple in front of us.

Selene nodded, as she lay her head against her boyfriend's chest.

"I won't let her," he said to their grandmother, and she nodded.

When the doctor came out, none other than Dr. Sharpay London, she looked over us all. Her eyes fell on me in shock, before she smiled knowingly. "Are you all Thea Cunning's family?"

"Yes," her grandmother answered as I helped her up.

"The bullet struck her liver, causing her to go into hypovolemic shock due to the loss of blood, which in turn caused her heart to give out. But she's in a stable condition now and is currently asleep. She will make it." She smiled. "A nurse will take you in to see her soon."

"Thank god," Her grandmother said and I looked towards

Sharpay. She smiled and nodded before she turned and walked back down the hall.

Taking a deep breath, I fell back onto the chair.

She was going to be fine.

THEA

"Urgh," I groaned as I tried to force my eyes open. It was a lot harder than normal, and when I did, all I felt was pain.

What the hell had happened to me?

My eyes adjusted, and as I looked around, I noticed the IV drip in my arm and the heart rate monitor that stood beeping next to my bed.

"What?"

I tried to move my hands, but looking down, I saw that Levi was there holding it. He was asleep, and dressed in a pair of scrubs. His hair was messy, and he had a thick layer of stubble under his chin. He looked beat down.

"You're awake," Selene smiled, as she came in with a pot of flowers.

She was wearing color! Not a single black item on her…

"What happened?"

"You thought you were superman, and threw yourself in front of a bullet," she snapped at me, as she put the flowers down to give me a hug. "Don't scare me like that. Grams is so angry with you."

"I'm sorry," I said, as my memories began flooding back to me.

She let go, and when she moved I noticed that Levi was now awake and sitting upright. He had a smile on his face with his arms crossed, half of his face was slightly red from sleeping on it, but I couldn't care less. He just kept smiling at me and as he stood up, I took his hand and squeezed it tightly.

"I'll give you guys a moment before I call Grams," Selene said, as she kissed my cheek and left.

She looked so different now, like she had grown up overnight.

"Are you alright? The pain, I mean?" He sat beside me.

His caressed my cheek with the back of his hand and I found myself so overwhelmed with emotion that I couldn't speak, I just nodded.

"Good, because I'm livid with you Thea Cunning. How could you be so stupid? How could you do that?"

He kissed my forehead before cupping my cheek. I was trapped in his green eyes, unable to move.

"I thought you were dead," he whispered, as a tear dropped from his face onto mine.

Reaching up, I wiped them away. "I'm sorry—no, that's a lie. I wasn't really thinking. I saw him moving towards you, I saw his intent and I just... But I'm glad I did. I'm glad I ran forward. You're always saving—"

"That is never the way I want you to save me, especially because you feel indebted to me."

"I don't," I said. Looking into his eyes I don't know why I didn't say it before. "I did it because I loved you... because I love you. I'd rather die than lose anyone I love."

The corners of his lips twitched and turned upwards, but he fought it. "You can't say that now. I still have a whole speech—"

"Later, Professor." I kissed him.

He kissed me softly... softer than any kiss we'd ever had before. It was as delicate as a first kiss, and all too soon he broke away.

"If you think you're running away from me now, then we should get your head checked too," he whispered, brushing back my hair.

I grinned. "Oh you have no idea what you're getting yourself into. I now have the *I-literally-took-a-bullet-for-you* card."

"Well I have the *I-helped-your-dad-get-out-of-prison* card," he said as he got up, and for a moment my heart rated quickened as I stared at the door.

Instead of my father, it was Selene, my Grams and another boy that I had never met before, who was holding on to Selene's hand.

"I don't understand," I told them as my Grandmother walked over to me and took my hand. She kissed it with a large smile on her old face.

"Just watch," she replied as Levi turned on the television.

The screen flickered once before turning on. Levi flipped through the channels and finally, there stood Tristan, making his way on to the screen and standing before a podium. The ticker underneath him read: *Odile Van Allen's SHOCKING confession.*

She sat behind the microphone, as beautiful and as regal as ever, with her head held high as she addressed the audience before her— "My name is Odile Van Allen, when I was twelve, my mother was murdered in a motel room in Woodstock, Connecticut. Her case made national headlines and our family was given an overwhelming amount of support from all of you... support that we didn't deserve.

"I was there when she went to go see her lover Ben Walton. She wasn't kidnapped, we drove there. And she wasn't raped, she loved him openly. The truth of the matter is that she was not murdered by Ben Walton.

"Her killer was my brother, Cole Van Allen, who I had called to come get me that night. For seventeen years, I've held my tongue and allowed an innocent man to pay the price for my brother's sins. And after seeing Cole's actions once again today in the attempted murder of Levi Black, I realized how far this has gone, and I feel that I can no longer lie for him.

"To Ben Walton's family, I'm so sorry for all the pain we have caused you and the rift we have left in your homes. Though my words mean nothing at this point, I will say it again for all of you to hear; Ben Walton is an innocent man and I urge the six court of Connecticut to free him."

"What?" I cried wiping my face, "I... why? How did you—?"

"Breathe," Levi whispered taking my hand, "it's over."

It's over.

"Oh my god!" I shrieked, as I latched on to him and cried.

It was finally over.

29

THEA

"We're late," I looked at my watch as Levi helped me into the wheelchair. It was the only way my doctor was willing to let me out for the day.

"Stupid press, now everyone wants to get a bloody picture," Selene mumbled, but I was more shocked at the bright yellow dress she wore, and how styled her hair was. At least one of us didn't look like a total mess.

Reaching up, I took her hand. "You look pretty. I'm sure he will think so too."

"I know I do," her boyfriend said.

Laughing, she smacked his arm and he wrapped himself around her waist. I couldn't help but stare at them being all lovey-dovey while we stood outside a prison. They were in their own little blissful world.

"You're glaring," Levi said as he knelt down beside me, making me feel like he was talking to a child or something. "It's hard watching little sisters rely on other people."

"I know, and what's worse is that I like him," I pouted.

He snickered as he wheeled me to the front of the building.

DeShawn White was about the same height as Levi. He was on both the basketball team, as well as the football team. In the spring, he played baseball simply because he enjoyed being active and he wanted to stay in shape year round. On the top of that, he was an honor roll student, whose top choice was Georgetown.

He treated Selene… well he treated Selene like Levi treated me, like all people should treat the ones they're with; like they were the most important person in the world.

"I'll be back," Levi said, and he softly squeezed my hand before he walked over to the press.

"Ladies and gentlemen, today is a profound day, because not only does a man get his life back, but he gets his family back as well. There are a lot of legal aspects to this case that need to be examined, but now is not the time nor the place for such a discussion. All your questions will be answered at a later date because all that matters right now is Ben Walton and his family. Thank you."

He backed away from them, and the police that were there kept them at bay. However it didn't stop them from hurling their questions my way.

"Ms. Cunning, how are you feeling?"

"Do you have any words for Odile Van Allen?"

"Will you be suing the state?"

"I just want to see my father," I replied to them, and Levi turned me towards the exit.

I sat up when the doors opened. I wanted to clap and cheer, but all I could do was watch as he got closer and closer to us. Until, there he was, chain free, in jeans and basic grey shirt. Even his hair was cut.

"Hi," he said to us, and Selene ran up to him, pulling him into a big hug.

He shook Levi's hand, and accepted all the cheers until his eyes fell on me.

"Hey Daddy," I managed to mumble.

He dropped his things, came over to me and hugged me tightly. "Thank you so much Thea Bear. Thank you for not giving up on me."

I looked up to the sky trying to keep my tears from overflowing, but I laughed at what I saw.

"Look up Daddy. Look at the rainbow."

PART THREE

FUTURE

EPILOGUE

LEVI

I had just washed the shampoo out of my hair when she pulled the curtains open.

"Hi," I said, a little stunned as the shower ran on.

"Why haven't you asked me to marry you?" she demanded, folding her arms over her chest. "It's been three years. Is this the whole milk-cow analogy? Because right now, I'm at a loss—"

Taking her by the hand, I pulled her into the shower with me, then closed the shower curtains.

"It was getting cold," I said simply, as I continued to rinse my hair.

"My hair, my clothes…" She glared at me. Her whole body was drenched, and her clothes clung to her.

I grinned. "You look hot."

"Fine." She stripped off her clothes and threw them outside the shower where they fell to the floor with a wet *plop*.

"Now you're just playing with fire," I said, as I pinned her up against the wall and kissed her.

She kissed me back, forgetting herself and her purpose for a brief moment. Then she stepped back and pressed her fingertips against my lips.

"I'm serious Levi, why haven't you asked me to marry you?"

"You've never brought up marriage once before. It took you months *and* a bullet to get you to finally admit that you loved me."

"I say it now!" She frowned at me.

I tried to kiss her again, but she wouldn't let me.

"You are twenty-six years old. You have a good ten years before you should be freaking out about marriage."

"What about you?"

"I'm a guy."

"Sexiest!"

"*Trustiest*."

That wasn't even a real word.

She rolled her eyes at me.

"Urgh! I can't talk to you like this." She climbed out of the shower. "I have no idea how we are going to have a child, when you're still one yourself!"

"Whatever—" I said, turning back to the shower.

Then I paused, as her last statement echoed through my mind.

"Wait, what?"

Grabbing a towel, I jumped out of the shower and dashed into our room where she was angrily yanking drawers open and slamming them shut.

"What did you say?"

"I called you a child, now if you'll excuse me, I need to get ready for our dinner."

She tried to go into the closet, but I followed her in. Grabbing one of my sneakers, I pulled out the small teal box and placed it in her hand.

"I bought you this a month after we got your father out of jail... with his blessings, as well as blessings from your sister, and your Grams.

"I told them that I was going to wait until you graduated

because I didn't want you to feel pressured, and I didn't want you to try planning our wedding while you were still in school. But most of all, I wanted to make sure that when we got married, it was something you truly wanted. So I told myself to wait, you were with me, you were alive, and I could wait."

She opened the box and a wide grin spread across her face as she stared at the teardrop shaped diamond.

"Now, would you like me to tell you how I had planned to propose, or are you going to tell me what it was that you just said?"

"This a good ring," she said, changing the subject.

"It's your *dream* ring. I spoke to Selene about it before I bought it. Now, out with it."

"Don't look at me like that! I've been dropping hints all week!"

"No you haven't."

She looked at me like I was insane.

"Levi there are baby books in your study!"

What, those? Those were her hints?

"I thought you were researching an infancy related case."

"Who thinks that?" She shook her head and threw her arms up into the air.

"I don't know, lawyers?"

"And the baby themed food I made last night?"

That was weird.

"Or the fact that I spelled out the word twice each time we played Scrabble? The bun I put in the actual oven! You missed it all? Some master thinker you are!" She snorted.

She wasn't even angry, she was just laughing at my oblivion, and at this point, so was I.

"Our course load at work has tripled in the last three years. This month has been crazy, honestly, I didn't notice."

Again, she crossed her arms at me, turning around. Hugging her from behind, I kissed the back of her head. "I'm sorry. But with stuff like that, just say it... like now, say the words."

"Levi, I'm pregnant," she huffed, melodramatically.

"And I'm happy," I whispered, tugging off her towel and kissing her soft smooth skin. She leaned against me as my hands traveled down the side of her…

"Levi, we need to get ready, everyone will be here in a few—"

The doorbell rang and I sighed.

"Later," she promised as she kissed my lips. "Or maybe not, because you've ruined my hair."

She put a towel to it when the doorbell rang again.

"I'll go, take your time," I told her. I was already fully dressed and she was still wrapped in her towel, working on her hair. Some things never changed with her, and I liked it.

"Thank you!" she called out from the closet, as I made my way to the front.

The second I opened the door, my legs were attacked.

"Uncle Lee!" Bellamy giggled, looking up at me.

"Princess Bellamy!" I picked her up. "How is the little princess?"

"Mad Mommy and Daddy took my princess wand." She pointed to them in the doorway, waiting for me get them.

"The horror!" I gasped at them. "Taking a princess' wand, how could you?"

"Yeah! How could you!" she yelled with me.

I was trying hard not laugh at the bored look on their faces as I let them in.

"When Princess Bellamy decides to hit everyone else in daycare with her Princess wand, Queen Mommy gets to take it away," Bethan said, taking of her jacket.

"Hey, you didn't give me the whole story there, kiddo." I looked to Bellamy as she hid her face in my neck.

"Not princess?" she pouted.

"Princesses don't hit people."

No longer her friend, she wiggled out of my arms and stomped over to the couch, where she took her seat on the throne.

"We are all against her," Tristan said, rolling his eyes.

I laughed, offering them something to drink. It didn't take much longer for my parents to show up. After the Savannah Van Allen case was over, they invited Thea and I out for dinner where they both apologized. It didn't need to be such a big deal, but it made them more comfortable to do so.

After them came Atticus and his boyfriend, along with Vivian who proclaimed last year at our dinner gathering that she never wanted to be asked about her relationship status.

Apparently it was something personal. I had no idea what that meant, but Thea seemed to get it. Over the years Atticus, Vivian and Thea had become close. As their former professor, and hopefully their future boss, I had a feeling they would be making waves soon.

"Sorry we're late!" Selene rushed in with DeShawn. Three years later and they were both at Georgetown and going strong. Thea said Selene has smiled more in the last three years than she had ever seen her smile in her entire life. The funny thing was that Selene had said the same thing about Thea. Their father wheeled in her grandmother, and it pained me to think that she might not make it to next year's get together.

The Ben Walton of now looked nothing like the Ben Walton that had left prison three years ago. He didn't look much different, other than new clothes, a decent haircut and a smile, but he was simply a different person. He was no longer in denial. Saying it was hard for him to come back into society was a stretch.

When we brought him back with us, he refused to stay inside during the day. He said in jail they were given one hour in a room with a window, so they could see the sun. But for seventeen years, he had never seen the outside.

Odile's confession had sparked wide range of backlash from every direction. Tristan had been able to keep her out of jail, but she moved to France with her son seeing as how my former business partner left her. He wasn't too pleased with all the bad press.

But then again, I didn't think he ever loved her. I doubted that Odile would ever be back, but I wished her happiness. Her father had died of a heart attack, and her brother was in prison: the Van Allen family had been shattered by Cole's actions, and on top of that, they had been ordered to pay a million dollars to Ben Walton for every year that he had been locked up.

"You okay?" Tristan asked, as he came up to where I was with a glass of whiskey.

"Just thinking."

"That's dangerous," he joked.

Other than Thea and her family, the person who had been most affected by the case had been Tristan. The only way he would become my business partner was if we didn't only help the rich anymore. We had received so many letters and calls from people who wanted us to look into their loved ones cases, but they just couldn't afford to get a decent lawyer. Being the numbers man that he was, he found a way to work out the cost so there was nothing left for me to do but agree. Black-Knox and Associates was thriving better than ever.

"You're really out of it," Tristan said as he waved his hand in front of my face.

"Are the hormones as bad as everyone says they are?" I asked him to change the subject.

He looked at up to me his brown eyes widened as he understood what I meant. Finally he grinned.

"That explains it."

"So, is that yes?"

"That is… good luck."

He kept snickering as he made his way over to his family.

"Professor Black?" Thea whispered, coming up behind me.

She was as beautiful as ever in her bright red dress. She took my arm and handed me my tie that I hadn't gotten the chance to put on yet.

"You haven't called me that in a long time," I told her.

It sounded even sexier now.

"I know, I've just been thinking about stuff."

"A penny for your thoughts?" I asked her.

"Only a penny, Mr. Black? What type of girl do you think I am?"

I grinned at her as I took her into my arms and kissed her soft lips.

"I don't care who or what you are, as long as you're mine." I spun her around and held her hands for a moment as I stared at her.

"What?"

Taking a deep breath I got on to one knee and she starting to shake her head at me even though a huge smile spread across her face.

"Oh my God," I heard my mother gasp from behind me, but I tried my best to ignore them as I took the teal box out of my pocket.

"Thea Cunning. Will you—"

"Yes! Shit... I mean shoot, yes... finish, sorry."

She was making me smile so much that my face ached.

"Thea Cunning," I waited to see if she would interrupt me again, "will you allow me to spend the rest of my life with you? Will you be my wife?"

"Yes!" She grinned.

Placing the ring on her finger, I stood as she pulled me into a kiss; all of our family gathered around us, clapping and whistling.

Who says dreams don't come true? Everyone deserves to have a 'Happily Ever After', and she was mine.

∼

THE END

SNEAK PEEK OF THAT THING BETWEEN ELI AND GWEN

CHAPTER ONE
Telltale Signs

Guinevere

I should have seen the signs that morning. They weren't massive, but they were there. I had almost slipped and killed myself coming out of the shower—okay, that one was a big, giant sign, but the others were pretty small. I couldn't find the left shoe to my favorite pair of red heels. The pearls *he* had given me slipped off my neck and scattered all across the bedroom floor. And when *he* did show up, twenty minutes late, Taigi would not stop barking at him…like my dog knew March 1st would be a day that would live in infamy for me.

Taking a seat in his brand new midnight blue Mercedes, he didn't say anything as we pulled out of the Hampton beach house. His knuckles were almost white as he gripped the steering wheel. The back of his hand rested just under his lips, something he had done hundreds of times in our three years together, but only when he was either really worried or upset.

"Bash?" I touched his leg and he jumped as if he had forgotten I was sitting next to him.

Turning to me, his light brown eyes met mine. "Yeah?"

"Are you okay? You look like we're going to a funeral, not a wedding," I joked, smiling. He shook his head and took hold of my hand.

"I'm fine." He kissed the back of my hand. "Just work stuff. I'm hoping we can do our rounds and get out of there before it gets too late."

Nodding, I looked back out at the beach as we drove. Sebastian —or Bash as I called him—was the owner and founder of both *Class* and *Rebel* magazines. It was the reason we had met, actually. He had attended one of my gallery openings and loved my photography. I had told myself I would never contract myself with any corporation or brand; I liked being a freelancer. I painted and shot what I wanted, what mattered to me. Yet there was just something about Sebastian Evans. No matter how many times I bluntly denied his request or ignored his emails, he never gave up. After all, no matter what Sebastian Evans wanted, he worked until it was his. Eventually, I agreed to shoot their spring cover. It was only supposed to be that one cover, but three years later I was a contracted photographer and his fiancée.

"Welcome to The Chateau Rouge," the valet said when we pulled up to a gated mansion. As Bash spoke to him, I found myself staring at the decorated landscape; everything was in beautiful greens and blues. Projected on the pure green grass were the initials E & H, and around them was a small orchestra, just for the arriving guests.

Only when I stepped out of the car was I able to see what had to be the icing on the cake: as if these people needed to prove they had money, there were even peacocks walking around.

I looked to Bash.

"What?" He looked at me, confused.

I pointed at everything. "Really?" was all I managed to say.

"You make it seem like you've never seen rich people before. You should have worn the red dress I picked out for you." He frowned and took my hand as we walked toward the seats for guests.

This was another point at which I should have seen the signs, but again, I was blind to it. I can still remember how cold his hand was as I held it. As we mingled with the rest of New York's elite during cocktail hour, I felt as if I were standing in the middle of the Arctic Circle in a bikini.

"Wow, she's beautiful," I whispered as the bride walked up the aisle, her makeup flawless to the point that her skin glowed. Her soft, honey-gold hair shined and her strapless heart-shaped dress clung to her every curve. Her blue eyes filled with unshed tears as she held her roses tightly, walking slow and steady. For a quick second I thought I saw her glance over to us.

I hope I look half as good as her on my wedding day, I thought, my eyes never off her as she made her way to the front.

It passed in a blur. One moment the pastor was saying something, and the next, Bash was no longer holding my hand.

"Hannah," he called out, moving to the center of the aisle.

She looked toward him, looked to her groom, and then back at Bash.

My Bash. *What...*

"Don't, Hannah."

What...is...this...?

"Hannah," Bash called to her.

Stop! My mind screamed.

But, to my horror, she let go of her groom's hands and ran toward Bash.

I couldn't breathe. I was up, knocking over my chair. "BASH!" I yelled.

But they were already running…hand in hand.

By this point, every other guest was up. Those around me moved away, allowing everyone to see the girl who'd just gotten dumped. I knew the only person who had it worse than me was the man up front. For the first time since I'd gotten there, I truly looked at him: tall, ivory skin, short dark hair, piercing green eyes watching his bride run from him. He stood there so still, so shocked, I almost forgot my own pain.

Why hadn't I seen the signs?

Eli

Even if I lived to be one hundred and fifty, I would never forget *that* March 1st. It was supposed to be one of the happiest days of my life. After two years of dating, I had finally asked *the* Hannah Michaels to be my wife.

We had met as medical interns at New York Presbyterian, and on the first day she'd had the attention of every straight male at the hospital. What was sexier than beauty and brains? She was dedicated not only to her work, but also to her patients. *The* Hannah Michaels... My Hannah was soft, sweet, focused, and precise. No matter what goal, she worked to achieve it; I liked that about her. Whenever we were around each other, we just clicked. She and I were so alike on so many levels, there were times we would end up finishing each other's sentences. We became close early on, but didn't actually start to date until we both became attendings.

I couldn't imagine dating anyone else.

"You nervous?" My younger brother, Logan, placed his arm around my shoulder as I stood in the dressing room.

I shrugged him off, fixing my cuff links. "Why would I be nervous?"

"Eli Davenport is finally taking the plunge. I just can't believe it. I thought you guys were never going to get married." He pushed me out of the way to fix his tie.

I smacked him over the head.

"Really? Even today you two fight?" My mother sighed, coming into the room. Her gray-auburn hair was cropped at her shoulders, and her soft green gown kissed the ground as she came close and pulled me into a light hug. The tears in her eyes were already starting to build.

"Ma, he's getting married, not dying." Logan chuckled.

She gave him a glare. "Now." She frowned, looking to me. "Are you sure about…this?"

"Mom." I held on to her shoulders; she was being ridiculous. "You like Hannah. I like Hannah. Why wouldn't I be sure? You're finally getting the daughter you always wanted."

"I know." She placed her hand on my chest. Even with heels, she was still a full head shorter than me. "I just can't shake this feeling. Who knew letting you go would be so hard?"

My mother and her dramatics, I'd thought. If only we had listened to her gut.

"You still have me," Logan added, proving he was more like her than our father.

We both looked at him before turning away.

"Wow! Okay, I see how it is," he muttered before walking toward the door, leaving our mother laughing.

"If your father was still with us, I'm sure he would have been proud of the man you've become, Eli. I know I am." She wiped away a few tears.

I wasn't sure what else to do but give her my arm. I was never the affectionate one, but that day I went through so many different emotions.

She held on to me tightly as we entered the grounds. She and Hannah had gone crazy with the decorations, but they really enjoyed it, and I honestly didn't care. I just wanted to skip to the important part.

I stood in front of all our family and friends with Logan to my left. Finally the music started, and my gaze shot toward the doors of the mansion, waiting for them to open. I had known she would be beautiful, but she was absolutely radiant.

God, I'm so lucky.

With every step she took, the grin on my face grew, until her hand was in mine.

"You look beautiful," I whispered.

She smiled, but didn't say anything in return. In that instant, as the pastor began to speak, all the moments we'd ever shared together played in my mind: the very first time we met...our first operation together...first kiss...first night... Everything ran though my mind like a movie, the highlights of our life.

And this is just the beginning of so much more. Today is—

"Hannah," someone called.

Hearing her name pulled me from thoughts. My head snapped to the man standing in the aisle with his hand outstretched to my soon-to-be-wife.

"Sebastian?" Logan questioned beside me.

Sebastian... The man calling out to my Hannah was Sebastian Evans, one of Logan's closest friends. We weren't close, but I knew of him.

"Hannah," he called again.

Enough! My mind hollered as I took a step forward, but it was too late.

Hannah released my hand. She let go and never looked back as she ran toward him.

I stood there, too shocked to move or speak. That moment was hell on earth.

For hours, I could not speak. My mind was blank. I tried to understand, but my brain, my heart—both were shot. I leaned on the balcony of the dressing room, staring out at the ocean until the sunset. Only then did I regain function of my body, and I ran. Stupidly, I ran out toward the front. All the guests, with the exception of family and the cleaning crew, had left. When I got outside, I saw my brother ripping the "Just Married" sign from the Bentley.

"Eli—"

"Keys." I walked around to the driver's side of the car. As I opened the door, I saw a woman dressed in blue step in front of me. She had long wavy brown hair and warm brown skin. Her brown eyes were now puffy and red, presumably from crying. She stood tall with her head held high.

"This is your number, right?" She pointed to the phone number on the RSVP card before quickly texting something on her phone and adding, "Please kick his ass." She turned toward her taxi without waiting for another word from me.

"Gwen!" Logan called out to her before groaning. "Jesus. He was her fucking fiancé."

Feeling my phone vibrate, I pulled it out of my coat pocket.

He left his email open on my phone. I got a confirmation for a room they just booked.

Prescott Hills

Montauk, NY

Room 1204

"Eli, don't—"

Ignoring him, I got into the car, and without a second thought I drove, the rage in me growing with each passing mile. I gripped the steering wheel, gritting my teeth as I thought. They were no more than twenty minutes away from the chaos they had unleashed on my life.

When I pulled up at the Prescott Hills, I was prepared to kick the door down. I immediately saw both of them walking toward me, completely oblivious, still holding those godforsaken hands.

"Eli!" Hannah gasped, no longer in her dress, now wearing jeans and a gift shop shirt.

Ignoring her, my fist collided with his jaw and he fell against the wall, but that didn't stop me. Grabbing him by the collar, I kept punching until my knuckles cracked on his face.

"STOP! Eli! Stop or I will call the cops, I swear," she yelled.

I wanted to kill him, but by some miracle, I managed to stop. "Call the cops?" I stood rigid, ignoring the pain in my hand and the fucker at my feet. "What's stopping you, Hannah? Make this day even more special!"

She hung her head, dropping to her knees beside him.

"I understand that you hate—"

"You understand nothing." I cut him off. I couldn't even look at them anymore. I turned to leave but stopped, pulling out my phone to take a picture of his bloody face. It gave me no real satisfaction, but what the hell. Maybe that other woman would get some peace of mind out of seeing it.

All I could wonder as I drove was, how? *How could this happen?*

~

Click here to order **BLACK RAINBOW** on your retailer of choice!

ALSO BY J. J. MCAVOY

Ruthless People Series
RUTHLESS PEOPLE
THE UNTOUCHABLES
AMERICAN SAVAGES
A BLOODY KINGDOM
DECLAN + CORALINE

Children of Vice Series
CHILDREN OF VICE
CHILDREN OF AMBITION
CHILDREN OF REDEMPTION
VICIOUS MINDS: PART 1
VICIOUS MINDS: PART 2
VICIOUS MINDS: PART 3

Single Title Romance
MALACHI AND I
BLACK RAINBOW
RAINBOWS EVER AFTER
THAT THING BETWEEN ELI AND GWEN
SUGAR BABY BEAUTIFUL
CHILD STAR

ABOUT THE AUTHOR

J.J. McAvoy first started working on *Ruthless People* during a Morality and Ethics lecture her freshman year of college. If you ask her why she began writing, she will simply tell you "They wanted to get their story out."

She is the oldest of three and has loved writing for years. Her works are inspired by everything from Shakespearean tragedies to modern pop culture. Her first novel, Ruthless People, was a runaway bestseller. Currently she's traveling all across the world, writing, looking for inspiration, and meeting fans. To get in touch, please stay contact via her social media pages, which she updates regularly.

Facebook

Twitter

Printed in Great Britain
by Amazon